w

THE BEST ASSASSINATION IN THE NATION

JOSHUA COHEN

Kasva Press

Make its
bowls,
ladles,
jars and
pitchers
with
which
to offer
libations;
make them
of pure
gold.

וְעָשִׂיתָ
קְּעָרֹתָיו
וְכַפֹּתָיו
וּקְשׂוֹתָיו
וּמְנַקִּיֹּתָיו
אֲשֶׁר יֻסַּךְ
בָּהֵן זָהָב
טָהוֹר תַּעֲשֶׂה
אֹתָם

St. Paul / Alfei Menashe

Kasva Press
Alfei Menashe, Israel / St. Paul, Minnesota

www.kasvapress.com
info@kasvapress.com

The Best Assassination in the Nation

ISBNs:
Trade Paperback: 978-1-948403-50-4
Ebook: 978-1-948403-51-1

M 10 9 8 7 6 5 4 3 2 1

To Marci, of course

THE BEST ASSASSINATION IN THE NATION

ONE

I spent July of 1952 tailing Eugene Bramble, president of Ambassador Tool & Die. His wife thought he was having an affair with her sister Myrtle and wanted me to find out one way or the other.

Her suspicions missed the mark, but only partially. Bramble was running around not with Myrtle but with Myrtle's husband, Floyd. The situation didn't come into focus for a couple of weeks. Eventually I caught the two lovebirds shacked up at a hotel in Akron when they were supposed to be fishing on Lake Erie. A few weeks later, after a modest payoff to Ambassador's night watchman, I sneaked into Bramble's office and found a desk drawer filled with cards and letters Floyd had sent to "Sweet Baby Gene."

"These so-called men," Mrs. Bramble said bitterly as she reviewed the dossier I'd assembled.

"At least it wasn't your sister," I said.

"I've kissed those same lips. I've... It makes me want to vomit."

"I'd try not to think about it that way."

"That man won't set foot in my house ever again. He goes off and does what he's been doing, then comes home and climbs into our bed."

"I'd really try not to think about it that way," I said.

"He's the one who won't want to think about it, when I get through with him."

I used some of the Bramble fee to buy a train ticket to Atlantic City. I planned seven days of rest and relaxation, but when it came time to board, I pulled my bag from the porter and left the platform. The prospect of going solo turned my anticipated vacation into an ordeal. I knew I'd find willing companions in the bars and on the beach, maybe get invited to a poker game or two. Inevitably, though, I'd end up back in my hotel room, alone, immersed in morose introspection over the personality flaws that left me without a traveling companion.

So I junked the junket. My vacation consisted of a visit to the aquarium, a fifth of scotch, and an afternoon sleeping it off on my living room sofa.

Judith Sorin came to see me Friday morning at the end of that week. I had no appointments scheduled for the day, which I intended to spend catching up on paperwork. I rode the bus downtown from my apartment in Cleveland Heights and walked from Public Square to my office in the Hippodrome Building. After only half a block, I peeled off my coat. A smoldering heat wave had gripped the city for the better part of a week. Three days in a row, the temperature topped out at over a hundred degrees. The newspapers predicted the streak would continue.

Sweat was dripping from my forehead as I entered the Hippodrome lobby. Jonathan, the dwarfish concierge, smirked as I passed his desk on my way to the bank of elevators. The building's management considered me to be an undesirable tenant, given the dubious nature of my clientele, and Jonathan fully committed himself to conveying that message.

"You're sweating up a storm, aren't you, Mr. Gold," Jonathan commented sarcastically as I wiped my brow with a handkerchief. "I'll have to have the maintenance crew out here with a bucket and a mop."

I loved Jonathan as much as he loved me. "You know, Pee Wee," I responded, "if you were just a little taller you'd be a bona fide midget."

I rode the elevator to the seventh floor and walked to my office at the end of the west corridor. My secretary, Mrs. Skokow, stood in front of her desk talking on the telephone. "Good morning," I said, to no effect.

I headed toward the door of my private office. "Just a minute," Mrs. Skokow said before putting her hand over the mouthpiece of the telephone. "You have a walk-in, Boss."

I looked at the empty sofa facing Mrs. Skokow's desk. "Where is he?" I asked.

"It's not a 'he'; it's a 'she'. And she's waiting inside."

"Who is she?"

"I didn't catch her name."

"What does she want?"

"Not sure."

"She might not be a 'walk-in' at all," I said. "Maybe she's selling encyclopedias. Why's she in my office and not out here?"

"I'm talking to my sister-in-law about a personal matter. I needed some privacy."

"Makes perfect sense," I said as I proceeded inside.

Judith Sorin stood in front of my desk, looking idly out the window facing Euclid Avenue. I immediately recognized her from the pictures in the newspapers after her old man's murder. She apparently hadn't heard the office door open and jumped a little when it clicked shut.

"Mr. Gold," she said. "I'm awfully sorry for showing up without an appointment."

"That's all right," I said. "Today's a slow day anyway. Very sorry about your father."

"You know who I am?"

I nodded.

"Thank you."

"Why don't you have a seat?"

I gave her the once-over as she put her purse on the floor and situated herself on the chair in front of my desk. She was tall and thin, with long legs, an ample chest, and thick black hair, which she wore down. Her face was pretty but somewhat severe, angling tautly down from her high cheekbones. Her fair complexion accentuated the shock of her red lipstick.

"I knew your father a little," I said after I sat down. "He hired me to do a couple of jobs when I first got into this business."

"I didn't know that."

"I worked as an attorney before the War. Your dad was the best."

"That's good to hear."

Maury Sorin had been the best. He was Cleveland's answer to Clarence Darrow, the underdog's champion who turned hopeless cases into stunning victories. He dominated the courtroom, mesmerizing jurors and judges with his eloquence and confounding opposing counsel with an unparalleled command of the law.

"The Rock," I said to Judith. She smiled sadly and repeated my words.

"The Rock" became Maury Sorin's nickname among his brethren in the Cleveland bar after his cross-examination of the prosecution's key witness in a trumped-up bribery case brought against a Negro city councilman. For a full day, Sorin demolished the witness's testimony, exposing exaggeration after distortion after out-and-out lie. Upon finishing the rout, he stepped away from the podium and headed toward the counsel's table. But then he abruptly pivoted toward the witness:

SORIN: One last question, sir.

WITNESS: All right.

SORIN: Where's the rock?

WITNESS: Pardon?

SORIN: Where's the rock, sir?

WITNESS: I don't understand.

SORIN: Where's the rock you crawled out from under to come testify here today?

Sorin's flourish got an ovation from the onlookers in the gallery. A few jurors stood and applauded, too, bringing an immediate motion for mistrial from the prosecution. The judge denied it, disgusted as he apparently was with the witness's testimony. The next day, the State dismissed its case, and the city councilman walked out of the courthouse a free man.

After a few moments of chit-chat, I got around to asking Judith why she'd come to see me. She said she needed help on her father's case.

"Your father's case?" I repeated. "I don't practice law anymore, Miss Sorin. If you like, I can recommend a couple of probate lawyers I know."

"This isn't about his will. It's about his murder."

"I thought the matter was closed," I said. "The guy who shot him was killed at the scene."

"He was killed, and they did close the case, but they didn't solve it. Make no mistake, Mr. Gold. My father was assassinated."

"Assassinated?"

"You may find it hard to believe, but it's true. He was about to blow the whistle on some very powerful people, so they had him killed."

"Do the police know about this?"

"The police!" she snorted. "They're in it up to their eyeballs."

I'd had crackpots come see me before. A plumber from Parma needed help in proving he was the bastard son of John D. Rockefeller. A lady thought the manager of her apartment building was fluoridating her water. Then there was the guy who believed his wife was conspiring with a dead neighbor to knock him off.

Judith brought a new float to this parade. Her father's murder had been a simple case — brutal and tragic, but completely lacking in conspiratorial intrigue. Sorin was walking to his office in the Standard Building on the first Friday in January. It was 6:45 in the morning, the usual time he got to work. A hophead named Warren Grubb was pacing in front of the building and blocked Sorin as he tried to enter. Grubb then pulled a .45 and demanded Sorin's cash. Sorin had no intention of resisting and went for his wallet, but apparently not fast enough for Grubb, who put the gun against Sorin's left temple and pulled the trigger.

An old lady on her way to the train station happened by just as the murder took place. Grubb panicked when he spotted her and turned the .45 in her direction. Luckily, an off-duty cop was also on the scene. He shot and killed Grubb before Grubb could rub out the old lady.

The Cleveland police investigated Grubb's motive for the murder. They thought he might've been a disgruntled former client of Sorin's or an adversary from one of his cases. He wasn't. They tried to find some other score he had to settle with the attorney, either personally or on behalf of some relative, friend, or associate. That was a dry hole, too.

The killing was exactly what it appeared to be. Grubb was a junkie in need of a fix he couldn't afford, and Maury Sorin had been his unfortunate victim. I could appreciate Judith's hard time in coming to terms with her father's murder. But what she needed was a headshrinker, not a shamus.

"This isn't the sort of thing I usually handle," I told her. "I know a couple of private detectives who used to work homicide. If you'd like, I could arrange for you to see one of them."

"You're uniquely qualified to handle my case, Mr. Gold," she said.

"You're being kind, but..."

"I mean it. I most definitely do."

"What makes me so special?"

"The masterminds behind the assassination," she said gravely.

Masterminds, I thought. She'd really gone off the deep end.

"And who is that?"

"Your in-laws."

"I'm not married," I said.

"Your ex-in-laws, then. The Forsythes. Elite Motors."

"The Forsythes killed your father?"

"Exactly," she confirmed. "And I have proof. Let me tell you..."

"Wait a minute. Wait a minute." I got up and walked over to open a window. "Why would the Forsythes want to kill your father?"

"Because he was handling a case that could've made them look very, very bad."

"What do you mean by that?" I asked as I sat back down.

"I can't be more specific."

"Have you spoken to your father's client about this?"

"No."

"Why not?"

"I don't know for sure who the client is," said Judith. "It's someone who works for Elite, or used to."

"What'd the guy hire your father to do?"

"File criminal charges against the Forsythes, I think. Possibly a civil suit."

"Was there anyone else involved?"

"I couldn't tell you."

"When did all this take place?"

"I don't know," she said. "Probably right before the murder."

Judith was a paranoiac, but not an especially imaginative one. Her assassination plot was nothing more than an amalgam of could-be's and maybe-so's.

Still, she had my stomach doing cartwheels. My ex-in-laws personified everything I hated in the world. They'd made life a living hell during my stint as the Forsythe son-in-law. Even after all these years, the mere mention of their names triggered flashbacks of the misery and recriminations.

"How'd you find out about what you know about the Forsythes?" I asked.

"My father's secretary."

"Who is she?"

"She didn't want me to use her name," said Judith. "She's afraid they'll come after her next."

Now there were two paranoiacs.

"Sooner or later you're going to have to tell me who she is, if you want me to help you," I said as I shifted sideways in my chair.

"Nancy Debevec is her name."

"What specifically did she tell you?"

"She said my father had an Elite employee as a client who wanted to blow the whistle on the Forsythes."

"Did she tell you anything more?"

"All my father said to her was that serious crimes were committed."

I pulled out a pack of Lucky Strikes from my top desk drawer and lit one up.

"All of this is so up in the air," I said. "I wouldn't even know where to begin an investigation, if I were going to accept the case, other than to interview this Nancy Debevec."

"I don't think that would be possible," said Judith.

"Why not?"

"Nancy left town in March, and she's not coming back."

"Where'd she go?"

"She didn't say. I told you she was scared. She wanted to vanish, and that's what she did."

I wanted Judith to vanish, too. I started to give her the brushoff, but she interrupted.

"I told you I had proof, Mr. Gold."

Judith opened her handbag and pulled out a rumpled sheet from a legal pad. As she unfolded it on the desk, I saw scraggly handwriting in bright blue ink.

"These are my father's notes," she said. "He took these when he was interviewing his client."

"Where'd you get this?"

"I found it among his papers at home, and Nancy explained what it was. I know it's my father's handwriting."

"What happened to the rest of the client file?"

"There wasn't one," Judith said. "That's what Nancy told me."

"How could there be no file?"

Judith shrugged.

"F.G.Z." I read from the top line of the page. "What's that?

"I think it's the client's initials."

"Any idea why your father didn't write out the full name?"

"No. None at all."

Judith deciphered the rest of the scrawl. Nothing specifically identified "F.G.Z.," but Maury Sorin had written down my former brother-in-law's name ("C. Forsythe, Jr.") and the name of the family business ("Elite M.C."). The rest of the page comprised short phrases, with no explanation: "unintended consequences"; "paid to keep quiet"; "didn't know what he was getting into"; "government contract"; "wife threatening to leave"; "expiate his sins"; "U.S. attorney"; "Cty. Prosecutor"; "willing to do time."

"Did you show these notes to the police?" I asked Judith as I ground my cigarette butt into the ashtray on my desk.

"I didn't. I told you they're complicit in this."

"Why are you so sure of that?"

"An off-duty policeman just happens to be on the scene when my father is shot, and kills the killer before anyone can question him? At that time in the morning? It's just too coincidental."

"You know he was protecting an old woman when he shot the gunman," I said.

"Please, Mr. Gold," Judith answered. "That was a convenient excuse. And by the way, what was that woman doing there, anyway?"

I didn't buy everything she was peddling. But her father's notes cast a new light on things. Their meaning wasn't completely clear, but their import was definitely sordid. "F.G.Z." had come to Maury Sorin with a guilty conscience. He'd done some insidious thing for the Forsythes — something that turned out to have "unintended consequences". "F.G.Z." hadn't realized "what he was getting into". The Forsythes were paying him "to keep quiet", but he wanted to "expiate his sins" by coming clean to the U.S. Attorney or the County Prosecutor, even if he had "to do time" as a result.

It was rational to assume "F.G.Z." was asking Sorin for help in making this happen. Doing so would've been a delicate proposition. The Forsythes weren't people to cross. Step on their toes, and they'd slit your throat. Do worse, and you'd wish they'd slit your throat by the time they got through with you.

Judith's deluded story wasn't necessarily so deluded, after all. That didn't thrill me, since it would make it harder to indulge my reticence about taking her case.

Judith had just finished reading her father's notes to me when Mrs. Skokow came through the door with two glasses of water.

"I see you finished your phone call," I said.

"As a matter of fact, I didn't. I put my sister-in-law on hold while I got you something to drink. You were so flushed when you came in, I thought you could use it. I got one for you, too, miss," Mrs. Skokow said as she put a glass on the desk in front of Judith.

"Thanks."

"Yeah, thank you," I said as I sipped the water. "It's already broiling this morning. It's hotter than hell out there."

Mrs. Skokow ordinarily would have scolded me for cursing, but she was craning her neck to read the notes I was taking. There wasn't much, but at the top of the page I'd printed, in large block letters, "JUDITH SORIN — M. SORIN MURDER."

Mrs. Skokow turned and stared at our guest. "You're Maury Sorin's daughter," she said.

Judith smiled. Mrs. Skokow took this as a green light to lean over and deliver a smothering hug.

"You poor thing," she said. "I saw your father shopping at Sterling Linder last October or November, before the… I'm pretty sure it was him. He was by himself and asked the saleslady about a red scarf."

Mrs. Skokow might've actually had some reason for sharing this reminiscence. Whatever it was, her yapping gave me a few moments to catch my breath. When she decided to explain precisely where she was when she heard about the murder, I seized the opportunity for an extended reprieve.

"You'll excuse me for a moment," I said as I got up and walked toward the front office. "I'm still a little sticky from the sauna outside. I think I'll go freshen up."

After shutting the door, I pulled a clean shirt from the top drawer of the file cabinet behind Mrs. Skokow's desk. Then I headed for the washroom.

The reprieve turned out to be no reprieve at all. Thoughts of my ex-in-laws cropped up like the outbreak of an angry rash. The Forsythes never let me forget that in their eyes, I was and forever would be the conniving, small-time Jew who hoodwinked their daughter into marriage. Elizabeth's father made a sport out of belittling me, whether we were alone or (preferably, for him) in front of others. As for my mother-in-law, she always had a disgusted expression when I was around, as though she'd just sipped spoiled milk or inhaled some noxious odor.

Judith Sorin's case hypothetically provided an opportunity to give my ex-in-laws what they had coming. Nailing them for Maury

Sorin's murder would be the ultimate retaliation. But it almost certainly was a pipe dream, even if I somehow managed to turn up evidence of their complicity. A different set of rules applied to people like the Forsythes. They literally could get away with murder, given the privilege and inside pull they wielded. Judith was picking a fight she couldn't possibly win, no matter what.

I was alone in the Excelsior washroom. I took off my shirt, and undershirt, too, and began rinsing off. The mirror showed how thin I'd become. The image startled me. In the bathroom of my cramped apartment, I never saw anything in the mirror beyond the part of my face I was shaving at the moment. But here I got the works — the bony arms, the scrawny neck, the protruding ribs. I was a six-foot-three, one-hundred-seventy-pound stick man. My appetite never returned after I came home from the Army, and now I looked only marginally better than the prisoners I'd seen in the camps.

Mrs. Skokow was back at her desk banging on her typewriter when I returned to the office. "I thought maybe you got lost," she said without looking up.

"What are you doing?"

"Preparing a contract for Miss Sorin."

"I haven't said I'm taking the case," I said.

"I don't know why you wouldn't," Mrs. Skokow replied as the keys continued to rattle. "That girl needs your help, and we certainly could use the money."

Judith was digging through her purse, searching for something or other, when I walked back into my office. I stood looking at her. She was an attractive woman, made more attractive by my realization that she didn't necessarily have a screw loose. I thought of asking her to dinner but instantly dismissed the idea as unprofessional.

My appearance in the washroom mirror also deterred me. Women who looked like Judith didn't go out with men who looked like me.

"Let's talk turkey," I finally said to catch her attention.

"Sure. Of course."

"First, I want you to know I find this whole assassination thing hard to believe. From what I've read, the police investigated your father's murder pretty thoroughly. I know you think they're in cahoots with the Forsythes, but it seems farfetched to me. I'll try to keep an open mind, but as of now, let's just say I'm skeptical."

"Okay," said Judith after a short pause. "If you'll keep an open mind."

"Also, this is going to be pretty expensive," I said. "You're not giving me much to go on, and I don't know what, if anything, I'll be able to prove. The key is finding this "F.G.Z." and getting him to talk. It really would make things considerably easier if you'd tell me where I could get in touch with Nancy Debevec."

"I don't know," said Judith. "Like I said — she just disappeared."

"Well, if you can think of any way we might be able to find her, pass it along. What she has to say is a shortcut to what you want to know."

"Okay."

I told her what I charged per day and said I needed a five-hundred-dollar retainer. She didn't flinch.

"Mrs. Skokow has a contract for you to sign," I said. "Leave your check with her, and I'll call you when I know something."

"Thank you, Mr. Gold," Judith said as she left my office.

When the door closed, I loosened my tie and undid the top button of my shirt. A few moments later, I was standing at the window watching traffic on Euclid Avenue when I saw Judith leave the building and head up the street.

Two

I spent the rest of Friday morning at the downtown library. In the reading room I perused stories on the Sorin murder in back issues of the local papers, from initial reports of the killing to the long obituaries that ran the day of Sorin's funeral.

I next headed over to the police station at 21st and Payne to have a chat with Lieutenant Monachino, the detective in charge of the case. Monachino was just returning from an early lunch when I arrived. A short, rotund fellow, he waddled rather than walked. The sweat on his bald head glistened in the lights outside his office.

"I don't know you," he said, chewing on an unlit cigar. "What are you here for?"

I couldn't tell the truth, since Judith believed the police were in on the plot to kill her father. So I said I was a freelance writer doing a piece on the Sorin murder.

"Oh yeah?" said Monachino. "A story for who?"

"*True Crime Detective.*" I pulled the name of the magazine out of my hat.

"Never heard of it. Why the hell do they want a story about the Sorin case? It's old news."

"You'd have to ask my editors."

"What else have you written, hot shot?"

"Nothing anybody has seen," I said. "Mainly squibs in trade publications."

"Oh, yeah? Then how'd you land this assignment?"

"Through my agent, Herb Zipken."

I went to high school with Zipken, who practiced podiatry in Mayfield Heights and who had never met a writer in his life, as far as I knew. For some reason, his name popped into my head as I fabricated my literary résumé.

"Which other writers does this Zipken represent?"

"Look, Lieutenant, if you doubt my credentials, you can call the magazine…"

"Take it easy, pal," said Monachino. "I'm just busting your chops. Far be it from me to keep *True Crime Detective* from getting its big story. Let me powder my nose, and I'll tell you what I can."

Monachino and I talked for half an hour. He gave me names and addresses of witnesses he thought I might want to interview. I already had most of that information from the newspapers.

I asked about Sergeant Vince Stuffleben, the off-duty cop who shot Sorin's killer. "He's a hero," said the lieutenant. "At least that's what everybody tells me."

"Don't you agree?"

"Sure I do."

"Well, what sort of a guy is he?" I asked. "You must know him, or know men in the Department who do."

"He's not one of ours," Monachino said. "Stuffleben's from the Mansfield P.D."

"Mansfield? What in the world was he doing in Cleveland?"

"Tracking a gambling ring, apparently."

"A hundred miles outside his jurisdiction at the crack of dawn?

That doesn't make any sense."

"The suspects apparently were running a dice game at one of the hotels," said Monachino.

"Which hotel?"

Monachino scratched his bald noggin. "I never asked," he said. "I'm homicide, not vice."

"A country cop doesn't come all the way to Cleveland to stake out a dice game."

"It didn't add up to me, either, to tell the truth," said Monachino. "But all that mattered for my purposes was he was on the scene when Sorin was shot, and he saved a little old lady from becoming victim number two."

Before leaving, I used a payphone to call the mother of Warren Grubb, the mug who shot Maury Sorin. I gave her the same song and dance about working as a reporter and asked whether she would talk to me. She said "yes," told me her address, and invited me to come right over.

Grubb had been a jazz clarinetist who got gigs now and then at some of the local clubs. He was into speed, so much so that he gave up music to devote himself full-time to it. During our conversation, Monachino had recounted Grubb's string of arrests dating back to 1948 for petty larceny, breaking-and-entering, and theft. Grubb committed these small-time offenses to feed his habit. Before killing Maury Sorin, he'd never threatened or hurt anyone. Nor had he used a gun in any of the incidents reported on his rap sheet.

It took the taxi about twenty minutes to get to the house, on a side street in Collinwood near the intersection of St. Clair Avenue and East 140th Street. The driver parked in front and agreed to wait for me.

I gave the place a quick inspection as I walked to the front door. It was well on its way to becoming an eyesore. The white paint job had turned gray, and even darker in some spots. Large chunks of the chimney had broken off. The only window on the second story was cracked and covered from the inside with cardboard.

The upkeep hadn't faltered on the 1951 Olds 88 sitting in the driveway. The car was fire-engine red and had its top down. It looked brand new.

A pudgy middle-aged woman with cropped hair and too much makeup opened the door immediately after I rang the bell. "You the guy from the magazine?" she asked.

"Yes, ma'am. I'm Benjamin Gold."

Grubb's mother showed me into her living room and offered me a seat on a decrepit brown sofa. The air was stale and warm and reeked of garlic and onions. A fat gray cat came in from the kitchen with its stomach dragging on the floor. It took one look at me, meowed, and plopped down on my feet.

"Bootsie loves company," said Grubb's mother.

"I guess so," I said. "Now Mrs. Grubb…"

"It's not Grubb. Hobbes. Rosemarie Hobbes."

"So you've remarried?"

"Common law," she explained. "It's a long story."

"Mrs. Gru…Hobbes. Where did your son live?"

"Here. With me."

"When did you see him last before the murder?"

"I heard him leave the house about 4:30 that morning".

"Do you know where he got the gun he used to kill Maury Sorin?"

Grubb's mother shook her head. "He never had no gun while he was living in this house," she said.

"Why are you so sure?"

"'Cause I cleaned his room twice a week. Cleaned it the day before he died, and there wasn't no gun."

I pulled a pack of cigarettes from the inside pocket of my suit jacket. Grubb's mother silently handed me a tin ashtray from the coffee table.

"You must've been shocked when you found out your son had committed the murder."

"Not really, to tell you the truth," she said. "He was off his rocker the whole week before."

"Was it the drugs?"

"It was always the drugs," she said, moving forward on her chair. "But the last week, he hit rock bottom. He was juiced up day and night, yelling like a madman."

"So he was worse than usual?"

"A lot worse," she said.

"What was he saying?"

"I don't remember. None of it made any sense."

"Did your son have a girlfriend?" I asked.

"The speed was his girlfriend."

"Any other friends?"

"I wouldn't know," said Grubb's mother. "He never brought anybody home, and he didn't say much, other than the gibberish."

I asked Grubb's mother whether she'd ever heard of the Forsythes or Elite.

"Sure, I heard of them."

"Did your son ever do any work for the Forsythes?"

"He was a musician, not a mechanic," she said. "Those Elite cars ain't too good."

"I can tell from the car out front that you prefer an Olds," I said.

"Warren bought me that, for Christmas, right before the..."

"Where'd he get the money?" I asked.

"I don't know. I assume he stole it."

"Did you ever tell the police about the car?"

"Nope," she said. "They didn't ask, and I didn't tell."

I finished my cigarette, then lit another. "So your son was pretty flush around Christmas time," I resumed.

"Seemed so."

"He bought you the car, and he was buying a whole lot of drugs, right?"

Grubb's mother nodded her head.

"Did you ever ask yourself why he was holding up Maury Sorin if he already had so much cash?"

"No, I never did," she said. "But that's no mystery. Warren went through money like nobody's business. He never had enough. He probably held up that Sorin guy because he spent everything he had and needed more."

After asking a few more questions, I tried getting up to leave, but the cat had my feet pinned. I sat back down.

"Scat, Bootsie," Grubb's mother hissed. The cat didn't respond. For a minute I thought it might've died on me. Eventually, my hostess went and got a broom and swatted Bootsie off my feet.

"When's the magazine going to publish your story?" she asked as we walked to the door.

"The magazine? Probably not for a few months, at least."

"Will they send me a copy?"

"I'll make sure you get two."

"Listen," she said as I headed toward the waiting taxi, "I really don't want to lose my car. I'd appreciate it if you wouldn't write that Warren bought it with stolen money."

I told her I wouldn't. Then I climbed into the backseat of the cab and gave the driver the okay. He started the engine, and we headed back downtown.

THREE

I SPENT FRIDAY evening at the Theatrical Grille drinking scotch. The Sorin case had me reflecting on the demise of my marriage, and I needed some anesthetic.

More than six years had passed since the divorce, but I hadn't fully come to terms with it. I'd known, of course, that Elizabeth and I were on thin ice, but she never told me why she called it quits when she did. For some reason, I wanted that explanation, and until I got it, she and I had unfinished business, as far as I was concerned.

She only came to see me once in the hospital after they shipped me back from Europe. I awoke one afternoon from a drug-induced stupor to find her sitting on the metal chair next to my bed. At first I didn't recognize her. She'd put on more than a few pounds in the two years since I'd seen her, and had dyed her curly blonde hair pitch black.

Once it registered who she was, I started bawling. I'd only been back a few weeks and hadn't progressed much in my recovery.

"I killed those kids, Liz. I killed those kids."

"Benny," she said, "take it easy."

"I did it, Liz. I killed them."

As I continued to rant, Elizabeth got up from the chair and back-pedaled toward the door. "Nurse, I need some help in here," she cried. "My husband's very upset. Nurse!"

The medical staff promptly descended. One orderly pinned my arms, another my legs, and an intern stabbed me with a hypodermic filled with liquid sleep. I conked out immediately. By the time I came to, Elizabeth had left.

Six weeks later, the hospital chaplain came to my bed and handed me a thick brown envelope. "It's over, son," he said. "The divorce is final."

"Divorce? What divorce?"

"They told me your wife divorced you. Perhaps I'm mistaken."

He wasn't. The envelope contained a final decree from a Nevada judge, a thirty-five-thousand-dollar bank check, the deed to our home, and the title to a 1942 Schooner sedan, the latest model Elite made before the War. The prize package also included a letter from Elizabeth's lawyer explaining the futility of contesting the settlement she'd negotiated with herself.

It was an ugly finish to an improbable marriage. I'd met Elizabeth after my second year of law school. A buddy of mine got me a part-time job as groundskeeper at Eastside Country Club, where I worked four evenings a week sweeping sidewalks, scrubbing the parking lot, and replacing divots on the golf course.

My assignment temporarily changed when a member accused someone on the restaurant staff of stealing an emerald necklace from her purse when she went to the lavatory. The theft almost certainly never happened — no waitress or dishwasher could have rummaged through the lady's pocketbook without being seen. Still, since the jewelry was pricey, and an all-Negro crew had worked the shift, they all got pink slips when the cops couldn't identify the non-existent culprit. The purge left the Club short of help for the weekend, so they drafted me as busboy for Saturday from noon till closing.

I wasn't jumping for joy at the prospect of moving inside. The Club was not a Jew-friendly establishment. I'd need to keep quiet and stay as invisible as I could.

Fortunately for me, the day passed uneventfully. But when we were closing down at a quarter till two, a ruckus broke out at the bar. A man was yelling at a woman in increasingly strident tones. After a momentary pause, I heard a slap followed by a shriek and another slap.

The bartender walked by as I mopped a table. "I'm not getting in the middle of that mess," he said.

I planned to ignore it myself. But then there was another slap and shriek, and I figured I'd better investigate.

I saw Elizabeth first as I approached, and was struck by the brightness of her golden hair. Then I got an eyeful of her escort, a swell-gutted behemoth with no discernible chin who was wearing a navy sport coat at least two sizes too small. They had the bar to themselves, and he was tugging at Elizabeth's breasts with both his mitts.

"Stop it," she said. "Please stop. Be a gentleman."

"You're a tease, Betsy."

Elizabeth pushed the Chinless Wonder's hands off her chest and pulled back from the table, earning her a fist to the forehead. Elizabeth wobbled for a moment, and then started whimpering.

"Can I help you folks?" I asked.

Chinless looked me over suspiciously. "You're not our waitress," he said.

"Right you are, sir. I only waitress on Tuesdays and Thursdays. Tonight I'm in charge of the split-pea soup."

"Beat it."

"Are you all right?" I asked Elizabeth.

"No...thanks," she slurred. "I'll be fine."

If the lady didn't want a knight in shining armor, I wouldn't insist. I turned to leave, but Chinless had something to say.

"You need to mind your own goddamned business," he told me. "What's your name?"

"Fred Astaire," I replied. "And I'll be dancing my way back to the kitchen."

"You do that. And tell your supervisor I want to talk to him."

"Whatever you say, sir."

I returned to the dining room and began clearing the last of the dishes. A few moments later, I heard a cry from Elizabeth: "Fred! Fred!" I didn't immediately understand she was calling for me.

"Mr. Astaire!"

I bolted back to the bar to find Chinless pulling Elizabeth toward the door by her hair.

"I said it was time to go, Betsy."

Elizabeth looked up as I entered the room. "Help!" she squealed.

Chinless released her hair and turned to face me. "Get out of here," he said. "Go back to your goddamned soup."

Chinless put his hands on his hips, striking a formidable pose but also providing me with an open target. I kicked him in his most vulnerable spot. He didn't react for half a second, then doubled over.

"You son-of-a-bitch," he wheezed. "You goddamned son-of-a-bitch."

"Why don't you come out front, miss?" I said to Elizabeth. She started walking toward me, but Chinless reached out with his left hand and grabbed her by the wrist.

"You're not going anywhere," he said. "This isn't over."

Chinless pushed Elizabeth backwards and lurched toward me. "Come here, you bastard," he said.

"You better sit down," I told him.

"Fuck you."

I threw three punches — one to his flabby gut, another to his right temple, the last to his jaw. Chinless went down in a heap.

Elizabeth straggled to the bathroom. When she returned five minutes later and kissed me on the cheek, her vomitous breath nearly knocked *me* out. I got a cab and rode with her to the Forsythe mansion. The Chinless Wonder, she explained, was the son of a department store magnate whom she'd been seeing intermittently during the summer.

After dropping her off, I walked all the way home. Our whirlwind romance began shortly thereafter.

Elizabeth was drinking heavily at the time, just as she was drinking heavily when I went into the Army and most of the time in-between. She rationalized the booze as her way of dealing with her parents. But if she hadn't guzzled so much, she would've been better equipped to stand up to them, to the extent she really wanted to.

I lost my wife shortly after losing my job. Grimm White & Dauer gave me the ax within a few weeks of my admittance to the psychiatric ward. The firm was strictly white-shoe — not the place for a Benny Goldstein, with or without his marbles. I got my position in the first place only at the insistence of Elizabeth's father, who figured if he had to have me as his son-in-law, at least I wouldn't humiliate him by working at some Jewish firm. Clayton Senior had to call in a lot of chits to get me on the payroll, even if he did rank among

Grimm White's most prominent clients. My exemplary marks in law school carried no weight. The firm wanted filet mignon on its menu of attorneys, not delicatessen salami.

I did well at Grimm White, winning almost every one of my cases. It made no difference. When the Forsythes withdrew their sponsorship, I got my walking papers immediately.

The heave-ho from the firm was a kick in the chops. But it was a loving caress compared to the blow landed by Elizabeth with her absentee divorce. Without my wife, I was alone. My parents had both passed away, and my brother had sworn never to speak to me again. I had no extended family, and I'd either fallen out of, or lost touch with everyone else who'd meant anything to me before my stint as the Forsythe son-in-law. I barely kept in touch with my army buddies, who'd scattered across the country. On the romantic front, I'd seen several women since the divorce, but only a few of them more than once, and only one that I really cared about. She was a cellist studying at the Institute who took a position with the Los Angeles Philharmonic while I equivocated about my feelings toward her. She eventually got engaged to a guy who wrote music for one of the film studios.

I had casual friends who'd go with me sometimes to a movie or a ball game. I'd kibbitz with the shoe-shine man, the guy who did my dry cleaning, and the regulars at the Theatrical and the other places I wet my whistle. I did the Jewish holidays with the Rosenthals who lived upstairs, and spent much of each workday conversing with Mrs. Skokow, whether I wanted to or not.

"Is that all there is?"

I posed the question to Max, the bartender at the Theatrical, who was filling the snack bowls with peanuts. "What happened to those cheese puffs I like?"

"We're out," he said. "The delivery man don't come till Tuesday."

"I demand to speak to the manager."

"You know he ain't here at this hour," answered Max.

"What the hell. Bring me another scotch-and soda."

"Are you sure, Mr. G? You've already had more than a few. I don't want to carry you out of here."

I glanced at my wristwatch. It was almost 8:30. I'd been wading through the muck of my former marriage for over four hours.

"You're right, Max," I said. "I didn't realize it was so late."

I settled up and proceeded out the front door. It had rained that evening and had come down pretty hard, judging from the size of the puddles. The sky had cleared, for the most part. It was still hot, but much less humid.

I walked up East Ninth to catch the streetcar. I was heading uptown, to Gleason's at Fifty-fifth and Woodland. I went looking for Rufus Prince.

FOUR

RUFUS WORKED AS Clayton Senior's valet back in the day, and often had inside dope on what his boss was up to. I was hoping he still had the job, still took Friday nights off, and still spent them at Gleason's. If so, I might convince him to tell me what, if anything, he'd heard about the Forsythes' involvement in Maury Sorin's murder.

It was a long shot, any way you looked at it, but I didn't care. Whether I found Rufus or not, the excursion gave me an excuse not to go home. My apartment was a dark and gloomy place — the ultimate testament to my descent down the ladder of success. I was already depressed from wallowing in memories of my marriage and divorce. Banishing myself to the apartment would only make things worse.

Gleason's, on the other hand, was one of Cleveland's better jazz clubs. The joint would be hopping on a Friday night. There'd be good music, and there'd be booze, so I could continue the binge I started at the Theatrical. Running down Rufus would almost be a bonus.

Rufus wasn't his real name. It was Dayton, which sounded too much like Clayton for the comfort of the Forsythes. I didn't know whether they just assigned him his new name or let him pick it for himself. He was an intelligent, articulate man who kept his job by suppressing any display of these qualities that might show up my ex-in-laws. Rufus treated me politely when we first met — politely but cautiously, the same way he dealt with everyone. Eventually, as my standing within the family deteriorated, he and I became confederates, sharing information about which Forsythe was doing what to whom.

Gleason's wasn't as crowded as I expected. I grabbed a stool at the bar and ordered a scotch on the rocks, then rotated my seat toward the stage. A Negro quartet was playing a Dizzy Gillespie set — "Salt Peanuts," followed by "Groovin' High" and "Flat Foot Floogie." When the music stopped, I lit a Lucky Strike and began surveying the room for Rufus.

He was sitting at a table near the back with a glass of beer in one hand and a half-smoked cigarette in the other. He was the same tall, slender man I remembered, though the nap on his head had thinned and grown a little grayer. With him sat a buxom woman with a towering coiffure. She had on a bright green dress and seemed to laugh at everything Rufus said. I didn't want to intrude, so I finished my drink and asked the bartender to bring me another. When the lady got up and headed toward the powder room, I made my way over.

"Rufus!" I said more loudly than I intended. The volume of my voice always went up a few decibels after I'd had a few. "I bet you don't remember me."

"Of course I remember, Mr. Gold. I don't believe I've seen you since you left for the service."

I extended my right hand, and we shook. I couldn't tell whether he was happy to see me or the opposite. His expression remained completely neutral.

"Listen," I said. "I know you're not alone, and I don't want to crash the party. But there are a couple of questions I'd like to ask you. It won't take long."

Rufus nodded without saying anything.

"I don't know if you know this, but I'm not practicing law anymore. I'm a private investigator."

"Miss Elizabeth had mentioned it."

"You're still working for the Forsythes?"

"I am."

"How often do you see Liz?"

"She's been living at the house, off and on, since you left," Rufus said. "Her brother moved back home about a year ago."

"Hail, hail, the gang's all here."

"Exactly, sir."

Rufus didn't invite me to sit, but I was teetering a bit, so I took a seat on my own. As I did so, Rufus got up.

"I'm going to find my friend and ask her to give us a few minutes," he said.

Rufus walked off, and I sat wondering what exactly he would tell me. If the Forsythes actually knocked off Maury Sorin, he'd probably heard about it, notwithstanding Clayton Senior's fetish for secrecy. The old man went to great lengths to ensure that competitors weren't bugging his office and refused to tell the missus anything meaningful about Elite's business, for fear she'd repeat it at the bridge table or on the tennis court.

In front of Rufus or his fellow servants, though, Clayton Senior became loose-lipped. He gave me inside stock tips in the presence of the chauffeur and expounded upon the company's involvement in a price-rigging scheme while the downstairs maid dusted the table nearby. I think he figured the help was too stupid to understand what they were hearing or too lackadaisical to care. He was wrong, especially when it came to Rufus.

"Did the Forsythes ever talk about Maury Sorin?" I asked after he sat back down.

"I don't remember specifically," he said. "His name may've come up at some time or other. Mr. Forsythe certainly didn't like the man."

"Why do you say that?"

"You know as well as I what he thinks of people with Sorin's point of view."

"I'm not arguing," I said. "I just want to know if you have some more particular reason for saying he didn't like Sorin."

Rufus shook his head.

"I'm asking because someone told me the Forsythes had Sorin killed."

Rufus had no visible reaction. "I never heard anything like that," he said, "but I wouldn't put it past them."

"Sorin got killed a few days after New Year's. Was there anything unusual going on around that time?"

"It was a horrible Christmas," Rufus answered. "There was some crisis with the company's design for one of its airplane engines."

"Airplane engines? I thought Elite only built cars."

"Apparently not, sir."

"What specifically was the trouble?"

"I never knew," Rufus said. "The elder Mr. Forsythe thought the company was going to lose its contract. He was on a rampage until the issue was resolved."

"That was at Christmas?"

"Christmas, till a few days after New Year's."

"So the crisis ended about when Maury Sorin was murdered," I said.

"That may be so," Rufus said. "I don't remember the timing exactly. But I can't say the one is connected to the other."

I stood up slowly. "I know I'm grasping at straws," I said. "The whole thing is pretty far-fetched, but I wanted to ask you."

Rufus silently nodded.

"Well, anyway, thanks for humoring me. You've got to let me buy you and your date a round of drinks."

"You needn't do that, Mr. Gold."

"I insist," I said. "Anything you want…"

What Rufus wanted was for me to scram. I thanked him again, then granted his wish.

Nothing ventured, nothing gained. That's how I assessed my outing to find Rufus as I stood in front of the club, smoking a cigarette. But then I began to wonder whether I'd made a big mistake in asking him so directly about the Forsythes' complicity in the Sorin murder. I'd taken a huge leap of faith in assuming he'd confide in me about his employers; his loyalties could very well have shifted over the years. Rufus was a master at self-preservation. More likely he would rat me out to the Forsythes than rat them out to me.

I stewed on this for a good five minutes, working myself into a pretty good panic before snapping out of it. Judith's unlikely hypothesis about her father's assassination probably amounted to nothing, whatever Rufus's sensibilities might've become. Even if he repeated our conversation verbatim to the Forsythes, nothing would come of it, other than adding "crackpot" to the list of pejoratives they used to describe me.

In the final analysis, I didn't think Rufus would end up telling my ex-in-laws anything. He detested them at least as much as I did back then. Hatred that profound didn't simply vanish, no matter how much time passed — not when it centered on people as immutably contemptible as the Forsythes.

"Need a ride, mac?" asked a cabby leaning against his hack parked on the street in front of me.

I shrugged while I ground what remained of my cigarette into the sidewalk. It was past 11:00, and I'd definitely had enough to drink, but I still didn't want to go home. Doing so meant being alone, and being alone meant renewed musings on my marriage and divorce, and my ex-in-laws. I intended to delay that inevitability as long as possible.

Desperate times called for desperate measures. I knew it was late, and I wasn't supposed to show up without an appointment, but I decided to go see Rosie.

FIVE

I KNEW A lot of hookers. I worked with them professionally, for surveillance purposes. Many of my assignments required me to catch husbands in the act. The job became that much easier if I knew beforehand where and when it would happen.

Most of the girls didn't think twice about selling out their johns. Rosie was an exception. I first approached her to get the dirt on one of her regulars, an optometrist from Lakewood, but she refused to serve him up. Rosie let me have it for even asking. She called me a "lowlife" and said her profession was downright honorable compared to mine. I was surprised a few months later when she called me with a job of her own.

Rosie had been plying her trade in Cleveland for twenty years since coming to town from Arkansas. She started at one of the city's biggest brothels. When Eliot Ness shut it down in his crusade to clean up Cleveland, she went out on her own and had been a sole proprietor ever since.

Her problem came out of nowhere. A pimp named Holiday stopped by one day and announced he was taking her on and gave her two weeks to capitulate. Holiday was bad news. He'd done a three-year stretch in Mansfield for cutting a guy up and then another five years for cutting up the guy's partner two days after his parole. He treated his girls brutally, using lit cigarettes instead of shivs to communicate his point of view. He worked them like dogs. Alleyways, phone booths, barroom toilets: any venue was acceptable to Holiday, as long as the customer had the cash.

"If the cops would only do their jobs," Rosie drawled, "that bastard would spend the rest of his life with his pals in the penitentiary." But she knew better than to count on the police. If they actually enforced the law, she would've had to close up shop long ago.

Rosie would move back to Hot Springs before she'd become Holiday's newest source of revenue. Before doing so, she decided to take a shot at making him back off. So she hired me to get the goods on him.

I worked the case for a week and a half. Holiday wasn't secretive in promoting his business. Everybody knew who he was, what he did, and where he sold his merchandise. I caught several transactions on film and got close-ups of the girls' burns and bruises. Clergy from a few of the local churches also gave me statements about what they'd seen and heard about Brother Holiday. I worked up a detailed report and sent copies both to the newspapers and to a guy I knew in the Prosecutor's Office. Holiday made it to page B-1 in the Sunday *Plain Dealer*. By Thursday, he was back in Mansfield, and Rosie paid me five hundred bucks.

I became a customer of hers a couple of months later, on what would've been my tenth wedding anniversary. The occasion put me in a black mood that grew frantic as the day wore on. By evening I was convinced that my loneliness put me on the brink of a return to bananaville, and that my only possible salvation would be reconciling with my brother, Jake. I'd considered a fraternal reunion before. Usually I let it pass. This time, though, I drove the fifteen minutes to Jake's home in University Heights and parked right in front. I told myself I'd knock on the door as soon as I caught my breath.

I could see right into Jake's living room through the open drapes. He was on the floor playing with his son, David, who was three or four at the time. Jake's wife, Miriam, walked in and spotted my car on the street. After coming to the window for a better view, she turned to talk to Jake. When they started for the front door, I took off. I was doing forty-five when I ran the stop sign at the end of their street and turned left toward downtown.

I sped to a dive I knew in Cleveland Heights where Jake would never find me (as if he were looking). The bartender brought a bottle of rye to my table in the corner, and I guzzled as much as I could as quickly as I could. With my panic chilled, I somehow got the idea to visit Rosie, and off I went.

Rosie lived in an apartment at East 30th and Woodland. I parked on the street and took the stairs up to her flat. When Rosie didn't answer the bell, I started pounding on the door with both fists.

"Rosie!" I cried. "Open up in the name of the law!" When no one came, I repeated the command. After the third time, Rosie cracked the door and peeked out.

"Dick Tracy, is that you?" she said in a half-whisper. "What in the hell you think you're doing?"

"I'm looking for my radio watch. I thought I might've left it here."

Rosie yanked me inside and closed the door, quietly but quickly. "You're touched," she said angrily. "You're absolutely touched."

I looked her over. She was wearing a sheer, low-cut negligee that hid exactly nothing. Rosie was firm and shapely, even though she was fifty, at least, and had a beautiful mane of red hair.

"You gotta git, Dick Tracy. You gotta git right now."

"You can't really mean that, after all we've meant to each other."

"I'm working, fool. I'm not alone."

I looked into Rosie's bedroom. Sitting on a divan in his underwear, scrambling to get his socks on, was a guy who looked just like Charles Coburn. His face was flushed and became even redder when he looked over and saw me staring at him.

"Don't mind me," I shouted. "I'm just her rabbi."

Coburn looked as though I'd poked him with a branding iron.

"If he leaves now, I don't get paid," Rosie said. "Your little escapade is costing me money."

"Don't worry. I'll cover it."

"Damn right you will."

"Will you take an I.O.U.?"

"You're not anywhere near as funny as you think, Dick Tracy."

Coburn preempted any further tirade by walking between Rosie and me on his way to the front door. He missed several buttons on his shirt, and forgot to tie his shoes, but was otherwise presentable.

"Aren't you a member of my synagogue?" I asked. "I thought I saw you there on Purim."

"I'm sorry about this," Rosie said to Coburn. "You call me tomorrow and we'll schedule a special date for the weekend."

"You were really great in *The Lady Eve*," I called out as he shuffled down the hallway. "Is Barbara Stanwyck really as nice as they say?"

Rosie had gone into the kitchen and was shaking her head at me when she returned. "What in the world are you babbling about?" she asked.

"He looks like Charles Coburn."

"Who in God's name is that?"

"Never mind. It's not important."

"If it's coming out of your mouth tonight, I can be sure it's not important."

The irritated expression on Rosie's face began to fade. "He was almost finished when you started banging on the door," she said. "From now on, any time he's with a woman, he'll be thinking somebody's fixing to burst in."

Eventually I got my turn in Rosie's bed. I had trouble getting started, given all I'd had to drink, but she knew exactly what to do. Afterwards, I was babbling my appreciation as she went into the bathroom to clean up.

"Shut up, Dick Tracy. The whole building doesn't have to know my business."

"I'm only congratulating you on a job well done."

"You're acting as though you just lost your cherry," Rosie said.

"As a matter of fact, I did. I lost it before, but this time it's for good."

"I think you're touched in the head," she said.

As I sobered up, I relapsed into the grievous state that'd brought me to Rosie's in the first place. She let me go on about it for an hour, filing her nails as I ranted.

"Your ex-wife's a bitch," was her final verdict. "But it was your own damn fault, 'cause you let her get away with it. Any husband worth having would've beat the tar out of her."

"How could I do that?"

"You're a man, aren't you?"

———

I went to Rosie's several times afterwards, always when I was in the dumps, but never without calling beforehand. I was playing long odds by just showing up after meeting with Rufus, late on a Friday night.

I had the cabbie let me off a few blocks from Rosie's. The air had cooled somewhat, and I thought the walk would clear my head. It didn't. I found myself thinking about Judith, wondering whether she'd disapprove of my commiserating with a prostitute. I shrugged off her anticipated objection.

Rosie answered her door after the second ring. When she saw it was me, I thought she was going to slam it shut.

"Not tonight," she said, frowning. "If I've told you once... You've got to call first."

"You working?"

"No. My Friday clients are out-of-town. But I'm working tomorrow, most of the day, and I'm going to the grocery beforehand. You've got to shoo. I need to get some sleep."

"I'm blue, Rosie."

"You're always blue, darlin'. You need to get yourself a different color."

"Please, Rosie."

"Jesus Christ," she said after a short pause. "Get in here."

Rosie brought me a bottle of beer, which I immediately downed. After she returned with another, I told her about the Sorin case and how it might implicate my former in-laws.

"You think those fat cats really had her daddy killed?"

"It's hard for me to believe," I said. "I hate those people, but this is coming out of nowhere."

"You should work them over for old time's sake."

"If I did what I wanted, I'd be the murder suspect."

Rosie stood and headed toward the bedroom. "Let's get to it, Dick Tracy," she said. "I've got an early morning."

"Let me stay the night, Rosie. I've had a miserable day."

She turned around sharply to face me. "No. Not a goddamned chance. I'm not a babysitter, hon. You know you can't stay."

"You don't have anyone else coming tonight."

"But like I told you," she said, "I've got a big day tomorrow, and I got to get my sleep."

I stood silently looking at her for around half a minute.

"Goddamn it, Dick Tracy."

Still, I said nothing. I said nothing, and Rosie cracked.

"All right. All right. You know what? You're pathetic. You can stay, but you're out at six A.M. and you're just sleeping. You'll not lay a finger on me. I don't want any part of you."

"Huh?"

"You want to sleep here, you're going to sleep. It'll be like a real husband and wife. Sleep and no nooky. You want nooky, I'll let you have that instead, but then out you go."

The disgust on Rosie's face finally registered. I got it through my thick skull just how much she wanted me to vacate the premises. Maybe the booze had obliterated the obvious. Maybe I was an idiot. Either way, I got the message.

"Now what're you doing?" Rosie asked when I began walking toward the door.

"I'm going to leave you alone, which is what I should've done in the first place."

"I just said..."

"I know what you just said, and I know what you said before. I shouldn't have barged in on you."

"You're crazier than hell, Dick Tracy."

"You've told me that before."

I laid three ten-dollar bills on the table next to the front door and bowed in deference. "Thanks for your patience," I said. "You're a true princess."

I shouldn't have bent over. The buzz from the alcohol had devolved into a ton of bricks on the left side of my skull, and when I lurched forward, it took me all the way over. I finished my somersault sprawled at Rosie's feet.

"What in the hell are you doing?" she shrieked. "Are you all right?"

"Yeah, I'm fine," I said groggily as I pulled myself up and headed for the door.

"You better sit down awhile."

"I've been here long enough."

I awkwardly reached out and shook Rosie's hand before exiting her front door. The whole interlude had been awkward, or worse. I'd made a forced entry into Rosie's apartment, invited myself to a slumber party, and performed an involuntary exhibition of free-style gymnastics — a true schmuck's trifecta.

Back outside, I stood under the light at the corner to check my watch. It was already after two, almost a quarter past. I'd been at Rosie's longer than I'd thought. In the meantime, Woodland Avenue had shut down. No one else was on the streets, and the only vehicle that passed was an ambulance heading slowly uptown with its siren off.

I pulled a cigarette from my pocket and put it in my mouth before realizing that I didn't have any matches. This was bad news, since a smoke was the only chance of settling my stomach. I had been slightly nauseous before taking my pratfall at Rosie's. Afterwards there was nothing slight about it.

I tore the cigarette in two and threw it into the sewer. I then broke out into a rousing chorus of retches, accompanied by intermittent commentary: "Shit…Goddamn…Goddamn it to hell…Fuck…"

I didn't feel that much better after I finished. My stomach was no longer threatening insurrection, but my head was a searing rock, and the slightest movement left-or-right, up-or-down triggered a shock of pain so intense that I thought my eyeballs would pop out. I determined to stand as still as possible until the taxi arrived to take me home.

I did this tin-man routine for about five minutes before it dawned on me that no taxi would be coming at all, since I'd forgotten to call for one. Without a call, there'd be no taxi — cabbies didn't venture into this part of Cleveland looking for random fares at this time of night. There was no place nearby I could use the telephone, and I certainly wasn't going back to Rosie's. The only thing I could do was to head back downtown. There'd be cabs at the hotels or, if not, I could call from there to get one.

I set out on my hour's trek to the Statler. I only made it two or three blocks before stopping. I wasn't tired, but my feet were aching. After another two stops to quiet the barking dogs, I decided the Thom McAn wingtips had to go. I took them off along with my socks, stuffed the socks inside the shoes, then removed my necktie and used it to tie the whole package in a bundle I could carry. It was an improvement, even if I did have to tiptoe around the broken glass and other debris in the street.

I was still shoeless as I approached the doorman at the Statler. He was standing on Euclid Avenue, enjoying a smoke and shooting the breeze with a taxi driver leaning against his cab. The two of them looked at me and grinned.

"A long night?" the doorman asked.

"You couldn't even imagine."

"Listen," said the doorman, "if you're here for a room, I'm not sure the hotel will take a guy in your condition…"

"Don't concern yourself," I interrupted him. "I'm not looking for a place to sleep. What I want is for this gentleman to take me to Cleveland Heights, if he's willing."

"I'll take you to Tipperary," said the cabbie, "if you've got the scratch."

"Not a problem."

"But you'll have to put your shoes back on before you get into the taxi."

"Fully intend to."

I sat down on the curb and tried to undo the knot I'd made with my necktie. It was easier said than done. After five minutes, I'd succeeded only in making the knot tighter.

"You think they have a pair of scissors at the front desk?" I asked the doorman.

The cabbie had anticipated my surrender. "Try this," he said, handing me a pocket knife.

"Thanks."

"Make sure not to cut yourself."

I supposed I deserved to be treated like an idiot. "Again, thanks," I said.

The doorman and the cabbie snickered as they oversaw my execution of the red polka-dotted number I'd bought at Higbee's a few weeks earlier. I didn't care at all they were yukking it up. During the walk from Rosie's, my mind gravitated back to the thoughts and memories I'd gone there to avoid. With the ghosts of my in-laws dancing in my head, and visions of Elizabeth keeping the beat, playing the fool was the least of my worries.

Six

I FINALLY GOT home at 4:15 Saturday morning. I wanted to climb into bed and sleep until Monday or Tuesday, but first needed to wash off the grime I'd collected on the night's travails. The bath was just right, not overly cool and not overly warm. I was too comfortable, in fact — after a few minutes, it was rock-a-by-baby. I woke up an hour later when I turned my head sideways and inhaled a snout-full. After I finished coughing, I saw I'd been marinating in water that looked like it came from a city storm sewer. I drained and scoured the tub, then took another bath to clean off from the first one. After that I was wide awake.

I waited until 9:30 to telephone Molly Bitka, the old lady who'd witnessed Maury Sorin's murder. I told her my name and said I was a freelance reporter doing a story on the case. After a few moments of conversation, she agreed to see me at two o'clock that afternoon.

Molly lived in a small house on East 69th Street, in the old Polish neighborhood. I showed up right on time. Molly led me from the front door through a hallway into the kitchen.

"Do you mind if we talk in here?" she asked. "I've got a cake in the oven, and I want to keep an eye on it."

I knew from what I'd read that Molly was in her seventies. She looked her age, with a wrinkled face and turkey neck, slumped shoulders, and faded gray hair worn in a loose bun.

Molly didn't bother to gussy up for our meeting. She had on a tattered gray robe with beige stockings rolled to her ankles. She wore no makeup, other than a faint smudge of rouge on each cheek. As her only other concession to vanity, Molly had doused herself with stale perfume that was so strong it had me breathing through my mouth.

For the first fifteen minutes, Molly was the one doing the interviewing. She wanted to know all about my career as a writer. She wondered where I'd grown up and whether I was married and had any kids. Which newspaper did I prefer? What were my favorite books?

Molly apparently didn't get many visitors, and she was determined to wring as much conversation out of me as she could manage. Her inquisitiveness put my flimsy alias as a reporter at risk. I hung on long enough to ask about the Sorin murder.

"I understand you were headed for Detroit that day."

"That's right. I was going to visit my sister."

"Did you actually make the trip?"

"No, not then," she said. "I was still at the police station when the train left. I ended up going in February."

"What time was the train scheduled to leave?"

She pulled a slip of paper from a white envelope sitting on the table and handed it to me. "Here," she said. "See for yourself."

It was a ticket to Detroit on the day of Maury Sorin's murder. The train left Cleveland at 10:43 in the morning and arrived at Michigan Central Station at 4:00 p.m. sharp.

"Didn't they make you exchange this for your ticket in February?"

"They were going to, until I told them what happened. They decided to let me keep it, as sort of a . . ."

"Memento," I filled in the blank.

"That's right. A memento."

"The murder took place around seven o'clock. Why were you downtown so early for a train that didn't leave until nearly 11:00?"

"I wake up at five o'clock every morning," she said. "Sometimes earlier. I packed the night before and was ready to go, so I got dressed and called a taxi."

"Where'd it take you?"

"Union Terminal."

"How'd you end up in front of Maury Sorin's building?"

"I checked my bag and decided to take a walk. It was stuffy inside the station, and I wanted to get some air."

Just then the timer on the oven went off. Molly shuffled over and pulled out her cake, which she placed on the table in front of me.

"I'm known for my chocolate cakes," she told me. "I bake one every couple of weeks."

"That's great," I said.

"The secret is the mayonnaise. Most people think it's just for sandwiches or salad dressing. But it keeps the cake moist."

"You don't say," I said.

Molly claimed to have made the cake especially for me. She said so a little later, after she'd frosted it and cut a huge slab for my consumption.

"That's so thoughtful of you," I said. "But really, I couldn't."

"Sure you can."

"I had lunch right before I left to come here."

"Then what'll I do with the cake?"

I scarfed it down the best I could. After singing its praises, I was able to turn Molly's attention back to the murder.

"That was the luckiest day of my life," she said.

"Why do you think so?"

"Because that guy with the gun was out of his mind. You should have seen his face. And the nonsense he was screaming. Thank God for that off-duty policeman. If he hadn't been there, I'd have been a goner, for sure."

"How close were you to the killer?" I asked.

"Pretty darn close."

"What was he saying?"

"I don't remember anymore. Something about needing money."

"You must've been terrified when you heard the first shot."

"I wasn't, at first," she said, "because I didn't know what was happening. But then I saw the lawyer on the ground and the crazy man waving his gun around. I'm surprised I didn't faint."

"How long did it all last?"

"It seemed like forever."

"And you didn't know the lawyer or the shooter?"

"Heavens, no," she said.

"How about Stuffleben?"

"Who?"

"The off-duty policeman."

"Never saw him before or since."

Molly was eying what remained of her cake in a way that made me nervous. Before she could slice off another chunk, I got up and carried my plate to the sink.

"You don't need to do that," she said.

"No bother at all," I replied as I started to rinse. "You've heard of Elite Motors, of course."

"What?"

"Elite — the car maker. You've heard of them, right?"

"Of course I have," Molly said. "Who hasn't? I once toured their factory in Lorain, years ago. It was very noisy."

"Did Elite ever come up in connection with the murder?"

"I didn't see the shooter in any car."

"I don't mean in that way," I said. "Did the police or Officer Stuffle-ben mention Elite for any reason?"

"No," she said. "That doesn't ring a bell."

"How about the name of Forsythe? Did that ever come up?"

"I certainly don't think so."

I asked a few more questions. Then I thanked Molly and got up to leave.

"I can hardly wait to read your story in the magazine," Molly said as she showed me to the door. "Call me if you have any other questions."

I knew I wouldn't. Molly Bitka might not have been as sharp as she once was, but she still essentially had her wits about her. The woman didn't know about any conspiracy to assassinate Maury Sorin. She'd had the misfortune of finding herself at a murder scene and narrowly avoided taking a bullet herself.

The interview was a bust. All I'd gotten from it was a bad case of indigestion. My stomach was gurgling as I drove back home.

SEVEN

MONDAY MORNING MRS. Skokow and I arrived at work at the same time. As we walked into the building, Jonathan was standing at the concierge desk, sorting through the mail.

"Good morning, Mr. Bratkowski," Mrs. Skokow called out to him.

"Bratkowski, eh?" I said. "I forgot that was your last name."

"What of it?" Jonathan asked.

"It's just I've never seen a Polish leprechaun before."

Jonathan gritted his teeth and turned red.

"Mr. Bratkowski is a neighbor of mine," Mrs. Skokow explained. "He and his mother live one block over."

"Our man Jonathan lives with his mom? Now isn't that sweet."

We stood in silence for ten seconds or so. Mrs. Skokow was looking at the floor. I stared straight at Jonathan.

"Nothing to add to the conversation?" I finally said to him. "I would've thought you'd be better at small talk."

"Ha ha."

"Maybe what I said went over your head. Everything else does."

Mrs. Skokow grabbed my left arm and began tugging me toward the elevators. "You've had your fun," she said. "It's time for us to get to work."

I enjoyed beating up on Jonathan, after spending the entire weekend beating up on myself. I picked up Saturday morning where

I'd left off Friday night after I left Molly Bitka's. A stream of retrospective newsreels began running through my head, cataloging a decade's worth of ugliness and heartbreak. It all came to life, as Time Marched Backward — my preposterous reinvention as a goy aristocrat, the fallout with my family, the abiding contempt of my in-laws, the disintegration of my marriage, and my abject cowardice in going through it all. I was a chiseler, a social climber, and a traitor to my race. One epithet rang as true as the next.

This, of course, was old news, a variation on a theme I thought I'd beaten to death in the hospital and on the analyst's couch. But Judith's assignment brought it back to life. I would've resented her for it, had I not been so smitten by her.

I sat in the dark on the living room couch, trying to sort out my schoolboy crush. It was all so lame and desperate. Judith seemed unattainable, with a capital U, so far beyond my reach that it made me angry to be thinking about her. She'd come up quite a bit in stature since she left my office the day before as a suspected fruitcake. My imagination imbued her with grace, intelligence, humility, and virtue — everything I'd want in a woman. *Compos mentis* was no longer an issue.

As for me, I was unworthy, with the same capital U, in bold type. She was the daughter of one of the country's most brilliant attorneys. I was a two-bit gumshoe — a so-so-practitioner in a low-life profession I'd taken up only after my breakdown left me no other choice.

I caught a few hours of fitful sleep, but the Sunday *Plain Dealer* sent me reeling again. The business section featured a full-page article about Elite and its airplane engines. The company had apparently gone into this line of work during the War and was now manufacturing the RTK-7 turbojet model for the Air Force. This engine, according to the newspaper, would permit travel "faster than the speed of sound." The article came with a photo of Clayton Senior and his designing engineer each smiling ear-to-ear, no doubt over the tens of millions the *Plain Dealer* said the Air Force was paying for the engine.

"We're proud to do our part," the old man was quoted as saying. Elite's "diversification was benefiting the country and shareholders alike."

I wanted to vomit. Why, on this day of all days, did the *Plain Dealer* run a story about the Forsythes and Elite? And why did it have to report such disgustingly good news? I took this as a dangerous omen, foretelling some terrible consequence from my connection to the Sorin case. This sense of dread gave way to dread over the return of my susceptibility to irrational fears.

I was feeling far too fragile. Humpty Dumpty had been back together again for a while, but I was teetering at a precarious height. By mid-morning on Monday, a crash landing seemed inevitable.

I closed the door to my private office and told Mrs. Skokow over the intercom not to disturb me. After pulling my address book from the top drawer of my desk, I turned to the B's and looked up the entry for "Braunstein, Dr. S." Braunstein had been my headshrinker back in the day. I hadn't seen or spoken to him in several years, but I saw no other alternative.

"Dr. Braunstein?" I said nervously when he picked up the phone. "It's Benjamin Gold. It's been a while…"

"Of course, Mr. Gold," Braunstein said. "It is good to hear from you. How have you been?"

"All right, for the most part, Doc. But the last few days have been pretty rough. I think I'm in need of a tune-up."

"Tune-up?" he repeated in his thick Austrian accent.

"I was wondering if you'd have time to see me. There are a few things I need to talk over."

Braunstein didn't immediately respond. The silence lasted so long I thought he might've hung up. But he hadn't.

"I do not think that would be possible, Mr. Gold," he told me.

"Really, Doc? I know it's August, and you're off this month. But..."

"It is not that," he interrupted.

"I've had a tough go of it, Doc. I wouldn't have called otherwise."

"Could you hold on for a moment, please?"

The break lasted two or three minutes. Again I wondered whether he'd ditched the call.

"Of course I will see you, Mr. Gold," Braunstein said when he finally got back on the line. "If you need to talk, I am someone who can listen."

"That's fantastic, Doc. When can we do this? The sooner the better."

"Perhaps this evening. After dinner, around 7:30."

"That'd be great," I said. "Should I meet you at the office?"

"Not the office. No," Braunstein said. "The office is unavailable. You live in Cleveland Heights, as I recall."

"That's right, Doc."

"Meet me at the Alcazar at 7:30. We will have coffee, and we can talk."

"That's fine, Doc," I said. "Thanks very much. See you then."

Just the prospect of seeing Braunstein considerably brightened my outlook. I probably should've known something was up when he arranged to see me at a hotel instead of his office. But all I could think about was my good fortune in getting an appointment so soon — during August, no less.

EIGHT

I TRIED TO get some work done on the Sorin case. I looked over the notes I took in interviewing Grubb's mother along with the scribbles from my conversations with Rufus and Molly Bitka. I'd come up with essentially nothing, other than the fact that Grubb somehow had enough cash to buy his mother a new car shortly before he held up Maury Sorin. He could've gotten the money from the Forsythes, as an advance payment for putting the hit on Sorin. It also could've come from a bet he won, some illicit drug deal, or any one of a hundred different sources. So far, on the Sorin case, I'd been chasing the breeze with a butterfly net.

When I looked up Braunstein in my address book, I came across Joe Brantley's name, and it gave me an idea. Brantley was a labor lawyer in town, and he at least formerly represented the United Auto Workers local at Elite. If he still did, he probably had a directory of the rank and file, and that directory might have a listing for "F.G.Z." I hoped I could convince him to let me take a peek.

I'd met Brantley during my days at Grimm White. He and I faced off in a nasty lawsuit over a strike at one of Cleveland's garment factories. As far as I was concerned, that was all water under the bridge.

"I thought you were killed in the War," Brantley said when I got him on the telephone.

"No. Really?"

"Somebody at the courthouse must've told me. Or maybe I just assumed you got what was coming to you."

I forced a laugh. Brantley said nothing.

"Let me get down to business. You're UAW's counsel at Elite..."

"Yeah. So what?"

"Do you have a membership list for the guys out there?"

"What do you think?" Brantley said.

"I think you do, and I need some information from it, Joe."

"You've got to be kidding."

"Why?"

"You're in the enemy camp," he said. "I'm not telling you a god-damned thing about any membership roll. You must take me for an idiot."

"You're way off base," I told him. "I'm not at Grimm White anymore. I'm not even practicing law. And if you think I'm connected to Elite, that's all in the past."

"I've got a long memory," he replied. "And from what I recall, you and your buddies couldn't tell the truth if you had to. So let's just say I don't have a membership roll and call it a day."

"Listen, Joe, you've got the wrong impression. I'm trying to pin something on Elite — something big. But I've got to find this one guy to do it, and I believe his name might be on that list."

"Don't you already have his name?"

"I only know his initials."

"If you're not a lawyer anymore, why are you trying to pin something on Elite?"

"I'm writing a magazine article," I said.

"Oh, yeah? What's this terrible thing Elite did?"

"I don't know."

"And how's this guy supposed to help you?"

"I'm not exactly sure," I stammered.

"You used to be a much better liar," Brantley said. "I don't know what kind of con you're trying to pull, but you'll have to find another sucker. I'll make sure to tell the union to be on the lookout."

"Wait a second, Joe…"

"Talk to you later, Gold," Brantley said. "Make that much later. The next time you decide to fling the shit, aim in another direction."

I tried not to dwell on Brantley's disappointment that I'd survived the War. But it only corroborated the self-perception that had traumatized my weekend. No ordinary putz could engender antipathy so enduring. My session with Braunstein couldn't come soon enough.

Mrs. Skokow opened the door to my office and stuck her head in. "I'm ordering tuna fish for lunch," she said. "Do you want something?"

"Yeah, I'll have the same. Tell them to hold the mayo. In fact, hold the whole damned sandwich. I'm not hungry, thanks."

Mrs. Skokow shook her head and shut the door.

I spent the afternoon trying to find someone else who might have a roster of local Elite employees. The people I called gave me the same brush-off I got from Brantley, albeit with less overt belligerence. One contact at Elite unconvincingly claimed he didn't have access to personnel records. Another said he'd never seen a comprehensive roster of company employees and didn't believe such a document existed. I took a chance and called a labor lawyer I'd known at Grimm White, Brantley's counterpart in negotiating the union contract at Elite. He just laughed when I told him what I wanted.

The rejections didn't surprise me. I was asking people I hadn't spoken to in years to stick their necks out for a purpose I couldn't reveal.

I thought of one other possible way of getting a list of Elite employees. Before leaving downtown for the evening, I stopped in to see Sig Danziger, a law-school classmate who had his own practice in town. Sig had once co-counseled a case with another lawyer who subsequently sued Elite for wage theft. My ex-father-in-law made his employees show up for work fifteen minutes early each day and wouldn't let them leave until fifteen minutes after closing. This off-the-clock time added up to three extra weeks a year, and Elite had a legal obligation to pay for it, under a worker-protection statute enacted as part of the New Deal. Sig's friend sued the company not just for his client, but on behalf of all afflicted Elite employees, and the court gave him the green light to proceed. The lawyer then sent written notice to all potential participants, inviting them to sign up.

The lawsuit ultimately crapped out. Elite overwhelmed the opposition, as it typically did, with its legion of attorneys. Still, I was hoping this lawyer had kept a copy of his employee mailing list, which might reveal the identity of "F.G.Z." I asked Sig if he'd check with the guy to see if the list was available.

"I'll look into it," Sig said. "But it'll cost you."

"You never paid me for the last job I did. Get the list, and we'll call it even."

"What you got going, Benny?"

"Get me the list, Sig, and I might tell you."

Louis Damiani was sitting on the building's front stoop when I got home that evening around a quarter to six. He was a fifteen-year-old who lived with his parents and younger sister in an apartment one floor above mine. I liked the Damiani kid. He was quiet and respectful but could tell you a lot about what was going on with the other tenants, if you could get him to talk.

"How you doing, Louie?" I asked as I started toward the door.

"Nothing much, Mr. Gold. How's tricks with you?"

"Got a hot date tonight. Looks just like Lana Turner. I think she may be the one."

The Damiani kid smiled politely. "Maybe she's got a younger sister," he said.

It was trite, but I still considered it a pretty good rejoinder for a kid his age. I patted him on the shoulder and went inside to change clothes for my meeting with Braunstein.

NINE

THE ALCAZAR WAS at the corner of Surrey and Derbyshire, about a ten-minute walk from my apartment. The hotel was a night-life hot spot for the city's upper crust. Elizabeth and I had been regulars during the first years of our marriage. We went less frequently later on, when her drinking became such that I preferred she do it at home.

I was halfway surprised Braunstein had even heard of the Alcazar. He was a serious man, not someone I could picture hoofing it in the fifth-floor dance hall or listening to jazz in the nightclub.

I really had no idea of what Braunstein did when he wasn't shrinking heads. I'd never seen him outside the office, and he revealed practically nothing about himself over the years. Sometimes, during our sessions, I would ask a personal question, but he never answered. I'd end up having to explain the reasons for my curiosity. If I persisted in asking, he'd analyze that, too.

What I did know about Braunstein I learned from others. He came to this country shortly before the War. He'd been some sort of bigwig in Viennese psychoanalytic circles and left Austria in 1938, just before the Nazis marched in. Colleagues in the United States brought him and his wife to Boston, where he worked at a clinic for unwed mothers. Mrs. Braunstein died unexpectedly in 1942 or '43, after routine surgery. The next year, he moved to Cleveland and began seeing patients.

The Army doctors recommended psychoanalysis for me only as a second choice. They really wanted to send bolts of electricity through my cranium. Shock therapy terrified me. Somehow I equated it with the torture meted out by the Germans. The docs humored me at first but lost patience when they saw I wasn't going to relent and let them flip the switch. The hospital needed beds, so when I showed some slight improvement, they proclaimed me fit to move. Shortly thereafter, I was back in Cleveland on Braunstein's couch.

I saw him at his office near University Circle five times a week at four o'clock sharp for just over three years. He would usher me in from a tiny waiting room through one door, and I'd exit through a different one precisely fifty minutes later. In between, I stretched out on a couch, with my head on a pillow and my eyes fixed on a preferred corner of the ceiling. Braunstein sat behind me and slightly to the left. There he became an invisible presence, directing my monologue and prodding me toward insights it always seemed he anticipated in advance.

It wasn't sweetness and light. I didn't have the option of skipping over the embarrassing associations or humiliating memories that came up in my stream of consciousness. If I tried, Braunstein somehow knew anyway. But that was the least of it. In those moments when some ugly suppressed truth would emerge, it was like having a rotten tooth extracted without Novocain. The shock and pain eventually wore off, but only eventually.

The Alcazar took up most of a block. It was built in the Spanish mission style and was a replica of some famous hotel in Florida, which itself was modeled on a castle in Seville. Whatever exotic intrigue the architecture once held had faded. The hotel seemed to meld naturally with the Georgians and Tudors that made up the rest of the neighborhood.

Braunstein hadn't yet arrived when I walked into the Alcazar lobby. It was still early on a Monday night, and the place was largely deserted. I took a seat on an empty couch and lit a cigarette. It was almost uncomfortably quiet. The clack of an elevator finally broke the silence. A couple emerged and headed for the front door.

It was ladies' night out for the two middle-aged beauties who entered the hotel a moment later. "Look at the tiles," commented one of them as she examined the walls of the lobby. "They're exquisite."

"I've read about this," said the other.

"And here's that fishpond."

"There's actual fish in there!"

They kept cackling all the way into the restaurant. The quiet returned.

I'd been sitting for around fifteen minutes when I decided to go outside to look for Braunstein. I spotted him standing on the corner, nervously checking his wristwatch. I headed in his direction.

His appearance hadn't changed much. Braunstein was short, maybe five-foot six, and extremely thin, with a full beard and curly gray hair. He was wearing a black suit with a white shirt and blue tie — his standard uniform throughout the time I'd seen him. Only the color of the tie varied. As I approached, I noticed he'd replaced his eyepiece with a pair of gold-framed bifocals.

"How you doing, Doc?" I said when I made it over to him. "Hope you haven't been waiting long."

Braunstein smiled as we shook hands. "Not at all, Mr. Gold. It is good to see you."

"Same here, Doc. Shall we get some coffee?"

"None for me now, thank you. Perhaps later. But if you want some…"

"I'm not that thirsty, either. Why don't we find a place to talk out in the courtyard?"

"Fine," he said.

We went through the hotel lobby to a door that let out to the patio. The place looked the same as ever, with its plush greenery, rose bushes, and tables with sun umbrellas. It was beautiful, but in an anomalous way — a garden oasis sitting at the center of a suburban hotel. It was like finding a sidewalk cafe in the middle of the forest — serendipitous, maybe, but puzzling in its presence.

I did a quick survey to see if there was somewhere Braunstein and I could talk privately. We were in luck. No one else was outside, other than a heavyset woman walking her black miniature poodle at the far end of the grounds.

I pointed to a bench facing the ornamental fountain at the center of the courtyard. "That looks like as good a place as any," I said.

"It is fine," agreed Braunstein. He followed me over to the spot.

I wanted to get straight down to business but couldn't, not with Braunstein sitting next to me. I couldn't imagine having to look him in the eye as I spilled my guts. By all rights, I should've stretched out on the bench, and he should've manned a post behind me in the bushes. Then we could've proceeded as usual. I was going to suggest it as a joke, but humor never played well during my time with him.

Braunstein, too, looked uncomfortable with the arrangements — his jaws clenched, and his arms crossed tightly across his chest. He looked as though he was preparing himself for a painful slap across the face.

"Mr. Gold, I must tell you something," he suddenly blurted.

"What is it, Doc?"

"You have asked to see me, and I came because I care about your welfare and did not want to leave you in the lurch. But you must understand I am not here as your doctor. My license to practice medicine has been suspended — temporarily, I hope, but for now, it is the case. So you must understand I can listen and comment, but only in an informal capacity."

"Jesus Christ, Doc, what happened?"

Braunstein looked at me without answering. He was pulling the same deaf-mute routine he used when I'd ask him a question during analysis, but I wouldn't have it.

"Come on, Doc. I really want to know."

Braunstein sighed. "The government is trying to deport me," he said. "They think I am some sort of subversive. The matter is not yet resolved. But the State of Ohio has determined I am no longer fit to serve as a physician."

I struggled to draw Braunstein out, but eventually he opened up. Two years earlier, he'd been arrested for lying about his political affiliations on his visa application. The government also accused him of reconnecting with the Communists after he'd emigrated. Braunstein denied the charges, but a hearing officer ruled against him. They just about had him on a boat back to Europe when a writ of habeas corpus brought a reprieve.

The reprieve was only temporary. The government took an appeal, which was still pending. In the meantime, the State Medical Board had decided to revoke his professional privileges.

"Did you ever actually belong to Communist Party?" I asked.

"Not that I knew of."

"I don't understand, Doc."

"In Boston, Freida and I belonged to several anti-fascist groups. One of them, I think, was run by radicals who may have turned the membership list over to the Party."

"So they may have signed you up?"

"If they did, we did not know about it."

"But the government doesn't care what you did or didn't know. Is that it, Doc?"

"Yes, it is part of it," he said. "They also accuse me of lying to them about being a Communist in Austria."

"You told them you weren't, but they think you actually were?"

"Precisely, Mr. Gold."

He told me about the organizations he belonged to in Vienna. There were several, and some had "Socialist" in their names, but Braunstein denied they had any formal connection to the commies.

"You had to know these were radical groups, Doc."

"I did not think that," he said. "We were mainly interested in fighting the Nazis."

There was a short pause.

"Listen, Mr. Gold. I know if I had not left Europe, I would not have lived for long. This country saved me. I am a loyal American. I never wanted to destroy the government, and I did not lie to get here."

I supposed Braunstein was telling the truth. Not that it mattered much. As things currently stood, you could sneeze funny and they'd nail you as a red. I myself had pocketed a decent chunk of change checking out suspected commies. It was the easiest money I ever made. Whatever the subject said or did substantiated the charge, even if it proved exactly the opposite. If they wanted to get you, they almost certainly would, one way or another.

"Why'd they come after you, Doc?" I asked. "What made you a target in the first place?"

"A woman I once treated called the FBI to complain. She said I solicited her to join the Party."

"Was there anything to it?"

"Of course not," Braunstein said. "It is a sad story, actually. The girl had a baby boy at the clinic in Boston where I worked. The baby died after just a few days, and she blamed me for what happened. Her fantasies turned me into a monster."

"What a mess. So where does the appeal stand, Doc?"

"Enough about me," Braunstein said. "We have been talking for half an hour and we still have not gotten around to the topic at hand. You said on the telephone you were in need of a 'tune-up'. Now you will say why this is so."

My problems seemed inconsequential after hearing about Braunstein's, but it didn't take me long to recapture the misery. I told him about Judith's visit to my office and the assignment to check out the Forsythes' possible complicity in her father's murder. I explained how taking the job triggered a revival of the crises from yesteryear — my sellout in becoming the Forsythe son-in-law, the estrangement from my family, the breakup with Elizabeth, and the suffocating loneliness that ensued. I recounted my interlude at Rosie's in painful detail. I admitted my schoolboy pining for Judith Sorin.

Braunstein was confused at first. Not knowing about my change in professions, he didn't understand why Judith had sought my services. After I explained, he sat back and listened intently.

"This was a nasty business, the murder of attorney Sorin, and you are asked to put yourself into the thick of it," Braunstein finally said. "Anyone could become agitated under the circumstances."

"There's agitated and then there's agitated, Doc. I thought I was past the point of becoming a basket case whenever anybody mentioned my ex-wife's family."

"She did more than just mention the name, the Sorin woman. She accused them of killing her father. In your fantasies, the Forsythe family was also complicit in killing your father."

"I blamed myself for that, too, Doc."

"Tell me," Braunstein said. "Did you know attorney Sorin?"

"Not really. I'd met him a time or two."

"What was your opinion of him?"

"He was the best," I said. "The absolute best. Maury Sorin took the right kind of cases and did them as well as they could be done. He was the lawyer I wanted to be like when I decided on law school."

Braunstein smiled. "Now there is something," he said. "Your ex-wife's family killed the lawyer you wanted to become. You could say it was a repeat offense."

I chewed on that for a while. "I see what you're getting at," I said. "But I'm frightened, Doc. I feel vulnerable, like I'll fall apart whenever I'm reminded…"

"Nonsense," said Braunstein. "You are well past the point of 'falling apart', Mr. Gold. But you cannot expect to have no reaction when something reminds you of the past, particularly when it happens so provocatively."

"Why am I so attracted to Judith Sorin?" I asked.

"Perhaps she is attractive."

I went back to whining. "I thought when I got off the couch, this was all resolved."

"Have you ever spoken to your ex-wife, or reconciled with your brother?"

"No."

"So everything is not resolved. I think you should take care of these matters. But that does not mean you will 'fall apart' before you do. Most people have unfinished business in one way or another."

Braunstein had never been so direct during analysis. Back then he only asked questions — the answers were up to me. Most of what he was saying now sounded obvious enough, though I'd thought of none of it myself. Obvious or not, I began to feel better.

We'd been talking for about an hour when I got up to stretch my legs. "I can't thank you enough for seeing me, Doc," I said. "I feel like the monkey's off my back."

"I did nothing," Braunstein said. "You are much stronger than you think, Mr. Gold. That has always been the case."

"Just the same, Doc. Thanks."

Braunstein looked at his wristwatch. "It is getting late. I think I will be going."

"Not yet, Doc."

"Naturally, if you still want to talk . . ."

"Not for me, Doc. I want to hear what's going on with your appeal."

Braunstein shifted uncomfortably. "There is not much to tell," he said. "The hearing will be in Cincinnati in October. After that, I should know what will happen to me."

"Your lawyer won in district court. What does he say about your chances on appeal?"

"The attorney I had is no longer on the case," Braunstein said. "I will have to handle the hearing myself."

"Without a lawyer? That's not a good idea, Doc," I told him. "That's not a good idea at all."

"I have tried to get a new lawyer," Braunstein said. "I hired one who resigned after a few weeks. I hired another who did the same thing. The FBI goes to their offices and tell them not to represent me."

"How do you know that?"

"They both told me so. I am out of patience with attorneys. And since I have not been working, I am out of money to pay them, too. I will argue for myself. The court will have to listen to what I have to say. It will be fine."

It wouldn't be fine, and Braunstein knew it. If he didn't, he either was supremely naïve or needed a psychoanalyst of his own to explore his susceptibility to self-deception. I figured that even with the best legal counsel, Braunstein would have only a so-so chance of retaining his citizenship. Without any lawyer at all, he might as well start planning for winter in Vienna.

"What happened to your first attorney?" I asked. "Did the Feds scare him off, too?"

Braunstein smiled queerly. "No, no, not at all. He was a fearless man, a man of great integrity. Very committed to helping me, I thought."

"Then why'd he bail? Was it a question of his fees?"

"Not that," said Braunstein. "And he did not 'bail'. He is no longer available."

"I don't understand…"

"My first lawyer is dead, Mr. Gold. His name was Maurice Sorin."

TEN

AFTER WE SAID our goodbyes in the Alcazar lobby, Braunstein went home and I headed for the hotel bar. I wanted a drink to calm my jitters before returning to my apartment. These weren't the same jitters I had when I arrived. Braunstein had convincingly explained why the Sorin case had thrown me so far off. As long as there was a rational reason for my irrationality, I could live with it.

Braunstein's connection with Maury Sorin was something else again. I wasn't really surprised the Doc had gone to him for help. Sorin had been one of the few lawyers in town willing to take on a commie-in-distress case. Still, it seemed more kismet than coincidence that after all these years, I came to Braunstein with a crisis precipitated by the very same incident that had thrown him into a crisis of his own. His tie to Maury Sorin somehow gave credence to Judith's suspicions about her father's "assassination," even though one thing had nothing to do with the other.

"Horse shit," I told myself as I sat at the bar. I didn't believe in fate or curses. Braunstein's revelation had spooked me because the Sorin case made me vulnerable to being spooked — that vulnerability had compelled me to call Doc in the first place. I wanted him to help me tighten the reins, and he'd done that. Or so I hoped.

I'd only planned on a drink or two, but a couple from Canton was celebrating their second anniversary and insisted on including me in a toast to their good fortune. Naturally, I had to reciprocate. Others joined the party, and one thing led to another. I didn't leave the Alcazar until after midnight.

Walking out, I realized I'd primed myself for one hell of a hangover. I decided to sweat out some of the booze, to avoid waking up with an anvil inside my head. I took the long way home, walking down to Cedar Road and looping back up to the apartment.

I was alone on the street once I got away from the Alcazar. My footsteps sounded exceptionally loud, so much so that in my tipsy state I worried I'd awaken people in the apartment buildings I was passing. Every few minutes, a car would come up the hill from downtown and scoot by toward the Heights. I knew my brother, Jake, went this same way on his daily commute. I thought about him and Elizabeth and the Forsythes as I continued on. I also wondered what I'd say to Judith if I had the chance to talk to her right then and there.

My mind eventually turned to Braunstein's immigration mess. I'd allowed myself to forget about it during my last few hours at the bar. The Doc was a goner if he went to court without a lawyer. Even if he got one, he was probably still a goner.

In a fit of selflessness, I vowed to steer Braunstein out of harm's way. I'd find the best available attorney willing to argue the case. I'd raise the necessary cash to cover legal fees. I'd...

As the buzz from the liquor began to wear off, my commitment to the cause yielded to what I charitably thought of as pragmatism. Braunstein had the prerogative to handle the appeal on his own, if he insisted upon doing so. I couldn't force him to accept my guidance. Best to leave well enough alone.

I'd worked up a pretty good lather by the time I stopped two or three blocks from the apartment to light a cigarette. The route in this stretch wasn't as deserted as it had been. A man was trying to walk his boxer, who made things difficult by exhaustively sniffing at every tree. A couple of teenagers parked in a convertible at the curb were giggling over something or other. A block behind me a car fitfully puttered along. The driver was apparently lost and looking for an address.

"Nice dog," I said to the man with the boxer.

"Says you," he replied as the hound pulled him along to the next tree.

I finished my cigarette, stomped out the butt, and resumed my walk home. I was in no particular hurry. The kids parked at the curb pulled out and tooted their horn as they passed. I waved at them, and they tooted again. Otherwise it was quiet.

My apartment was on the opposite side of the boulevard. I started my cross about half-a-block away. I was jay-walking but didn't think anything of it. The traffic consisted of me on foot and nobody else. As I sauntered across the street, I noticed a light in a window on the top floor of the building and began wondering whose apartment it was. I hadn't yet figured it out when I saw the car.

It was the same car I'd spotted crawling along when I stopped for a smoke — the lost driver's. He'd apparently decided on his destination, because he was going fast now, maybe thirty-five or forty, and accelerating.

His destination was me. When the car was about sixty feet away, I realized its headlights were fixed squarely on my mid-torso. Then the driver floored it, and the car came barreling forward. He'd caught me right where he wanted me, in the middle of the road.

But he pulled the trigger just a little too soon. When I saw what was happening, I took a step forward and launched myself onto the median that divided the boulevard in two. It was a frantic, visceral move, nothing I had time to think out or plan. I belly-flopped hard on the concrete but avoided the more serious collision. The side mirror nicked the heel of my right shoe as the car sped past. Otherwise the driver missed me completely.

I heard the car screech to a halt. Nothing happened for a second or two, which was good for me, since I was desperately sucking wind. I still hadn't regained my breath when I heard the car coming back toward me in reverse. I couldn't figure what the driver had in mind, now that I was on the median, but I wasn't going to wait to find out. Wind or no wind, I got up and limped as fast as I could toward the entrance to my apartment. After I'd gone up half the steps to the front door, I turned around to find my assailant. The car was driving off by then.

I made it up to my apartment as quickly as I could, locked myself in, and went to telephone the police. My hands were trembling as I picked up the receiver. It took me a moment to remember the number, but when I did, I started dialing.

I never finished. I decided against it when I realized all the questions I wouldn't be able to answer. I hadn't gotten a good look at the driver and didn't know whether he was young or old, white or Negro. He could've been a she, for all I knew. I also couldn't describe the make or model of the car. The most I could say was it was a dark sedan, probably black or blue. Thousands of cars in the city fit that description.

No one had witnessed the incident, which left no physical evidence. After hearing this, the cops would ask whether I'd been drinking, and I'd have to recount what I'd consumed at the Alcazar. Then they'd recommend an ice bag for my head and remind me to look both ways the next time I crossed the street.

I sat down and tried to make sense of what had happened. Within a few moments, a primary suspect emerged for the attempted hit-and-run. Only days ago, I'd exposed Eugene Bramble as a flit and an adulterer, and his wife was threatening to take him to the cleaners. She could wreck his life, depending upon how brutal she was about it, and I'd made it all possible. It was no surprise if Bramble wanted to exact vengeance on me.

I'd previously had naughty husbands take a poke at me after I'd investigated them. Others sent me threatening letters or left profane messages with Mrs. Skokow. No one, though, had gone to this extreme. Bramble didn't come across as the violent type, but you couldn't tell what a guy might do in his predicament.

Bramble drove a blue '51 Kaiser, if I remembered correctly. That car was larger than the one that tried to do me in had looked. But it could've been him, I supposed, and probably was. Bramble was the only person I could think of who'd want to flatten me into a flapjack.

For an instant, I wondered whether the Forsythes were behind it all, trying to end my inquiry into Maury Sorin's murder. I quickly dismissed the notion. Judith's case was a tempest in a non-existent teapot. My ex-in-laws were bastards, but they weren't going to rub me out for investigating nonsense. Besides, they'd have to know what I was doing before they tried to kill me for it. Of the people I'd interviewed, only Rufus could have ratted me out, and I didn't believe he'd done so, given what I knew about him and how he felt about the Forsythes.

It took me about an hour to get over the shakes. I'd been terrified, but eventually I became angry. Bramble would get his, if I had anything to say about it. I considered driving over to his factory in the morning and confronting him. By the time I fell asleep at

6:30 A.M., the whole incident started to seem slightly unreal and more than a little ridiculous.

I awoke to a ringing telephone four hours later. "It's late, Boss," Mrs. Skokow bellowed over the line. "Why aren't you here?"

"I'm painting my toenails," I told her. "I'll be right in."

Eleven

WHEN I GOT to the office, I called Eugene Bramble. He didn't give me the warmest of greetings.

"You're a goddamned son-of-a-bitch," he said. "They ought to shoot peeping toms like you."

"Or run us over. That was quite a stunt you pulled last night."

"I don't know what you're talking about," Bramble said. "Fuck you just the same."

"Save the sweet talk for your brother-in-law. I'm just calling to warn you the next time you try something that stupid, I'll break your neck."

"Fuck you, Gold," Bramble repeated. Then he hung up.

Mrs. Skokow buzzed me over the intercom a few minutes later. "Somebody's on the telephone," she said in a teasing voice. "It's Judith Sorin..."

Somehow Mrs. Skokow had figured out that I was carrying a torch for our newest client. In her own good-hearted, tactless way, she was giving me the business for it.

"I've got good news, Mr. Gold," Judith told me after I picked up the receiver.

"Great."

"You remember I told you about Nancy Debevec, my father's secretary. She left town to protect herself from the Forsythes. You said she'd be the easiest way to find out who 'F.G.Z.' is."

"I think she would be," I said.

"Well, I've got a telephone number for her. She's in Chicago."

"Did you try to call her?"

"I thought I'd leave that up to you," Judith said.

Fifteen minutes later, I was introducing myself, person-to-person, to Nancy Debevec. "I know who you are," she interrupted me. "Judith told me she was going to hire you to look into her father's murder. The two of you are playing with fire."

"You really think Elite had something to do with Mr. Sorin's murder?"

"Whether I do or don't," said Nancy, "I'm not taking any chances."

"Your boss had a client with the initials 'F.G.Z.' who was involved with Elite. Do you remember who that was?"

"I don't want to get mixed up in this business. I thought I made that perfectly clear to Judith."

"Miss Debevec…"

"How'd you get this number, anyway?"

"You're one of the few people who can help me find out what actually happened to your boss."

"That's exactly my point, Mr. Gold," she said. "You know that, and they know that. I'd just as soon keep my mouth shut."

"At least tell me how to get in touch with 'F.G.Z.' —"

"Good luck with that," she said.

"Is it true your boss didn't keep a file on this case?"

"I've got nothing to say," she said.

"Well, that's saying something in itself."

"You're grasping at straws, Mr. Gold," she said. "You'll have to get your information elsewhere." With that she hung up the telephone.

I wrote out a memo of the conversation and put it in the file. The content wouldn't have varied much had I interviewed a lamppost. I did note that Nancy Debevec seemed genuinely frightened of Elite, and clearly suspected the company of having a hand in Maury Sorin's murder. That deduction didn't amount to much. She could've been susceptible to conspiracy theories, for all I knew. She could've been just plain wrong.

My star witness wasn't talking. If the Forsythes had killed Maury Sorin, their secret was safe with Nancy Debevec.

TWELVE

I HAD AN APPOINTMENT on Wednesday to interview Stuffleben, the off-duty cop who'd killed Maury Sorin's killer. He agreed to meet me at his apartment in Mansfield at 5:15, after his shift ended. It would take a couple of hours to get there, so I left the office around 2:30.

I turned on the radio once I got out of downtown, but it didn't hold my interest. I was thinking about Dr. Braunstein for the umpteenth time since our meeting at the Alcazar.

I owed the man a lot. He'd managed to reassemble my life when all the parts seemed irreparably broken. While I didn't really get to know him during my time on the couch, I hardly saw him as some duplicitous bomb-throwing Bolshevik. Still, he was going to be deported on those grounds, sure as shooting, if he didn't hire an attorney. There was no such thing as do-it-yourself justice, especially in a case like his. The government would be loaded for bear at the Sixth Circuit, and would present its arguments before sympathetic judges. Braunstein would have to find counsel almost as good as Maury Sorin to have any chance of sticking around.

I told myself I couldn't really help him. But that was a self-serving lie. I could scout out lawyers who might be willing to take on his case. I could help him cover the legal fees he'd have to pay in getting new counsel, and solicit others to do likewise. If worse came to worst and Braunstein ended up representing himself, I could assist in preparing his argument.

Helping Braunstein, however, would put my own neck on the line. In the current climate, sympathizing with a suspected Communist was just as bad as actually being one. The government couldn't deport me, but it could make my life miserable in any number of ways if I got branded a fellow traveler.

I had no interest in martyring myself for Dr. Braunstein. Fortunately, he hadn't asked for my assistance. He expected nothing from me. I could walk away with a clear conscience.

But my conscience wasn't clear; by doing nothing, I felt I'd be throwing Braunstein to the wolves. I was annoyed that I just couldn't let the matter drop. I wanted to do — or not do — as I pleased without debating myself over the right and wrong of it.

It was already after 5:00 when I finally pulled into Mansfield. I didn't know the town too well and had only a vague idea of where to find his apartment. Somehow I ended up in the right neighborhood, and asked for directions from a lady who recognized Stuffleben's address. I arrived just about on time.

The place had seen better days. It was a rectangular brick box, with two chimney stacks that were stubs of their original selves. The exterior was covered with thick black soot. Some of the windows had no shutters, and at least a fourth of the wood shingles had disappeared from the roof. A sign reading "Rooms Available" hung crookedly from a post on the front lawn.

I had to step over a bicycle with two flat tires on the way to the front door, which was unlocked and part-way open. No one answered the bell. After the third ring, I just went in.

"Hello!" I called. "Anybody home?"

Right then a brown and white chihuahua came prancing down the hallway from the back of the house. The dog's nails made quite a racket on the wood floor. The pooch stopped about six feet in front of me, paused for a moment, and then let out a high-pitched yip-yip-yip that curdled my blood. As it turned to make its exit, a tall gray-haired woman came toward me with a spatula in her hand.

"All right, Victor, all right. What's all the fuss?"

"I'm the fuss," I said.

"Who are you?"

"I'm here to see Sergeant Stuffleben."

"You that reporter fella he was telling me about?"

"That'd be me," I said.

"How'd you get in here?"

"The front door was open. I just came in."

The woman grunted. "Somebody must've forgot to shut it," she said.

She told me which room on the second floor was Stuffleben's. On my way up the stairs, she asked whether I was staying for supper. "It's meatloaf and succotash," she said. "That's what we have on Wednesdays."

"I'll have to let you know," I said as I ascended the stairway.

"It's a buck and a quarter. Paid in advance."

Stuffleben opened the door before I reached his room. "You Gold?"

"That's me," I said.

"I heard you walking down the hall. Come on in."

Stuffleben apparently had just gotten out of the tub. He was barefoot and bare-chested, with a towel wrapped around his waist. He looked to be about my age. He was average height and extremely muscular in his upper half. His shoulders were broad and thick, so much so they made his head seem small by comparison.

"You drive down from Cleveland?" he asked.

"Yep."

"How long'd it take you?"

"A couple of hours. I stopped once."

"No one believes me, but I once made that drive in an hour and thirteen minutes. Without the sirens and the flasher."

"Semper fidelis," I said as I pointed at the growling bulldog tattooed on Stuffleben's left bicep under the letters "U.S.M.C." When he didn't respond, I asked whether he'd seen action during the War.

"I was never in the service," he said. "They wouldn't take me, on account of a heart murmur."

"Then why...?" I dropped the question before finishing it.

I inspected the apartment while Stuffleben put on the suit he pulled from his closet. It was a dirty, dingy one-room flat with a rusted tin sink. Cigarette butts and ashes lay everywhere on the torn green carpet. A half-smoked cigar sat on the nightstand next to a half-full bottle of beer and an issue of *Argosy* with part of its cover torn away. The bed was unmade. Stuffleben's pillow had no pillowcase, and his sheets were yellow-tinged and paper thin. The place needed a good airing out. It smelled like the washroom at a bus station.

"How long have you lived here?" I asked Stuffleben.

"Since I joined the Mansfield force. Two years next month."

"Where were you before?"

"Galion Police Department."

"That's right next door," I said. "You didn't have to move too far."

"I didn't move at all," Stuffleben said. "I still got my house in Galion. I'm there on the weekends with the wife and kids."

"Why this place, then?"

"It's easier for me to stay in town when I'm working. Plus I'm closer if they need me for an emergency."

I spotted a .45 on the dresser next to a ring of keys and some loose change. I asked Stuffleben if that was the gun he used to shoot Grubb.

"Grubb? So we're starting the interview. Yeah, that's the gun I used."

"Was he the first man you'd ever shot in the line of duty?"

"He was the third," said Stuffleben. "But only two of them died. Aren't you going to take notes for the story?"

I'd momentarily forgotten about my alias as crack reporter for *True Crime Detective*. I pulled a pencil and notepad from my inside coat pocket and scribbled something down. Then I asked Stuffleben to describe what had happened the morning Maury Sorin got killed.

"I was lucky," he said. "I just happened to be in the right place at the right time."

"How close were you to the gunman?"

"Pretty damn close. Maybe twenty feet."

"You could've gotten shot yourself."

"I wasn't thinking about that," Stuffleben said with a stiff upper lip.

"Did you actually see Grubb shoot Mr. Sorin?"

"I saw the whole thing."

"What exactly did Grubb do?" I asked.

"He was screaming at the guy. He said he wanted all his cash and told him to fork it over. Then he took his gun and shoved it right against the guy's head."

"Did you have a chance to shoot Grubb before he killed Sorin?"

"I suppose maybe I did," Stuffleben said after pausing. "But by the time I figured out what was going on, they were too close together and I didn't think I had a clear shot, so I yelled at Grubb to stand down instead."

"That's interesting, and it's an exclusive for the magazine. Did you tell the police about it?"

"I'm sure I did. I must've."

"I wonder why they left it out of their report. What specifically did you yell at Grubb?"

"I told him to drop his weapon, I think," said Stuffleben.

I knew from what I'd read that Stuffleben had told the police he was up the block when Maury Sorin got shot, and came running when he heard the gun go off. Most likely, the revised version he was feeding me now was just his attempt to embellish his heroics for the pages of *True Crime Detective*. It was a meaningless lie, but I didn't feel like letting it slide. I'd already decided I didn't like Stuffleben.

He walked over to his dresser and pulled nearly half an inch of papers from the top drawer. "You should take a look at these," he said, handing over an assortment of clippings, snapshots, letters, and commendations celebrating his valor in gunning down Grubb.

"I've seen most of these already," I told him as I shuffled through the stack. "You're going to be the star of our feature, too. I'm just asking about the stuff that wasn't in the newspapers. I'm looking for a fresh angle."

"Okay, I guess."

"You were in Cleveland that morning on assignment?"

"That's right," he said.

"You told the Cleveland police you were staking out a dice game a Mansfield gambling ring was running."

Stuffleben nodded.

"Did the game go all night?" I asked.

"They were still playing when I left in the morning."

"Why'd you leave?"

"I'd seen what I came to see," he said.

"Did you ever arrest the guys you were trailing?"

"Not yet," Stuffleben said. "The investigation's still going on."

"These must be some high rollers," I said.

"Those mugs? They're penny-ante punks."

"Where was the game?"

"At one of the hotels near where the shooting was," said Stuffleben, crossing and then uncrossing his arms.

"Do you remember the name?"

"Not offhand," he replied curtly.

My reaction to Stuffleben's tale was the same as when I'd heard it from Lieutenant Monachino at the police station. A country cop doesn't leave his jurisdiction overnight chasing small-time gamblers without making a pinch. Stuffleben might have been in Cleveland for recreational purposes, or he might have come for romance. But he certainly wasn't there on any sting operation.

As Monachino had conceded, the Cleveland P.D. hadn't necessarily bought Stuffleben's cock-and-bull story, but Stuffleben's reasons for being in town didn't make any difference to them. The Cleveland cops just wanted to know what happened at the murder scene, regardless of the circumstances that brought Stuffleben there.

Stuffleben sat at the foot of the bed polishing his shoes as the interview continued. He told me he'd immediately diagnosed Grubb as "high on reefer" and "liable to do anything", and weighed all his options before shooting to kill. He said he'd desperately tried to resuscitate Maury Sorin and bloodied his hands in the attempt. Stuffleben gave his spiel with the flair and sincerity of a door-to-door

Bible salesman.

"Are we about done?" he asked when he came up for air. "I've got an appointment at 6:15 and can't be late."

"Almost," I said. "I wanted to ask you about Elite Motors..."

Stuffleben dropped the oxford he was putting on his left foot. "What?" he said.

"Elite Motorworks. I wanted to ask—"

"Is that what this interview's really about? I should've known, goddamn it."

Stuffleben walked over and pushed me in the chest with two hands.

"You're a roach, pal," he said. "Elite Motors! There's nothing to that story and never was. You made a big mistake trying to snow me."

I gathered myself, walked up to Stuffleben, and pushed him twice as hard as he'd pushed me. Stuffleben fell back on the bed.

"You need to calm down, buddy boy," I told him.

"Fuck you." Stuffleben started to get up, but I pushed him down again.

"That was a long time ago," he said, "and it was all a bunch of rumors. Nobody had anything on me."

"What in the hell are you talking about?"

Stuffleben looked at me for a good fifteen seconds without saying anything. I looked right back at him. His face had turned bright red, and beads of sweat showed on his forehead.

"You really don't know?" he asked.

"I haven't a clue."

He paused for a moment, then exhaled loudly. "Hey, pal, sorry about that," he said. "That was a big mistake. I lost my head."

"What did you think I was asking you?"

"I misunderstood, man. It's nothing that has anything to do with this."

"Sounds like somebody put you through the ringer."

"I don't want to talk about it," he said. "I got accused of something I didn't do. It was pure garbage. Why were you asking me about Elite, anyway?"

It took me a while to answer. "It's a little embarrassing," I finally said. "I was trying to impress you. I married into the family that owns Elite, and I wanted to let you know about it. Showing off, I guess."

It was a lame excuse, but it was the best I could come up with on the fly. Fortunately, Stuffleben was thick enough to believe it.

"Yeah. I've heard of Elite," he said. "That must be pretty sweet, having access to all that dough."

Stuffleben morphed into a simpering brown-nose before my very eyes. He lost all interest in his 6:15 "appointment" and practically begged me to stay and have a drink with him. When I said no, he offered to take me to dinner. "We can go any place you like," Stuffleben said. He clearly wanted to make sure his fit of temper didn't jeopardize his hero status in the upcoming article.

I thought better of asking directly about his tie-in with Elite. The man obviously didn't want to tell me, and just as obviously had a short fuse. He also had a well-used .45 sitting on the dresser. I wasn't willing to risk what he'd do if I accurately implicated him in an assassination conspiracy.

"You're not going to mention our little shoving match in the story, are you?" Stuffleben asked when I told him I was leaving.

"I've already forgotten it," I said. I took a rain check on the dinner invitation, shook his hand, and started out the door.

Stuffleben followed. "Let me know if there's anything else you need," he said as we walked down the stairs.

"Will do."

I was sure I'd get rid of him at the front door, but he followed me out. I thought for a moment he was going to walk me all the way to the Schooner.

"So long," he called after I started the engine. The moron was actually waving as I pulled away from the curb and headed out.

Thirteen

I drove to the only restaurant I remembered in downtown Mansfield and took a table at the back. When the waitress came, I ordered the special without knowing what it was, along with two martinis.

"Two?" she asked. "Are you expecting someone else?"

"No," I said. "Just thinking ahead."

I was drinking to wash away the creeps from talking to Stuffleben. He was a slithery louse, someone who seemed constitutionally incapable of doing anything on the up-and-up. He was lying when he gave his revised version of shooting Grubb. He was lying when he explained his reasons for being in Cleveland that day.

And I was sure he was lying about Elite. When I asked him about the company, it was as if I'd jabbed a red-hot poker into an open wound. He'd been part of some scandal involving the company; at some point, he'd done something with or for Elite that put him under the gun. This made it at least conceivable that Stuffleben was again doing the Forsythes' dirty work when he shot Grubb. If so, Judith was on to something in suspecting the Forsythes as her father's killers.

The special was nothing special — lamb chops and mashed potatoes. I concentrated on the two martinis and ordered another to keep them company. Afterwards I was feeling no pain. But I'd drunk too much. I realized it when my neck collapsed from the weight of my head.

I hadn't intended to overindulge, given the long drive back to Cleveland that was awaiting me. I assured myself that I wasn't going to spend the night in Mansfield, no matter what...then it took me three tries to light a cigarette, and I started having doubts. When the waitress brought the check, I garbled my thanks and managed to make it out of the restaurant without bumping into anything. Back on the street, I staggered to the Schooner and stretched out on the back seat.

I thought I'd rest a few minutes, then get up and walk it off. A couple of times around the block, I figured, and I'd be good to go. But I dozed off trying to think of words that rhymed with "Stuffleben" and didn't awaken until hours later, when a policeman tapped on the windshield with his nightstick.

"Sir. Sir. You need to get up."

"I'm up, officer," I answered groggily. "I was just resting for a few minutes."

"You've been out for more than a few minutes. I've been watching."

"What time is it?"

"Almost 9:15."

"Damn," I said. "I'd better be on my way."

"You been drinking?"

"I had a highball at dinner."

"Got a bottle in the car with you?"

"Nope. You can check if you want."

"That's all right," he said. "I looked around in there before waking you up."

As we spoke, I tried to gauge how tanked I was. The prognosis was decent. I felt a little sluggish but otherwise all right.

"Know where I can get some coffee?" I asked.

"There's a diner three blocks up the street. Place called Earl's. He's open till 10:30, unless he closes early tonight."

I got out of the back seat and walked to the front of the Schooner. I must've been teetering a little, because the cop asked whether I was really all right. I promised that I was, plopped down in the driver's seat, and departed.

I found the diner and had three cups of joe. With them came political commentary from the man behind the counter, who considered it his civic duty to explain all the reasons why I had to support the Eisenhower/Nixon ticket in November. I only managed to slow the guy down by telling him I was Canadian and couldn't vote for Ike no matter how much I liked him. When my new friend started complimenting the Prime Minister's fight against the Red Menace, I paid my tab and left.

FOURTEEN

IT WAS AFTER 10:00 when I finally got on the road. I was wide awake now, and impatient to get home, but it started raining, so I had to go easy on the gas pedal. The radio didn't help pass the time. All I could find was Kay Starr spinning her "Wheel of Fortune" and Vera Lynn chortling "Auf Wiederseh'n." I could take that for only so long.

I was left to speculate about Stuffleben's connection to Elite. The more I thought about it, the more skeptical I became about its actual significance. Stuffleben was an oafish thug. He might've run a penny-ante flimflam for some Elite dealership or parts sup-plier, but I couldn't envision anything more elaborate than that. The Forsythes never would've trusted someone like him to execute a sophisticated caper — not with their riches and reputation on the line, as they would have been if they'd orchestrated the assassination of Maury Sorin.

This concession to reality was more a relief than a disappointment. While it would be nice to pin something on Stuffleben and my ex-in-laws, I'd just as soon be done with the whole business. Judith Sorin's assassination story had brought back demons I thought I'd vanquished forever. Although Braunstein had brokered a tenuous truce with them, there was no guarantee what my state of mind would be ten minutes from now. The sooner I could put this case behind me, the better.

The rain had stopped by the time I got back to Cleveland. I saw no point in heading to my apartment — after my extended snooze in the back seat, I wasn't going back to sleep anytime soon. I wasn't going to a bar, either. I'd consumed enough booze for one day, and I felt like working anyway. So the office became my destination. I figured I'd dictate a memo on the interview with Stuffleben and see if Mrs. Skokow had left me any messages.

The night watchman didn't want to let me into the building. "Who is it you say you are?" he asked through his dentures.

"Benjamin Gold. Gold Investigations."

"Sixth Floor?"

"Seventh."

"Why you coming to work now? It's one o'clock in the morning."

"No rest for the weary, Pop," I said. "Sorry to disturb you."

"You ain't disturbing me," he said. "I just don't know why you fellas can't get your work done during the daytime, like normal people."

I rode the elevator up and headed toward my office. They'd polished the floor that night, and it was still a little slippery. Making my way down the hallway, I was thinking that at least there'd be no distractions working at this hour. Then I realized I wasn't alone.

My office door was unlocked and slightly cracked. Peeking in, I saw flashes of light shooting sporadically from the direction of my private office into the unlit anteroom. I opened the door halfway and stood as quietly as I could to listen. I didn't hear any talking, but I could definitely tell there was someone inside.

I rarely carried my gun, which was locked in a safe in the inner office. This was one of the few occasions I regretted not having it on me. Mrs. Skokow, however, kept a pistol in the drawer of her desk. She insisted on doing so, as protection against the "undesirables"

I sometimes attracted as clients. I let her have the gat, but only for show — no bullets allowed. I didn't want her gunning down the delivery boy when he brought the wrong order for lunch.

I slipped off my shoes and tiptoed to her desk. Mrs. Skokow only selectively followed the instructions I gave her. Sure enough, her Colt .32 was fully loaded.

The desk drawer creaked when I opened it, and I thought I'd given myself away. But then my visitors started talking. I could tell they thought they were alone.

There were two of them. "Found anything yet?" asked Number One in a loud whisper.

"Nothing. You?"

"Nothing. These files smell like a dead rat."

"It's the mildew," said Number Two.

The door to my office was about a quarter open. I sneaked over and peeked in. They were working with flashlights at opposite ends of the file cabinets lined up against the far wall, removing one folder at a time and shuffling through a few pages before returning it and taking out another. I could see them because they'd turned on the small reading lamp on my desk.

"How are these things organized?" asked Number Two.

"Alphabetical by year, Einstein," said Number One. "What in the hell have you been looking at?"

"Hands in the air, assholes!"

I barked out my command after slipping into the office and sidling my way along the wall to the light switch. My visitors definitely had not heard me enter. The one on the right threw the file he was holding straight up when the lights came on, as if it were about to explode. Papers scattered everywhere. The one on the left keeled over and grabbed a cabinet handle to keep from collapsing entirely.

They'd already collected themselves by the time they turned to face me. "Looks like you caught us, Mr. Gold," the one on the left said nonchalantly. He was Number One. Number Two was smiling smugly at me.

I couldn't figure out who these guys were. They were dressed more like junior executives than burglars: dark suits, white shirts, shiny black leather shoes. Number One looked to be in his mid-forties, Number Two about ten years younger. Both were slim and clean-shaven and around six-feet tall.

I alternated my aim of the Colt .32 between one man's noggin and the other's. "You need to be careful with that thing," said Number One.

"I still haven't decided whether I'm going to shoot you."

"Nobody's shooting anybody," pronounced Number Two.

"You guys carrying guns?"

They both shook their heads.

"Take off your coats so I can see."

"Listen," said Number One. "We've obviously made a mistake. We're in the wrong place. We haven't taken anything."

"Take off your coats," I repeated.

"Our briefcase is on the desk. You can see it's empty."

I fired a shot into the file cabinet three feet to the right of Number One. Then I shot another bullet three feet to the left of Number Two.

"What do you think this is?" I said. "I'm not a total idiot. I don't know what you came to steal, but you came for something. The police can sort it out when they get here. In the meantime, I intend not to get shot. Take off your goddamned coats so I can see what's underneath."

94

This time Number One and Number Two followed orders. In doing so, they each exposed a leather shoulder holster cradling a gun.

"What do you know," I said. "You're liars as well as thieves."

I motioned toward Number Two. "Take off your buddy's gun and slide it over to me. Then he'll do the same for you."

"Come on," said Number One. "Do you really have to...?"

"We've been through that."

With the holsters in hand, I had Number One and Number Two lie on their stomachs while I went to unlatch the window fronting Euclid Avenue. Once I got it open, I pitched their weaponry down toward the street.

"Now that that's taken care of," I said, "I can arrange for your ride to the precinct."

"You shouldn't have done that, Mr. Gold," said Number One grimly.

I directed my guests to sit with their backs against the wall and their hands in front of them. Then I went to my desk and picked up the telephone.

"You ought to think twice before making that call," said Number Two.

"Oh yeah? Why?"

"Because you're making enemies you'd rather not have."

"I don't know," I said. "You seem like a couple of two-bit hoodlums to me, even if you are well dressed."

"Keep joking," said Number Two.

"Look what's in the pocket of my coat," said Number One. "Maybe then you'll get the picture."

I was sure he was stalling, but with the situation under control, I could afford to play along. There was nothing in the outside pockets.

From the inside I pulled out a badge that read "Federal Bureau of Investigations." At first I thought it might be a prop, although it looked real enough. My skepticism began to fade when I looked over at Number One and Number Two and studied their humorless, impassive expressions. They could've been G-Men, at that.

"The FBI," I said. "What could you possibly want from me?"

"Don't play dumb," Number Two said.

"Obviously, we're looking for your client's file," said Number One.

"Which client?"

"Look, Mr. Gold, you've stayed out of trouble till now, as far as we can tell. And you might have the best of intentions in taking the case. But it's a sucker's move."

"What in the hell are you talking about?"

"Braunstein," blurted Number Two. "Dr. Stanislav Braunstein."

"We understand you're arguing his case at the Sixth Circuit," said Number One.

"Braunstein was my doctor..."

"We know that," snapped Number Two.

"You guys are a couple of geniuses. Braunstein's not my client. I don't even practice law anymore. Look at the door: 'Benjamin Gold — *Investigations*.'"

"You still have your law license, don't you?" asked Number One.

"So what?"

"We know you met with Braunstein. We know you met with the daughter of his former lawyer. We think she came to see you on Braunstein's behalf."

"You guys don't miss a trick," I said. "Next you'll tell me what I had for breakfast."

"Don't let Braunstein talk you into anything," said Number One. "Don't let him tell you it's all some big mistake. He was a member of the Communist Party, both in Europe and in Boston. He may still belong. You can't trust him."

"He probably lost China," I said.

"There's no way Braunstein's walking out of that courtroom," said Number One. "He's a menace, and the quicker he's deported, the better off we'll all be. No need for you to go down with the ship."

"I can't get off a ship I'm not on," I said. "Braunstein never asked me to represent him. I'm not his lawyer, or anyone else's."

"Who are you kidding?" said Number Two.

"Do you honestly believe Braunstein's some subversive radical? Because if you do, you're probably in need of his professional services."

"Now I'll ask you one," said Number One. "Can you absolutely guarantee me that Braunstein is as innocent as you think he is? That he's not still a Communist? That he's not involved in some plan to blow up a factory or assassinate a senator?"

"I'm going to call the police," I said.

I said it, but I was waffling on what to do. I worried that if the cops actually came, Number One and Number Two would identify themselves and explain that they'd broken in to get evidence on a radical subversive I was aiding and abetting. The police would probably end up grilling me.

I sat down at my desk and spent a few moments trying to decide how best to proceed. Number One tried to engage me in conversation, but I ignored him. Eventually I picked up the telephone and dialed the number for time and temperature, just to see how my visitors would react. If they were afraid I was calling the police, they didn't show it.

Ten minutes passed, or maybe more. Finally, I got up and gathered their suit coats off the floor. I removed Number One's badge from his inside coat pocket and got Number Two's from his. Then I returned to the desk, stuffed the coats into the black satchel Number One had called a briefcase, and closed it.

"That bag's bigger than it looks," I said.

I walked to the open window where I'd disposed of the G-Men's guns. "Bombs away," I said and sent the satchel flying.

"You can pick up your things downstairs," I announced. "You're free to go."

"You're a real jerk," said Number Two.

On the way out, Number One pointed to the badges lying on the corner of my desk. "What about those?" he asked.

"My secretary will drop them in the mail first thing in the morning. FBI, Washington, D.C. — Attention Mr. Hoover. It should give your careers a big boost."

I used the .32 to escort the G-Men to the elevator. A few minutes later, I watched out the window as they collected their belongings and headed west on Euclid toward Public Square.

I went to the file cabinets to survey the damage I'd done with my shooting. One of the drawers I'd hit had been practically empty. In the other, I'd murdered the J's through N's from the past three years.

I realized I was still walking around with the Colt in my hand. I removed the magazine from the pistol, cleared it, and returned the gun to Mrs. Skokow's desk drawer. Just then I heard someone coming down the hall. The bottom fell out of my stomach. I figured Number One and Number Two were coming back to thank me for my hospitality.

But I was wrong. Only one set of footsteps was clacking on the tile, and the gait was too slow to belong to either of them.

I opened the office door before the night watchman had the chance to knock. "You all right?" he asked. "Two fellas from that accounting firm thought they heard shots. Said it was coming from your office."

"Shots? Here? In the middle of the night?"

"That's what I thought. Those buzzards must've been drinking. But I thought I'd better come see for myself."

I raised my arms over my head. "No bullet holes here. You're welcome to look around."

"Forget it. You ought to go home, like they did." The old man was shuffling toward the elevator as I closed the door and went back inside.

FIFTEEN

I SPENT THE rest of the night at the office composing a letter to the head of the FBI field office in Cleveland. That's where I decided to send the badges confiscated from Number One and Number Two. The first draft read like a legal brief on illegal searches prohibited under the Fourth Amendment. I tore it up. Then I wrote a blow-by-blow account of what had taken place. I tore that up, too, after getting to the part about the sniper attack on my file cabinets. In the next version, I vehemently denied having anything to do with Braunstein or his court case. I realized I couldn't send that one, either, since it corroborated the pariah status the G-Men ascribed to the Doc.

In the end, I decided to return the badges without any correspondence. The FBI didn't need my commentary to realize its agents had botched the operation.

Their biggest mistake was casting me as Braunstein's new attorney. For all intents and purposes, I hadn't practiced law since I left for the Army nine years ago. I'd been planning on resuming my career at Grimm White upon returning from Europe, but I got the ax, and the crackup prevented me from doing any work at all for the next several years. After Braunstein finally got my head on straight, I applied for positions at more than thirty firms in Cleveland, but got the cold shoulder at each. The word had obviously gotten around that I was damaged goods.

So I hung out my own shingle. Despite my best efforts, I managed to land only one client — a Coast Guard seaman charged with assault and battery after defending himself against an off-duty policeman in a barroom brawl. The case seemed straightforward enough, but trial work wasn't like riding a bicycle. My skills had seriously atrophied in the years since I'd last set foot in a courtroom. Atrophied — or vanished completely. My examination of witnesses was ponderous and dull, my arguments and objections dull and often practically unintelligible. As the deputies led the seaman out of the courtroom in handcuffs at the end of trial, I saw my legal career exiting with him. I'd lost my edge, and it wasn't coming back.

I still had to earn a living. Not working and the cost of psychoanalysis had depleted my savings and then some. If I didn't find a source of income soon, I'd be back replacing divots at the Country Club.

As fate would have it, I received a call the next week from Sig Danziger, my law-school buddy with his own practice. "I've got an assignment for you," he said. "It's a little unconventional."

"At this point, I'll take anything."

"I've got this honey of a case, and it's leaving town on me. Literally."

"What do you mean?"

"My client got hit in a crosswalk by the wife of a stockbroker," Sig explained. "A real muckety-muck from Chagrin Falls. An eyewitness saw the whole thing. I've got her dead to rights."

"So what's the problem?"

"The eyewitness ain't gonna show for trial," said Sig. "The stockbroker got to him. Instead of testifying, the witness and his wife will be in Havana for the week, all expenses paid plus plenty of pocket change."

"How do you know this?"

"The guy straight-out told me. He's not the brightest."

"You could have him subpoenaed."

"Subpoena nothing," said Sig. "He's gonna lose his memory if I drag him into court. He'd have no incentive then but to stick it to me, the lawyer who robbed him of his sweet payday."

"So what are you going to do?"

"They bought him off, so I've got to up the ante," said Sig. "I've gotta make it worth his while to take his vacation right here in sunny Cleveland and show up in court. The case is worth that much, Benny."

"I presume you know what you're doing."

"It's got to be done. I've figured it from all angles."

"So what do you need from me?"

"You've got to do the deal," Sig said. "I can't be the one, and he can't know I'm behind it. His ignorance is my bliss."

"How stupid is this schmuck? Who besides you would pay him to stay in town and testify?"

"You're right," Sig conceded. "But so what if he knows, as long as I use a cutout? He ain't gonna volunteer that information on the stand, and the opposition ain't gonna ask about it, even if it leaks. They're in the payoff business themselves, so they won't be in any hurry to bring up the topic in court."

"That may be, but —"

"But nothing. I want to stay one step removed. I need a stand-in, and I'm offering you three hundred bucks to be that guy."

I wasn't shocked by the move Sig was planning. My time at Grimm White had shattered any lofty notions I had about the sanctity of the justice system. For all I knew, my former firm had cut the deal Sig was intending to trump.

The payoff may have been business as usual, but I still didn't like the idea of serving as a bagman. The right and wrong of it were easy to figure. But unfortunately, so were the dollars and cents of it. Sig offered me the assignment because he knew I desperately needed the cash. I didn't really have the luxury of turning him down.

I contacted the witness easily enough, and negotiated our agreement over his fifteen-minute lunch break at the bowling alley where he worked. Sig was a satisfied customer, so much so that he funneled other odd jobs to me over the following weeks. I photographed the narrow apartment hallway where one of his clients tripped on the carpet and broke her hip. I took statements from victims of food poisoning at a catered banquet in Rocky River. I tracked down a deadbeat who moved house overnight without paying what he owed Sig's cousin for cleaning his carpets.

This work enabled me to meet my expenses. I did even better than that after Sig gave my name to other attorneys who called me with jobs of their own. Within a year, I opened my own small office with "Benjamin Gold — Investigations" painted on the door.

The G-Men had confused me with my former self in thinking I was taking over as Braunstein's counsel. Even at that, they mistook me for the kind of lawyer who could handle a situation like his. My experience at Grimm White hadn't included immigration disputes. The cases on my résumé were about money, and money only — not citizenship rights, due process, freedom of association, or any of the other higher notions that occupied Maury Sorin's attention.

Any similarity between his practice and mine had been remote and purely coincidental.

I wondered if I ever could convince the FBI of the reality of the situation. Number One and Number Two seemed doctrinaire and dogmatic. They wouldn't be satisfied until I forswore further involvement in a case that wasn't mine, betraying a client who'd never hired me in the first place.

It was almost nine o'clock when I concluded my abortive letter-writing campaign to the local FBI chief. Mrs. Skokow sashayed in about fifteen minutes later.

"Good thing I loaded that gun," she said when I told her about the late-night invasion.

"Load it again," I said, "and the next time I'll use you for target practice."

"You don't mean that. Let me go see the damage you've done to our files."

Mrs. Skokow headed toward the cabinets at the back of the office. I grabbed my hat and headed for the door.

Sixteen

On Thursday night I met Judith for dinner in Little Italy. Mrs. Skokow had arranged the date. Judith called the office that morning around 11:00 to see whether I'd made contact with Nancy Debevec. Mrs. Skokow told her I was "indisposed" and didn't know when I'd be available. The conversation went back and forth, one thing led to another, and Mrs. Skokow somehow worked the situation around to dinner at 7:15.

I went home intending to clean up and get a couple hours of shut-eye before returning to the office. But I never made it back downtown. After Mrs. Skokow let me know about my evening rendezvous with Judith, I went to the barber shop for a trim, then headed to the May Company to buy a new shirt and tie.

I was more than a little ashamed of myself, primping for the meeting like a schoolgirl getting gussied up for the senior prom. But my crush on Judith hadn't abated over the course of the week. If anything, it had gotten worse. I continuously replayed our conversation in my office, looking for signs she was as interested in me as I was in her. I imagined heartfelt conversations between the two of us, imbuing her with all the fineness and intelligence and compassion I associated with her father. This was a fantasy, of course. I knew that, but I was holding out hope it would somehow come true.

Mrs. Skokow had reserved a table for us at the Golden Bowl. It was probably the best place in Little Italy, and certainly my favorite, but it wasn't an appropriate choice for the evening. The restaurant's configuration and its large Friday-night crowd would make it hard for me to keep tabs on the FBI agents I expected to crash the party. I figured I'd be under regular surveillance after the early-morning festivities at my office. That didn't make me happy, but I didn't see any way of preventing it. The best I could do was keep an eye on whoever was keeping an eye on me.

Angelini's on Murray Hill would better serve my purposes. It had a large dining room but not many tables — Mama Angelini ran the kitchen by herself and could only handle so many orders at once. No matter where we sat, I'd be able to see everyone who came and went. The food wasn't half bad, either.

I would've called Judith to tell her about the change in venue, but I didn't have her number at home and didn't think to call the office for it until after Mrs. Skokow had left for the day. Angelini's was just a short way up the street and around the corner from the Golden Bowl, so I figured I'd meet Judith out front and we could walk over.

Little Italy spanned a few blocks on the near east side, right next to Western Reserve College. It was only about a five-minute drive from my apartment. I found a parking spot on Mayfield near Euclid, then worked my way back up to the restaurant.

It was another warm evening, but a steady breeze coming off the Lake made it tolerable. Waiting for Judith, I looked around for possible G-Men. No one I saw fit the bill.

Judith pulled up in a taxi right at 7:15. I started walking over as her legs swung out of the back door. I could see she wasn't wearing any stockings.

"Miss Sorin," I said. "Thanks for meeting me."

She had on a light blue blouse and a red skirt that billowed to her knees. Her hair was down and topped by a white straw bucket hat, which she had tilted to the left.

"I'm hungry," she said as she headed for the entrance of the Golden Bowl. "Let's get a table."

"Slight change in plans," I said. "We're going somewhere else."

"Pardon?"

"Angelini's is a short walk from here. I think you'll really like it."

"Isn't that place a dive?" Judith asked.

"Only to the uninitiated."

"Mr. Gold, I fully intend to pay for my own meal, and yours, too. We're meeting for business."

I took her left hand in both of mine. "It isn't the money," I told her. "We need to go somewhere else. I'll explain it to you during dinner."

Dark shades covered the windows at Angelini's, which occupied one corner of a stand-alone building with apartments on the second floor. The door to the place was small and made of unpainted wood that was warping. The sign above was chipped and faded — only someone who knew beforehand what it said could decipher it. Two of the rubbish cans in the alley next to the restaurant had tipped over. A thick brown liquid oozed from one of them.

"It doesn't look like this place is even open," Judith said.

"It's open."

We went inside and walked down a short hallway decorated with beer signs and autographed photos of presumptive celebrities who patronized the place. I didn't recognize any of them.

The lights were dimmed in the dining room. There were twelve tables arranged symmetrically in three parallel rows, each with a checkered tablecloth and a red centerpiece that looked like a distended candlestick. Two of the tables were occupied. Toward the back, an older couple almost certainly from the neighborhood sat silently waiting for their dinner. In the middle row, three college-aged girls were negotiating who-owed-what on the check.

The headwaiter was Mama Angelini's brother-in-law, a short, fat man who'd worked there since the place opened. He approached Judith and me in no particular hurry.

"Evening," I said to him. "Got a table for us?"

"I think I can squeeze you in."

He sat us at the front, in the row furthest from the door. From that vantage point, I wouldn't have to crane my neck to see who came and went.

The headwaiter handed us menus. "We've got linguini with clam sauce tonight for $1.75," he said. "I'd stay away from it. Those clams didn't smell so fresh to me."

"Thanks for the warning," I said.

"You want a bottle of wine?"

"Sure."

"White or red?"

I looked to Judith for an answer, but she didn't say anything, and her face gave no hint of any preference.

"Red, I guess. What have you got?"

"I'll choose," said the headwaiter. "You spending a lot or a little?"

"What the hell," I said. "Let's go for broke."

"I'll be right back."

"I don't think they'll be moving much linguini tonight," I said as the headwaiter walked away.

"Why are we here, Mr. Gold?" Judith responded. "Do you really have a reason?"

"Do you know a psychiatrist named Braunstein?" I asked. "He was a client of your father's."

"What's that got to do with it?"

"Everything, actually."

"I didn't know my father's clients," Judith said. "He never discussed his work with me."

"So you haven't spoken to Braunstein about finding a lawyer to replace your dad?"

"I told you. I don't even know the man."

"I'm glad to hear it," I said. "That makes this mess a little less messy."

I explained who Braunstein was and how her father had saved him from deportation. Then I told her about my meeting with the Doc earlier in the week and the FBI break-in at my office.

"They specifically mentioned you," I said. "They somehow know I'm doing a job for you, and they think it might have something to do with Braunstein."

"That's frightening," Judith said. "We're living in an honest-to-God police state."

"From here on in, I've got to assume that where I go, they go — at least till I can convince them I've got nothing to do with Braunstein's case. I need to be in places where I can tell who might be listening. That's why I wanted to come here instead of the Golden Bowl."

The headwaiter returned to the table and began opening the bottle he'd brought with him. "You want to sniff the cork?" he asked me.

"Not especially."

"Some people insist."

The headwaiter poured a glass of wine for Judith and one for me, then took our order. As he waddled toward the kitchen, we resumed our conversation.

"Maybe I should help Dr. Braunstein get a new attorney," Judith said.

"Why would you do that?"

"It might reflect badly on my father if one of his last clients had to go into court on his own. I think Dad would expect me to help the man."

"It'd be best all around if you stayed out of it. Trust me."

Judith didn't seem convinced. She took a perfunctory sip of wine and repositioned the napkin on her lap. There was an uncomfortable silence.

"Let's talk about your case," I said. "Mrs. Skokow said you wanted to know about my conversation with Nancy Debevec."

"You spoke to her. Good."

"Not good. She refused to talk to me."

"Okay," said Judith curtly as she shifted in her chair. "I don't know why you couldn't have told me that over the telephone."

"I probably could have, but there are a couple of other tidbits to report. Grubb — the man who shot your father — came into a lot of dough right before the murder. Even bought his mother a car. He didn't need to be pulling stick-ups for cash."

"What did the police have to say about that?"

"Apparently they never found out about the money or the new car."

"Your in-laws must've paid him . . ."

"Ex-in-laws," I corrected her. "He could've won the Irish sweepstakes, for all we know. But it is curious."

"He didn't win the Irish sweepstakes," said Judith.

"I interviewed the old lady who was at the scene, but that was a zero. She didn't know anything. It was different with Stuffleben. I went to talk to him yesterday."

"Who's Stuffleben?"

"He's the cop who killed the killer," I said. "When we first met, you told me there was something phony about his being on the scene of your father's murder."

"Uh huh."

"Well, there was. He's a Mansfield cop, not a Cleveland cop. He said he was in town that morning doing undercover work on some Mansfield gambling racket. But he's not a detective, and even if he were, he wouldn't have come all the way here to stake out a dice game."

"The Cleveland police must've realized that."

"I think they did," I said. "They probably figured Stuffleben was in town seeing his girlfriend or something. It didn't matter to them why he was here. He was the hero of the story: He shot a vicious, crazed, maniacal killer."

"So we're nowhere with him, too."

"I haven't told you everything yet," I said. "When I was finishing the interview, I asked whether Elite was mixed up in the shooting. Well, as soon as I mentioned the company's name, Stuffleben blew a gasket. I mean he really lost it — came across the room and shoved me hard. Said the story about him and Elite was a lot of hooey and wanted to bean me for bringing it up."

"What story?" Judith asked.

"I never got that out of him. But it shouldn't be too hard for me to find out."

"Maybe it's my father's murder."

"That wasn't what was on Stuffleben's mind," I said after taking a sip of wine. "But who knows? He's got some history with Elite. Maybe the murder's wrapped up in it."

"He's at the murder scene and he's tied in with Elite. It couldn't be pure coincidence."

"Yeah, it could," I said. "I need to do some more digging."

Right then our meals arrived from the kitchen. I'd ordered the veal, she the lasagna. I wasn't hungry but felt obligated to eat, given the praise I'd heaped on the restaurant. Judith worked on the lasagna tentatively, slicing small bits with her fork and knife and chewing them longer than seemed necessary.

"What's the verdict?" I asked.

"Actually, it's better than I thought it would be," she admitted.

"Get out! You're not welcome here no more!"

The headwaiter was yelling at a kid with slick black hair who'd come in with a hot blonde hanging on his arm.

"Come on, Tony," said the kid, who was maybe twenty years old. "I've been eating here forever."

"Not no more you ain't, not after what you pulled the other night."

"Tony —"

"Why don't you take your date to niggertown?" the headwaiter said. "I'm sure they got some fine restaurants over there."

"The place is practically empty. We're just going to take a table in the back."

"Listen, and listen good," the headwaiter said. "This is the last thing I'm gonna tell you. You got ten seconds to turn around and go out that door. If you don't, I'm going in the back to make a telephone call. Then you'll take your teeth home in a doggy bag."

The kid paused for a minute, then turned to leave. "Goddamn it, Tony. You're out of your fucking mind." He and the hot blonde walked out the door.

"What was that?" I asked the headwaiter when he came by our table.

"You wouldn't believe it," he said, "but last Saturday night, that punk brought a shine in here. The place was packed, and he walks in with a big black buck."

"What happened?"

"Nothing. There were too many people for us to do what should've been done. We just fed them and got them out of here as fast as we could."

"I'm glad nothing happened," I said.

"The kid knows better," Tony grumbled as he walked away. "He's lived here his whole life."

Judith was fuming. "That's outrageous," she said. "This isn't Alabama or Mississippi. We should leave."

"Where would we go? It's like that everywhere in Little Italy. The neighborhood's not safe for Negroes. If they come here, there's going to be trouble."

"And you're all right with that?" Judith asked indignantly.

"Of course not. But that's just the fact of the matter."

"I wonder what they'd do if they found out I was Jewish."

I laughed. "They like Jews fine," I said. "Besides, you may be able to pass, but with this nose and face, everybody's got me pegged."

Judith stared at me for a good five seconds without saying anything. Then she looked down at her plate and meticulously cut another sliver of lasagna.

We sat without talking for a few minutes. Then I said, "So I take it you're not voting for Strom Thurmond in November."

"He's not running," Judith replied sullenly. The silence returned.

The headwaiter brought a fresh bottle of wine. He poured me a full glass, which I promptly drank and refilled. Then I tried to break the ice again.

"Read any good books lately?"

She took the question literally. "I'm reading children's fiction at the moment," she said. "I'm looking for stories for my class."

"Class?"

"I'm a fourth-grade teacher at Taylor Elementary, in Cleveland Heights."

"I didn't know that," I said. "I think my nephew goes there."

I expected some response, but she didn't even grace me with a perfunctory "that's nice" or even an "oh." If the woman wasn't talking about her case, she didn't want to talk to me at all. At first I'd thought the change in restaurants had soured her mood. But that wasn't it. Judith was clearly signaling her desire to end the evening as quickly as possible. That revelation inspired me to finish the second bottle of wine post-haste.

"Let me ask you a question, Miss Sorin," I said when I got to the bottom of my third glass. "Why do you find my company so distasteful?"

Her face turned bright red. "I don't know what you're talking about, Mr. Gold."

"Sure you do. Sorry to be so blunt, but you're obviously not enjoying yourself. You don't know me well enough to dislike me as much as you seem to. I just want to know what I did or said."

"I think you're an excellent detective," she said as she straightened in her chair. "You've made good progress on my case, and I'm sure you'll continue to do so. And if I didn't say it before, I'll say it now: I very much appreciate your efforts."

"So you think I'm good at my work. Aside from that, I'm a refugee from a leper colony."

"That's not what I said."

"There's no point in denying it, Judith."

"...Since you insist on asking," she said, "I feel like I was roped into this dinner. Your secretary's not very subtle. She let me know in no uncertain terms that you had more on your mind than just my case, and that was supposed to make me jump for joy. I hate having to go through all this just to talk about what I'm paying you to do."

"Don't you ever go out to dinner?" I asked. "Are you interested at all in men?"

"...Some men," she said. "But I'm selective in whom I see."

"And if you were selecting, you wouldn't be here with me."

"Quite frankly, no."

"Which leads me back to my original question..."

"Why do you care what I think?"

"Because I have more on my mind than just your case. You said so yourself."

"Mr. Gold, you have to know I'm not the only person who's critical of your past," Judith said with her head bowed.

"What the hell is that supposed to mean?"

"Come on," she said. "Everybody knows your story: a kid from the neighborhood who changes his name and converts to Methodism so he can marry into the richest family in the city and take a job where it's 'No Jews Allowed' for everybody else. And you had the audacity to talk to me about 'passing'."

"I was kidding about you passing," I said. "And I never converted."

"The word was that you were on the board of trustees of your church."

"They needed someone with a legal background," I said. "I didn't convert."

Judith stared at me with a disgusted look on her face.

"You might find this hard to believe," I said, "but I loved my wife very much."

"You must've absolutely worshiped her to do what you did."

"The marriage was a mistake," I said. "A horrible mistake that hurt me in ways you can't imagine. Quite frankly, I would've expected more sympathy from a daughter of Maury Sorin's."

"I wouldn't bring him into this," she said. "It doesn't help your case."

"Why do you say that?"

"Because he was a man of principle. He never would have done what you did."

"No disrespect to your father, but everybody makes mistakes," I said. "Even men of principle."

"Of course. But there are certain lines men like my father won't cross. It's a question of integrity — like the Hollywood writers who went to jail rather than informing on their friends."

"So you think I'm the type who'd name names?"

"I don't know what you would do," she said unconvincingly.

"You're talking about ancient history," I said.

"People don't change. Not really."

So there it was, in plain English. I was a gold-digging traitor, a sell-out, a man with a cash register for a heart. When I'd asked what the trouble was, I knew Judith wouldn't respond with a testimonial to my manifest virtues, but I hadn't expected this. She'd had her mind made up about me before we even met, and had no interest in hearing my side of the story. There *was* no "my side" as far as she was concerned.

Now I was the one looking for a quick exit from our little get-together. I caught the headwaiter's eye and motioned for him to come over.

"You two hardly touched your dinners," he said. "If the food was bad, I'll take it back..."

"Not at all," I said. "It's just that we both had a late lunch. The food was fantastic — even better than usual. Tell Mama Angelini I said so."

"She ain't cooking tonight, on account of swollen ankles. It's her cousin Rosalee."

"Well, then, tell Rosalee. And while you're at it, could you bring us the check and call a cab for the lady?"

As he walked away, I looked across the table at Judith. Half of me wanted to pop her in the kisser. The other half wanted to do much worse. She'd performed her hatchet job with an iciness that would've done my ex-father-in-law proud. I briefly thought of quitting her case but dismissed the idea. I didn't want to give her the satisfaction of knowing she'd upset me as much as she had.

I paid the check when it came, then I walked Judith out of the restaurant. Her taxi was waiting.

"I need more money from you," I said coldly as she got in. "I did a lot of work on the case this week, and I went through the retainer and then some."

"Send me a bill. By all means, I'll pay it."

"Great," I said. "It's been a wonderful evening."

Judith pulled the taxi door shut. I watched as the cabbie drove away, then I dragged myself to the Schooner and sat behind the steering wheel for a good ten minutes. Judith had landed some brutal punches. From what she'd said, I wasn't an incorrigible fink only in her eyes — apparently I had a wide reputation for it. It felt like I had no place to hide.

I briefly considered going to Rosie's for some sympathy and understanding, but my humiliation from the previous week was still too fresh. Talking with Dr. Braunstein also crossed my mind, but I decided against that, too. Any conversation with him would be complicated by the obligation I felt to help him with his legal problem. And I didn't like the thought of making two emergency calls in the course of four days, after being out of touch with him for all those years. I decided to just head home.

The telephone was ringing when I walked into the apartment. I could think of only one person who might be calling at that hour: Judith, with some lame, insincere apology she thought she had to offer. I wasn't interested. I didn't answer.

Ten minutes later, the phone rang again. I was already in bed, trying to forget I ever met her. This time she waited eighteen rings before giving up.

Her persistence persisted. When the phone began ringing five minutes later, I grabbed it from the nightstand. "What?" I shouted nastily into the receiver.

"Benjamin?" The voice definitely wasn't Judith's, though at first I wasn't sure whose it was.

"Who is this?"

"Benjamin Gold?"

"This is he. Who are you?"

"Nietzsche said that 'without forgetting, it is quite impossible to live at all.'"

"Jesus. Is that you, Junior?"

"It's me," Junior said. "It's Clay Forsythe."

"Oh my God. Did Elizabeth die?"

He laughed. "No, she's very much alive."

"Then why in the hell are you calling me?"

"You've been asking questions about Elite," Junior said. "Benjamin, we need to talk."

SEVENTEEN

I SAT ALONE in the lobby of Elite Motorworks' executive offices, watching the minutes tick by on the old grandfather clock in the corner. It was past nine o-clock on Monday morning. Junior was more than half an hour late for the appointment we'd made on Thursday night. If he was trying to annoy me by having me cool my heels, he was succeeding.

I recalled my first visit to the office all those years ago. I'd come at the request of Clayton Senior, about a week after I rescued Elizabeth from the clutches of the Chinless Wonder. At the time, the old man didn't know she and I had become an item...

The romance began the day after the showdown with Chinless. I returned home from a doubleheader at League Park to find a brand new Elite sedan parked outside. When I came upstairs into our apartment, Elizabeth was sitting on the living room sofa talking to my father.

"Wash up, Benny," my mother called from the kitchen. "It's time to eat, and we've got company."

I pieced together what had happened from the mealtime conversation. Elizabeth had showed up around three, and asked if she could wait when she found out I wasn't home. My father quizzed her about the redesigned engine Elite was putting into its new line (as if she would have known anything), then showed her a family photo album. With dinnertime approaching, my mother invited her to eat with us, and she accepted.

During the meal, Elizabeth asked my mother how she'd prepared the salmon croquettes, then teased my father about something or other. She was sweet and charming and funny and completely oblivious to the fact that my mother wasn't eating, to make sure there would be enough food for the company. I was mostly holding off, too, for the same reason.

Elizabeth helped clear the table and sat with my father and me while my mother did the dishes. Later, in the living room, she asked my parents about where they'd grown up and how they'd met. My brother Jake wandered in, and he and Elizabeth spent twenty minutes discussing a girl he knew who'd gone to high school with her at Hathaway Brown. It was after eleven o'clock when I finally walked Elizabeth to her car.

I couldn't figure out why she showed up as she had. Only in the movies did country-club debutantes fall for the hired help. Make the hired help a *yid*, and the scene wouldn't survive the cutting room.

Elizabeth picked me up at the Club after work the next night and drove me home. We spent two hours parked in front of the building while she laughed at my self-deprecating jokes. She picked me up again later in the week, and then another time. That last evening we went to an unoccupied servants' cottage next to her parents' mansion and had at it. It was a revelatory night for Elizabeth. She'd never before seen a circumcised penis, though I was pretty certain she'd seen the alternative. She kept talking about my "Jewish thing," as if it had celebrated its own bar mitzvah and fasted on Yom Kippur.

〜

On my first visit to Elite's offices, Clayton Senior had thanked me for coming to his daughter's aid and told me I was a "credit to my race". I knew I wouldn't get the same compliment from Junior this go-round, but I really had no clue as to what he was going to say. Certainly he wouldn't tell me directly how he'd found out about my investigation and why he gave a damn. I hoped, though, that I'd at least get a sense of where things stood from whatever he did deign to share with me.

I was looking forward to it. The nastiness with Judith on Thursday night had lowered the stakes on her case in my mind, and made me less spooked by thoughts of the Forsythes. Seeing Junior would be a diversion of sorts, like taking in a freak show at the circus.

〜

"Come this way, Mr. Gold."

Just when I thought Junior had forgotten about me, a sour-pussed secretary emerged from the door behind the receptionist's desk. I followed her down a long hallway past a string of open offices, each with the same guy in the same gray suit sitting behind the same desk, talking on the telephone or shuffling papers. We arrived at a door with a sign that read "Board Room". When the secretary opened it and turned on the light, no one was there.

"Where's Junior?" I asked.

"Who?"

"Junior. Clayton Forsythe the Younger."

"Mr. Forsythe is finishing up a call," said the secretary. "Can I offer you something to drink?"

"Sure," I said. "Pineapple juice, freshly squeezed if you have it."

"I don't believe we do, sir."

"Freshly squeezed?"

"Pineapple juice, or juice of any kind."

"Not a problem at all. How about a Cel-Ray Tonic?"

"Sir?"

"Dr. Brown's Cel-Ray Tonic. Surely you have…"

"No, sir, we don't."

"Disappointing," I said. "Just bring me Junior, then."

The Board Room looked as big as a basketball court. I counted forty two seats around the stained oak conference table in the middle. There were no windows, and the light emanating from the crystal chandelier had an artificial, antiseptic feel. On the far wall hung a mammoth portrait of Clayton Senior, wearing his signature smirk. The air was stale and warm. I felt a trickle of sweat drip down the back of my neck.

I looked up to find the old man himself standing in the doorway. "They told me you were coming," he said. "I came to see for myself."

Clayton Senior had not aged gracefully. He'd lost a lot of weight since I'd last seen him, and was walking unsteadily. The lenses of his eyeglasses looked as thick as pancakes.

I approached him and extended my hand. He just looked at it, as though I were offering him a rotten tomato.

"Is it Gold or Goldstein now?" Clayton Senior asked.

"Gold. Benjamin Gold."

"Didn't go back to the maiden name, eh?"

"Correct, sir."

"Fine, fine," he said. "I understand you're no longer practicing law."

"No, sir."

"Lose your license?"

"No, sir. Just switched professions."

"Now I remember," he said. "You're some sort of private detective now, is that it?"

"Yes, sir."

"Kind of a dirty business."

"No dirtier than practicing law, when it comes down to it."

"Like being a peeping Tom for a living."

"Tell it to the Pinkertons."

Clayton Senior bellowed a phony guffaw. "Fine, fine," he said. "If you say so."

"...So, did Therese Laramie ever call the house?"

"What?" The old man wasn't guffawing now. "Who d'you say? Therese Laramie?"

"That's right," I said. "Therese Laramie. She called my office last Tuesday and asked for your home phone number. Thought I was still married to Elizabeth."

"And you gave it to her?"

"Sure. I figured it was all right, since she's a family friend. She said she was in town for her cousin's wedding and wanted to catch up with you and Mrs. Forsythe. Your number's not in the book, but she found mine."

All the blood had drained from Clayton Senior's face. He didn't seem to realize I was lying through my teeth.

Therese Laramie worked as a hatcheck girl at some dinner club in Akron before the War. Clayton Senior knocked her up and paid a tidy little sum to keep her quiet about it — fifty thousand dollars in cash, plus a swanky new house in Los Angeles and the cost of getting rid of the baby. The old man tried to keep the incident under wraps, as he had all the other times. I only found out about it during one of my undercover reconnaissance missions through the Elite files at Grimm White. I distinctly remembered the prickly letter from Therese Laramie's attorney, demanding an extra thousand dollars for the "perversions" she'd had to endure.

"Our number's unlisted for a reason," Clayton Senior said. "We don't want the Therese Laramies of the world calling our house."

"But she knew so much about you and Mrs. Forsythe. She thought for sure you'd want to catch up, and hear about the twins."

"The twins?"

"Yeah. She said she had twins. Just celebrated their tenth birthday. She acted as though you'd met them."

Clayton Senior was wobbling as he turned to go. "Junior will be along shortly," he said.

"I wanted to ask about Elizabeth..."

"She's fine," he said distractedly. "As well as can be expected."

"Please give her my best."

I probably overdid it with the bit about the twins. Clayton Senior had been a shrewd cookie when I was still in the picture. Unless he'd completely lost it, it wouldn't take him long to figure out that I was pulling his leg. Even then, though, he'd wonder how I knew anything at all about Therese Laramie — and what else I knew that I wasn't supposed to. I hoped it worried him. I hoped it worried him a lot.

Junior showed up around ten minutes later. He entered the Board Room with an entourage: a mousy secretary carrying a stenographer's pad, a middle-aged business type in a black suit, and a six-foot-four, muscle-bound gorilla, wearing gray slacks and a tight-fitting blue sport coat.

The years hadn't been as hard on Junior as they'd been on his father. I noticed only a slight paunch and a few flecks of gray on his head. Otherwise he looked pretty much the same as I remembered.

"Good God, Benjamin," Junior greeted me. "You're skin and bones."

"It's nice to see you, too, Junior," I said. "I know you're doing well. I read about the airplane engines you're building for the Air Force."

Junior smiled. "A lot of people saw that article," he said.

"What's next? A rocket ship to the moon?"

Junior ignored my sarcasm. "This is Miss Beckert," he said, pointing to the mousy secretary. "And this is Tom Thomas, our attorney from Grimm White. I've asked him to join us."

"Pleased to meet you," I said. "I don't think you were at the firm when I was there."

The lawyer gave me an expressionless nod.

"Is your name really Tom Thomas?"

He nodded again.

"Thomas Thomas?"

He finally spoke. "Yes."

"Not particularly creative of your parents," I said. "I won't ask your middle name."

"Have a seat," said Junior. "Let's get down to business."

I pointed at the Gorilla. "Who's he?"

"That's Mr. Stanley. He's the security detail."

"What — are you expecting the boys in the mailroom to riot? Since when do you have a security detail?"

"Since we became a public company," said Junior. "There are protocols for everything. We're not just a family business anymore."

"That's right," I said. "I completely forgot. *Mazel tov*. Elite Motorworks has made it to the New York Stock Exchange."

"Twenty-five hundred stockholders at last count," said Junior.

"You must've made a bundle on that. How much of Elite does the family still own?"

"Fifty-one percent. My mother and father each own seventeen percent. I own eleven, and Elizabeth has the other six."

"Good for Elizabeth. If she gets up the gumption, she can start an insurrection and kick you and your father right out on your duffs."

"I don't think so," said Junior. "Her shares are held in trust."

"Who's the trustee?"

"I am."

"Jesus. Isn't that a little incestuous, Junior?"

"Good God, Benjamin," he said. "That's vile."

The vehemence of his reaction surprised me. I obviously hadn't meant what I said literally.

"Why should a grown woman be under the thumb of her little brother?" I asked.

"You should know the answer to that better than anyone."

I turned to the lawyer. "Did your parents ever explain why they named you Thomas when your last name was already Thomas?"

"Why are you asking about that?" he countered.

"Because I can't get it out of my head. It might've dawned on them they were being a little redundant. Was one of them a parakeet?"

"You're a real comedian," said Junior. "Let's talk about why you're here."

"It's your show," I said.

"We understand you've been asking questions about our company in connection with the murder of Maurice Sorin." Junior looked down at the paper in front of him on the table and pretended to read the last part of what he said — as if he'd never heard of Maury Sorin before this morning.

"I don't know what you mean," I said.

"Yes, you do," said Junior. "You've been claiming to be a reporter and asking people whether Elite had something to do with the Sorin case."

"Who's 'people'? You mean that Stuffleben buffoon from Mansfield?"

"So it's true…"

"What's true?"

"You've been going around implying that Elite Motorworks was somehow involved in the unfortunate death of Mr. Sorin," said Thomas Thomas.

"…Well?" asked Junior when I didn't respond.

"I was just waiting," I said. "I thought Tom-Tom might repeat himself."

"Up yours," said Thomas Thomas.

"You're a Grimm White attorney, sir," I said. "At least say it in Latin."

"You're defaming my company, Benjamin," said Junior. "If you think you can dance your way out of it, you're dead wrong."

"Is he allowed to talk?" I asked, pointing to the Gorilla. "Because he hasn't said a word. Neither has Miss Whosit. I'd like to hear what they think of your lawyer's name."

"The complaint's already prepared," said T-Squared, waving a stack of papers in my direction.

"Complaint? For what?"

"For slander," he said. "For insinuating that Elite Motorworks and the Forsythes killed attorney Maurice Sorin."

"I never insinuated any such thing," I said. "But I certainly thought it."

"We're filing today," Thomas Thomas continued, "unless you agree in writing to cease and desist."

"You know, slander is Junior's favorite tort," I announced to the room. "He once sued a guy at the Club who told his golfing buddies Junior was a . . . well, it's not polite to say in mixed company."

"Stop it, Benjamin," said Junior.

"Turns out the guy himself was exactly what he accused Junior of being . . . We got a nice settlement in that case, didn't we, Junior?"

"Are there any other family confidences you plan on revealing, Benjamin?"

"As a matter of fact . . ." I got up and walked to the corner where the Gorilla was standing. "He's going to think I'm telling you some dark secret," I whispered in his ear with my hands cupped around my mouth. "It'll drive him crazy."

"He told me nothing," the Gorilla said as I went to sit back down.

"Smart boy," I said. "You'll have a better chance of keeping your job if you can convince Junior of that."

"What game are you playing, Benjamin?" Junior asked. "You're in no position to defend a defamation case. We know you have no money. We know the FBI is hounding you."

"How do you know about that?"

"Don't say anything more, Mr. Forsythe," advised Thomas Thomas.

"A slander suit will kill your little business, even if you somehow manage to win in court. Elite Motorworks will go on, no matter what. But you'll be finished, and so will everyone who's associated with you. Think of your brother and his family."

"My brother?" I said. "He and I don't even have the same last name. Suing me for slander has nothing to do with him."

"Still," said Junior, "you're taking a big risk."

Junior presumably knew Jake and I were on the outs, since he seemed to know everything else. That hadn't deterred him from making his threat, and I didn't appreciate it — not one bit. It was one thing for Junior and his lawyer-lawyer to work me over; it was quite another to include my brother, who had nothing at all to do with the matters at hand. It was a sobering reminder of the Forsythes' fundamental ruthlessness.

My chair toppled as I jumped to my feet and slapped the table with my open palm. "You're sick," I said, staring right at Junior.

"Benjamin —"

"You say you're going to sue me?" I interrupted. "Go right ahead, gentlemen. I'll walk over to the courthouse with you right now so you can file the papers while I watch. Let's take a picnic lunch to celebrate the occasion."

"Benjamin..."

"You're not going to court, Junior. You're not going to sue me or anyone else, you little shitbag. You're just bluffing." My voice got louder with each sentence.

"We'll see about that," Junior said.

"You're not going to sue me, because a courtroom's the last place you want to be. Truth is an absolute defense to slander. Here in your own boardroom you can huff and puff all you want, but in court you'll have to answer my questions about what you did to Maury Sorin. You'll have to answer under oath and confront the evidence, and that's something you just can't do. I don't know how, I don't know why, and I'm not sure I even care — but I know for sure you assholes are mixed up in some way with the murder."

"That statement itself is slanderous, Mr. Gold," T-Squared opined.

"So sue me, goddamn it!" I said. "Go ahead and sue, and prove to me that this morning wasn't just some pathetic charade. I'm dead serious. Let's walk over to the courthouse and file. Show me how a powerful public company protects its rights."

Junior fidgeted in his seat. He folded his hands on the table, then removed them to his lap before returning them to their original position.

"We've heard quite enough," he said, as calmly as he could manage. "We've warned you about the consequences of your actions. Mr. Stanley, please escort Mr. Gold to the door."

"I knew it, Junior," I shouted. "I knew you and your idiot lawyer were just playing games."

"Mr. Stanley . . . ?"

The Gorilla walked over and grabbed me by the shoulder. "Let's go, please, Mr. Gold," he said.

"I'm going. I'm going. No need to rumple the suit."

At the elevators, I smiled at the Gorilla and asked him to tell Junior to give his sister my best regards. He looked at me as though I were speaking a foreign language.

EIGHTEEN

I LEFT DOWNTOWN and drove straight to Jake's home on Brockway Road in University Heights, parking three houses away on the other side of the street. I'd staked out the place more than once since my brother moved there several years earlier, trying to catch a peek of him without being noticed.

This time I came to see whether my ex-in-laws had already blown Jake's house to smithereens. I took Junior's threats against my brother seriously — if the Forsythes really had a hand in Maury Sorin's murder, they'd do anything and everything to deter my investigation. Jake created an obvious vulnerability. He was my only remaining family, our estrangement notwithstanding. The Forsythes knew they could get to me by going through him.

I sat for a few minutes watching Jake's house and assured myself that everything was in order, at least for the time being. With no obvious disaster in progress, I got ready to leave. But then Jake's son, David, came down the driveway on a two-wheeler. He'd gotten noticeably taller since my last visit. The bike was bright red and slightly too big for him. I figured it had been a birthday present.

David pedaled on the sidewalk until he was beyond the view of his parents' front window. He then began bolting into the street for one-house intervals, going down one driveway and up the next. I smiled. This was what passed for derring-do for a six-year-old.

David worked his way up to Cedar Road in this fashion, then turned around and headed back. He was three houses closer to home when I saw a blue Buick Roadmaster turn onto the street. I didn't think much of it, and still didn't when I saw David make another foray into the street. The car was at least fifty feet behind him on the opposite side of the road. The Buick, however, blasted its horn for a good three seconds after coming to a screeching halt. The commotion made me jump and bang my head on the roof of my car.

The driver of the Buick hit his horn for another two-count before emerging. He was a short old man with white hair whose posture was distinctly hunched. He wore a pea-green cardigan sweater, which he had buttoned despite the summer heat.

"What in the hell were you doing?" he screamed at David. "You nearly got us killed."

David dropped his bike on the sidewalk and faced the old man, as motionless as a statue.

"I've seen you around," the old man snarled. "You live on this street."

David said nothing, which made the man even more irate.

"Goddamn it, boy. I don't know why you were in the street, but your parents and I are going to have a talk about it."

"That's enough, grandpa."

I'd gotten out of my car and walked over to the scene of the phantom crime.

"Who are you?" asked the old man.

"A disinterested bystander," I said. "I saw the whole thing. Nothing happened."

"The boy darted out in front of me. I had to slam on my brakes."

"You weren't anywhere close to him," I said.

"He's a troublemaker, that kid."

"Troublemaker? He's six years old."

"He nearly caused an accident."

"You were on the other side of the street," I said. "Maybe you're too old to be behind the wheel."

At this point David turned and made a beeline for home, leaving his bike where it lay. The old man shook his head disgustedly. "Now I'll have to find him," he said.

"Why don't you go run over a puppy instead?" I said. "*Farbissiner.*"

"What did you call me?"

"*Farbissiner. Alter kacker.* Nasty old fart."

"I understand what you're saying, smartass."

"You must be Jewish then," I said. "That makes me an anti-Semite *and* a smartass."

The heady repartee continued a little while longer, until Jake's wife, Miriam, came down the street with an infant cradled in her arms.

"What happened, Mr. Levine?" she asked the old man.

"That was your boy, wasn't it?"

"I'm sorry to say it was."

"He was riding in the street and came out of nowhere. I had to hit the brakes to avoid a collision."

"Nonsense," I said. "The kid was barely in the street, and this guy was a mile away."

Miriam shot me an incredulous look. "Don't lie, Benny," she said. "That doesn't do David any good."

"You know this guy?"

"Not really," said Miriam. "He's my husband's brother. He didn't expect me to recognize him."

"A *disinterested bystander,*" sneered the old man.

"He thought he was helping," said Miriam. She apologized for David after apologizing for me, and asked the old man whether he'd been hurt. He used the opening to give a detailed description of his gallant struggle with sciatica and arthritis. Miriam listened sympathetically and then promised a hard time for David when Jake got home. It was music to Mr. Levine's ears. He got back into his car and drove off — slowly — a contented man.

"He doesn't like children," Miriam explained.

"Apparently not," I said. "How do you know who I am?"

"I've seen your picture, and we've seen you around. For a private investigator, you're not much of a spy."

"What do you mean?"

"You think I haven't noticed when you're out on the street watching the house? It's been three times at least."

"I know you saw me the one time," I said. "Jake must've seen me, too."

"He didn't, but I told him you were there, and I insisted we invite you in. Then you drove off like a madman."

The baby whimpered.

"This is your niece," Miriam said. "Rachel, say hello to your Uncle Benny."

"She's beautiful."

"Take a good look. The way you and Jake are going, you won't see her again until God-knows-when." The kid squirmed and kicked as I leaned over to give her a kiss.

"Help me take the bike back home," Miriam said. "Then you can tell David who you are."

"Does he know he has an uncle?"

"Sure." Miriam smiled. "We talk about you all the time. 'Uncle

Benny used to pick his nose just like that.' 'Your room's a pigsty, just like Uncle Benny's.'"

"It's nice to be remembered," I said.

When we got to the house, I rolled David's bicycle into the garage and joined Miriam on the front stoop. "Come on in," she said.

"I don't think I'd better. Jake wouldn't like it."

"Maybe not. But he's at work."

"Why doesn't David come out here to say hello?"

"Have it your way."

Miriam called to her son through the screen door. When he came outside, he hid behind his mother's hip after shaking my hand. I understood why he was a little afraid after hearing me joust with Mr. Levine.

Miriam handed me the baby after David went back inside. "Take her for a minute," she said.

"Miriam…"

"For God's sake, Benny, she's not a china doll. Just sit down and hold her in your lap. She won't break."

I did as I was told. Miriam reached into the front pouch of her apron and pulled out a pack of Winstons. "You can give her back in a minute," she said after lighting up.

I was extremely uncomfortable. It felt like I was cradling a lump of jello that might slip away at any second. Every time the kid fidgeted, I tensed up and fought the impulse to hold on for dear life. Somehow, the baby and I both survived until Miriam finished her smoke.

"Seriously, Benny, when are you and Jake going to put an end to this?" Miriam said. "It's time already. Kids grow up fast, and you're going to miss it. It's not fair to them. I have just the one sister, and she lives in Philadelphia. You're their only family in town."

"This isn't the way I want it," I said.

"Then do something. I've tried with Jake, but he won't make the first move. You're the big brother. You're going to have to do it."

I shrugged my shoulders.

"Or you could just go on spying on each other for the rest of your lives," Miriam said. "That makes a lot of sense."

"What do you mean, 'spying on each other'?"

"Just what I said," said Miriam. "You sneak over here, checking up on us. And Jake's got that Damiani boy watching you."

"The Damiani boy? Luigi?"

"Jake calls him 'Louis'. Thirteen, fourteen-year-old who lives in your building. He gets a few dollars a week to let us know what you're up to. You had to have known."

"I didn't. The kid's a better dick than I am."

"It's been going on for at least two years," said Miriam.

"I can't believe I never picked up on it."

The Damiani kid had seriously fooled me, but not nearly as much as Jake had. A full decade had passed since my brother and I last spoke. I'd had no reason to believe he knew where I was living or what I was doing, much less gave a damn. Miriam's revelation raised a glimmer of hope about the prospect of reuniting with him. Then again, Jake might've been keeping tabs on me just to celebrate how crummy my life had become.

"So what's it going to be with you and Jake?" Miriam asked. "Is this nonsense going to continue?"

"I just don't know, Miriam. I just don't know."

"Here, I'll make it easy for you," she said. "We have *Shabbos* dinner every Friday night. Just the four of us — Jake, David, Rachel, and me. I'm not going to set a place for you, because if I did it would be a whole production with Jake. But I'll expect you. It can be this Friday, or any Friday. You'll be expected. I mean it, Benny."

I started to give Rachel a kiss on the forehead, then thought better of it. "Jake is very lucky," I said as I got up to go. "I hope he won't be too hard on David."

"Jake's a marshmallow," she said. "I'm the enforcer in the family."

I laughed at hearing that. "Then you go easy on David," I said.

I patted Miriam's shoulder and headed to my car. She smiled as I passed her on my way up the street.

NINETEEN

I ENTERED THE Hotel Cleveland from Euclid Avenue and walked up the big flight of stairs to the lobby. I was half an hour early for my nine o'clock meeting with Nancy Debevec.

She had called the previous morning to tell me she was in town for her nephew's baptism. "Well, it's good weather for it," I said.

"I thought maybe we could get together and talk."

"You said you weren't interested."

"I might've changed my mind," she said. "It just so happens I haven't worked since Mr. Sorin was killed. The bank account's running low, so if you're willing to pay for the information you want, we might be able to strike a deal."

"You said you didn't want to get mixed up in this business," I said.

"I'm not particularly thrilled about it. But I'm less thrilled with the idea of going broke. So what do you say? Are you interested?"

"I think I'm interested," I said. "It depends on how much you want."

"One hundred fifty dollars for one hour's talk."

"That's pretty steep. What if we run over?"

Nancy started to make up some contingency plan, then realized I was just giving her the business. It would be Judith's money, not mine, and I didn't really care about being economical on her account.

The Hotel Cleveland was one of the city's nicest. All day long I wondered why Nancy had chosen to stay at this place, with its pricey rates, if she was short on cash. Maybe her family was paying for her stay. Then again, maybe she wasn't really as broke as she said she was.

I ordered a scotch and soda at the hotel bar and took a table at the back where I could keep an eye on who came and went. There weren't any potential G-Men in the place, or much of anyone else. Two business types in shirtsleeves were having a good-natured argument about the relative talents of Lemon and Wynn and Garcia, and whether the universe could survive without Bob Feller on the mound. A lady with a cocktail glass was standing and chatting with the bartender, who was polishing something or other with a white rag. At the far end of the bar, an older man silently stared down his shot glass, then abruptly lifted and drained it.

The debaters left after fifteen minutes. I went to the bar for a second drink. "The man wants another," announced the lady as I approached. The bartender nodded. "Well, set him up, and be quick about it, Sammy," she said as she winked at me. I went and sat back down.

By 9:30, I'd finished the second scotch and soda and was considering whether to order number three. I decided against it. I was going to give Nancy five more minutes. Then I was walking.

Just before the grace period ended, the lady at the bar let out a tremendous laugh. "Sam, you're something!" she said as she stroked the bartender's cheek. The room was too dark for me to make out the subtleties of his reaction, but he did lean forward and whisper something in the lady's ear.

"That's sweet of you," she said. "But I've got business to attend to." With that, she turned directly toward me and walked up to my table.

"I'm Nancy Debevec," she said. "You must be Gold."

"Yeah, I am. You just figuring that out?"

"I knew it the minute you walked in."

"Why didn't you come over earlier?" I asked.

"Why didn't *you* come over earlier?"

"I didn't know you were you."

"I'm the only woman here, Gold. Who else could I be?"

I thought of several choice responses to that question. None of them was likely to get our conversation going in the right direction.

Truth was, she had completely fooled me. I didn't recognize her voice from the telephone, and her demeanor was night-and-day different from the frostiness she'd conveyed during our two brief calls.

She also looked nothing like I'd envisioned. I was expecting a wizened spinsterish sort, a woman approaching retirement age with her hair in a bun and a pair of spectacles perched at the end of her nose. But Nancy Debevec couldn't have been more than my age, and she was still a hot number — tall and curvaceous, with her rounded hips snugly encased in a bright yellow skirt. Her hair was light brown and mussed, and her blue eyes glistened — maybe more than usual, given how tight she was.

"I could use another," she said, pointing to her empty glass.

"What are you drinking?"

"Highball."

I went to the bar and watched Sam pour our drinks. "So what can you tell me about your boss's client?" I asked after I sat back down.

"Not much for small talk, are you?"

"I thought you'd want to get this over with as quickly as possible."

"The night is young, Gold."

"Do you think you could keep your voice down?"

"The night is young, Gold." This time she whispered it.

"So when did you get to town?" I asked.

"Monday afternoon."

"When's the baptism?"

"Sunday. Want to come?"

"I think I'll pass," I said. "I haven't been to a baptism since my own."

"You're kidding, right?"

"Obviously. Buddhists don't have baptisms."

I pulled out my Lucky Strikes and extended the pack toward her.

"No, thanks," she said. "Not my brand."

I lit one up for myself and grabbed an ashtray off the next table.

"Got my money?" she asked.

"Oh. I almost forgot."

I reached inside my coat pocket and pulled out an envelope that I handed to her. She barely looked at it before stuffing it in her purse.

"Five hundred dollars, just like we discussed," she said with a devious smile.

"Your memory's a little off."

"You can't blame a girl for trying."

Nancy was in a chatty mood. She told me how homely her sister's kids were, and how her brother-in-law had pawed her under the table at dinner the previous night. "I finally stabbed him with a fork to make him stop," she said. "Right in the thigh. Honest to God."

"I have no trouble believing it," I replied.

She described the street in Columbus where she grew up. She told me about the other attorneys she liked talking to during her time with Maury Sorin and those she didn't. She'd expound on almost any subject, except the one I was paying to hear about. Every once in a while, I tried to steer the conversation toward "F.G.Z." She either ignored me or told me "not now."

I didn't really mind. I was having a good time. Nancy gave as good as she got, and had a brain in her head. This was absolute heaven after the horror I'd endured with Judith Sorin in Little Italy.

"Two ginger ales, Mac. No ice in either." Number One placed the order as he and Number Two passed the bar and sat down at the table next to Nancy and me.

"You didn't think we forgot about you, did you, Mr. Gold?" said Number One.

"After last week, I expected the two of you to spend the rest of your careers getting cats out of trees."

"Who are these guys?" asked Nancy.

"The Keystone Cops."

"We're from the Federal Bureau of Investigation, ma'am," said Number One. "This man is making it his life's work to obstruct the government from deporting known subversives."

"His life's work? What do you mean?"

"He's representing —"

"Keep your paranoid fantasies to yourself," I interrupted. I didn't want the G-Men to tip Nancy they were hounding me about one of Maury Sorin's former cases. If she showed any familiarity with Braunstein, it would've seriously complicated both her life and mine. The two super-sleuths might have already known who she was. But I got the sense that they didn't, and I wanted to keep it that way.

"I'll apologize for these two gentlemen, *Phyllis*, but they aren't really gentlemen. They're never going to leave us alone to continue our conversation. I know you've had a long flight in from Kansas City, but my office is only a few blocks from here, and — "

Nancy was quick on the uptake. "You forget, cousin, I have a room upstairs."

"Are you sure it'd be all right?"

"For God's sake, Benjamin, we're family. And Mom should be back from her dinner date within the hour — she's looking forward to seeing you."

I went to the bar and paid her tab and mine. Then I told Nancy to give her room number to the agents to save them the trouble of trying to figure it out.

"It's either 813 or 814. You'll have to check at the front desk. It's under the name of my mother's new husband. Finkleston, with an F."

"Good work, Phyllis," I said after the doors of the elevator closed.

"Never a dull moment, eh, Gold? What was that all about?"

"Remember a client of Sorin's named Braunstein? He's a suspected commie the government's trying to deport."

"Yeah. I think so…" Nancy said. "Sure. Why do you ask?"

"I know him, and those guys have got it in their heads that I've taken over his case."

"How can you do that?" she asked.

"I'm an attorney, and I still have my license even though I don't practice anymore. But I never agreed to represent Braunstein, and I'm not going to. Try convincing them of that."

"Saul Schwartz is handling that matter," said Nancy. "He took over most of Mr. Sorin's cases. I'm sure I sent the file to him back in January."

"Yeah, well, apparently it didn't work out. At any rate, I'm now on the FBI's dance card."

We got out on the eighth floor. "What's your real room number?" I asked Nancy.

"Fourteen-thirteen."

"Damn. We'll have to walk up the six flights."

"Can we just wait a few minutes and take the elevator?"

"No. They'll be watching."

"Please, Gold," she pleaded.

"Listen — the more time we have before they pick up the scent, the better."

Nancy shrugged her shoulders. We found the stairwell and began our climb.

"Hold on a second," she said when we reached the landing on the twelfth floor. After I turned to face her, she stepped toward me. "There's something about you, Gold," she said as she stood on her tiptoes and put her arms around my neck. She smiled, then pressed her lips against mine.

It was a long, unhurried kiss. She closed her eyes, so I closed mine, too, and curled my left arm around her waist. I could feel her breasts pressed firmly against my chest. Her jasmine perfume tickled my nose.

"That was unexpected," I said.

"That's all you have to say?"

"Unexpected but nice."

"Really? I'm glad you think so," said Nancy.

"You sound surprised."

"I don't know ... some men only want to make time with twenty-year-olds."

"I'm a lover, not a kindergarten teacher," I said. "Besides, you're still looking pretty good yourself."

"Thanks, Gold." Nancy smiled and moved in for another kiss.

TWENTY

WHEN WE GOT to Room 1413, Nancy handed me her key, and I opened the door. The room was nicely done but on the small side. There was a bed, a dresser, a nightstand with a small lamp, and an upholstered chair in the corner, which Nancy was using as a repository for various shopping bags from the downtown department stores.

"Excuse me a minute," I said. "I'd like to wash up a little."

I walked into the bathroom and shut the door. I'd worked up a pretty good lather, but it wasn't just from the stairs. The kisses had me flustered...the kisses, and finding myself alone in a hotel room with an attractive woman who thought there was "something" about me. As I rinsed my face, I wondered whether what I thought might happen actually would happen. I also wondered what Elizabeth would have to say about it if it did happen — even after so much time and so much water under the bridge.

Judith Sorin crossed my mind as well. She wouldn't approve of her father's secretary consorting with a reprobate like me. A week earlier, before our disastrous dinner date, I would've wanted to find myself alone with *her* in a hotel room. The realization was at once titillating and repulsive. I washed my face a second time.

When I came out of the bathroom, Nancy was sitting on the side of the bed facing the door. I sat down beside her, and she handed me a folded sheet of hotel stationery.

"Here's what you came for," she said. "'F.G.Z.' — name and address, best as I can remember."

"Thanks."

I began to unfold the pages, but Nancy took hold of my hands to stop me. "Not now," she said.

"Whatever you want."

What she wanted was to kiss me. Nancy put one hand under my chin, closed her eyes, and went to work. As we sat there necking, I tried to pace myself and not move too far too soon. It was becoming an increasingly difficult proposition when Nancy abruptly pulled away and stood up.

"I'm thirsty," she announced. "I'm going to get some water."

Nancy took two glasses sitting on top of the dresser and headed for the bathroom. She closed the door just far enough to prevent me from seeing what she was doing.

Her sudden retreat confused me, but in my present state, I quickly gave up trying to figure out what it meant. I took the opportunity to see what she'd written on the note:

Frank G. Zimmer

Master Electrician — Elite Motors

3616 Glencairn

Shaker Heights

I was trying to recall exactly where Glencairn was when I heard the faucet turn off. When I looked over, Nancy was standing in front of the bathroom door with her hands on her hips, wearing nothing but a slinky half-slip and a gold anklet that I hadn't previously noticed above her left foot. She'd put on fresh lipstick and brushed her hair. She shook her head at me.

"I guess you didn't really go to get a drink of water," I said.

"Nope."

"You seem to have forgotten your clothes in the lavatory."

"I didn't forget anything, Gold," she said. "Why don't you come keep me company?"

"I would if I could walk," I said.

Eventually I made my way over. She undressed me from behind, her arms wrapped around me, meticulously unknotting my tie, unbuttoning my shirt, pulling the BVD undershirt over my head, and unzipping my trousers. When she finished, she spun me around by the shoulders and kissed me. Then she slipped off her slip and took my hand.

"Follow me, Gold," she said as we headed toward the bed.

Afterwards, Nancy propped her head up on one hand while she stroked my cheek with the other. Within a few minutes, she lowered her head on my shoulder and nodded off, using me as her pillow and her teddy bear. I dozed too, for a while, but awoke about an hour later to her snoring and a numb tingling in my shoulder where her head was still resting.

"Hey, you. Time to get up," I said in a half-whisper.

"Mmm. Why?"

"I need to get going."

Nancy lifted her head. "Why?" she asked, more alertly than before.

"Because the longer I stay, the more likely it becomes that the boys downstairs will figure out you're not my cousin from Kansas City via the eighth floor."

"They're long gone, don't you think?"

"Not a chance."

I got up and started to dress. Nancy watched intently, as though I were performing some sort of magic act.

"Before I go," I said, "I've got to ask you some questions about the mysterious Mr. Zimmer."

"You looked at the name."

"Yeah, I did, while you were in the bathroom. How many times did he come by the office?"

"Just once, for the first appointment," Nancy said. "After that he insisted Mr. Sorin meet him in public."

"Like where?"

"They met once at a high school football game," she said. "Another time at the art museum. I can't remember all the places."

"Why wouldn't he just come in?"

"He was sure he was being followed. He was terrified of being seen going into or out of an attorney's office."

"So he figured they were on to him," I said.

"Mr. Sorin always said that Zimmer was a little unhinged. But after they killed him, we —"

"Hold on. Hold on," I interrupted. "You say they killed him?"

"I forgot. You didn't know."

"No, I didn't. When the hell did that happen?"

"The day after Christmas," she said. "About a week before they got Mr. Sorin."

"Another shooting?"

"No, this one was a hit-and-run driver, when Zimmer was walking home from the Rapid Transit."

"So you're just assuming it was Elite..."

"Mr. Sorin was pretty sure," she said.

"They ever catch the driver?"

"He ran his car into a tree about an hour later and killed himself."

"How convenient."

"That's what Mr. Sorin thought," Nancy said. "The guy was a known rummy."

"Just like Grubb was a hophead."

"Huh?"

"Never mind," I said. "Was there anything in particular that made Sorin believe that Elite arranged the killing?"

"He'd met with Zimmer five or six times by then. They were going to see the prosecutor just after the holidays. Mr. Sorin said that when that happened, Zimmer would go to jail — but the Forsythes would go to the gas chamber."

"Did he tell you specifically what he meant by that?"

"He never explained."

"The Forsythes couldn't have known where things stood between your boss and Zimmer."

"Don't be so sure," she said. "Mr. Sorin believed they'd tapped Zimmer's telephone. And people from work really were following him. They definitely knew he was up to something."

"Why do you say that?"

"They threatened his wife once, right in their driveway when she was going out shopping," she said. "Told her that her husband better keep his mouth shut for her sake. And their son at Ohio University — they pulled him aside on campus and told him the same thing. The kid had no clue what was going on."

I hadn't either. That's what I realized as I recalled my game of tag the previous week with the black sedan on my way home from the Alcazar. I'd quickly anointed Eugene Bramble as the one and only suspect. I hadn't seen my ex-in-laws as possible perpetrators, mainly because I regarded the accusations against them as likely nonsense and didn't want to believe my old pal Rufus had ratted me out.

But now I knew hit-and-run was part of the Forsythes' *modus operandi*. They'd used it once on Frank Zimmer, Maury Sorin's mystery client, seemingly as a prelude to killing Sorin himself. The assassination theory was looking far more plausible than I'd originally thought. As for Rufus, I hadn't seen him for years. I'd taken a big chance in assuming I could still trust him, and apparently I got burned.

Eventually I finished putting back on most of what Nancy had taken off me. I climbed on the bed next to her and stretched out. She patted me on the stomach, then laid her arm across my chest.

"Did Sorin go to the police after Zimmer was killed?" I asked her.

"He decided not to. He wanted to keep his appointment at the Prosecutor's Office instead, after New Year's."

I could tell that talking about Maury Sorin's murder upset Nancy. I kissed her gently on the forehead.

"Why wasn't there a file for Zimmer?"

Nancy laughed. "That file was an inch and a half thick. Mr. Sorin wrote out a bunch of notes after every one of their meetings, and Zimmer gave him a stack of papers."

"Where's the file now?"

"Gone," she said. "We kept it in the safe, but it wasn't there when I returned to the office a few days after Mr. Sorin's funeral. Somebody got it open somehow. Nothing else was missing."

"Did you ever see the documents Zimmer gave your boss?"

"Only to take them from one folder and put them into a bigger one, a Redweld."

"What were they?"

"I can't say specifically. But I know at least some of them were very incriminating. Mr. Zimmer took them without permission from Elite. He didn't think anyone at the company knew he had them. Mr. Sorin said they were a 'smoking gun.'"

"But you don't have any notion of what these documents actually were?"

"I'm sorry, Gold," she said. "I just couldn't tell you."

I kissed Nancy again, this time on the lips. "Your friend Judith told me her father had one page of notes and nothing more," I said.

"That's what she thought, because that's what I told her."

"Why?"

"If I'd been quicker on my feet, I wouldn't have told her even that much. She found those notes at her father's house in a stack of papers. She caught me by surprise when she brought them up and started cross-examining me."

"Like father, like daughter," I said.

"Yeah... Well, I told her as little as possible, and after I did, I left town within two weeks. I knew she was going to press the issue — and when that happened, the Forsythes might come looking for me."

"I'm wondering when they first got wind that Judith was making inquiries. It may've been earlier than I thought."

"I guarantee they've known for a while. Judith went to almost every P.I. in town before she came to you, and she wasn't particularly quiet about it."

"I didn't know she'd shopped the case around."

"She didn't want to use you," Nancy said. "She thought you'd be biased in favor of your ex-wife's family. But in the end, she didn't have any other options left."

"She told me that my history with the Forsythes made me 'uniquely qualified' to handle the case."

"She was trying to flatter you, I guess."

"Why didn't anyone else want the job?" I asked.

"I'm not sure," she said. "Maybe it was too much work, or maybe Judith came across as a little too crazy. Maybe they didn't want to make enemies of the Forsythes."

"All very good reasons," I said.

We sat quietly for a moment. Nancy turned on her side to look at me as I thought about just how much I wanted to strangle Judith Sorin. Nobody liked to be played for a stooge. She'd sought my help in spite of — not because of — the one thing she said made me perfect for the job. And the con had worked. It probably never occurred to her that taking on the Forsythes might revive a part of my past I'd just as soon forget — and if it did occur to her, she didn't care. She'd gotten what she wanted: the degenerate renegade was doing her bidding even though she couldn't stand him, and would remind him of that every chance she got.

I stayed with Nancy for another half an hour. She'd told me everything she knew about Zimmer, leaving us to small talk that was both stilted and halting. It didn't help that the tipsiness from earlier in the evening had dissipated. I, for one, had a clear-headed appreciation of the awkwardness of the situation — being in the most intimate of settings with someone I didn't even really know.

"Talk about hit-and-run, Gold," Nancy said when I finally stood up to leave.

"I'm sorry," I said, and meant it. But I resisted the temptation to speak of a future rendezvous. I wasn't sure I wanted one, for one thing; and I didn't even know if one would be possible, since Nancy presumably intended to high-tail it back to Chicago after the weekend with her family.

She watched me as I walked across the room and opened the door. "Goodbye," I said, and headed out.

TWENTY-ONE

I FOUND A BACK way out of the hotel, which I managed to navigate without running into Number One or Number Two. Once outside, I walked east on Euclid and made my way to the Hippodrome Building. It was already a quarter till five, close enough to daybreak to pass on taking a trip home.

The night watchman was not happy to see me. "You fellas are making a habit of this," he complained. "Don't know why people can't get their work done in the daytime."

I shrugged.

"You just missed those fellas from the accounting firm," he said.

"What?"

"Same boys who were here the other night when you were. They left about fifteen minutes ago. Said they were working on a special audit or some such thing."

"I don't know why people can't get their work done in the daytime," I said.

"That's my point. Same goes for you, mister."

As I rode the elevator to the seventh floor, I wondered why the G-Men had returned to the scene of the crime. I had a hard time believing they came back looking for the Braunstein file. They couldn't have expected me to keep it in my office after their first break-in.

They might've come just to ransack the place, to pay me back for making monkeys out of them when I gave them the slip at the hotel. Number One and Number Two could pillage at will, confident in the knowledge that I was occupied elsewhere, reminiscing with my K.C. cousin. I braced for a shock as I unlocked the office door.

But I'd worried needlessly. My FBI friends broke and entered that night on their best behavior. The office was pretty much as I'd left it the night before. I could see Number One and Number Two had gone through the cabinets next to Mrs. Skokow's desk and rummaged through the papers on mine. But nothing was destroyed. Nothing was seriously out of place.

They'd left a note taped to one of the office windows. It told me just how far Nancy and I had thrown them off with our performance at the bar:

Your "cousin": Elaine Mencken — Room 831
Providence, RI
Tell her we will be visiting tomorrow
Hope you enjoyed "catching up"

I stretched out on the sofa across from Mrs. Sokow's desk and dozed off. It took me a moment to get my bearings when I woke up around an hour later. Eventually I walked to the telephone and dialed the number of the hotel.

"Hotel Cleveland. How may I help you?" said a young man's voice.

"Elaine Mencken, Room 831, please."

"Sir, do you know what time it is?"

I looked at my wrist watch. "Yeah . . . past six, around 6:15."

"I can't disturb our guests at this hour," said the Hotel Cleveland.

"This is an emergency, sonny. Please connect me."

"Are you a member of Mrs. Mencken's family, sir?"

"No," I said. "But trust me — she's going to want to talk to me."

"Sir, at this hour I simply can't."

"It's not *that* early."

"It is at the Hotel Cleveland, sir."

"You're making a mistake. In an hour, hour and a half, FBI agents are going to show up at Mrs. Mencken's door, and it won't be pretty."

"FBI agents, you say? Can I assume Mr. Hoover will be one of them?"

"This isn't a joke," I said.

"Oh, come on, sir. Next you're going to ask if we have Prince Albert in a can."

"By lunchtime, you're going to wish you'd listened."

"Ring back then, sir, and I'll tell you," said the Hotel Cleveland before hanging up.

The best I could do was call my "cousin" again in a couple of hours. Maybe it wouldn't be too late. Maybe the schmuck at the front desk would drop dead in the meantime.

I waited only until 7:30 to call Judith Sorin. It was a conversation I didn't want to have, so I decided to get it over with as quickly as possible. I couldn't avoid talking to her — as my client, she had a right to know what I was finding out on her dime. I was still irritated, though, about what had happened on our dinner date, and I liked her even less after learning about the bull she'd served up to convince me to take her case in the first place.

Judith picked up after the fifth ring. "Hello," she said in a feeble, scratchy voice. I'd obviously awakened her.

"Miss Sorin, it's Benjamin Gold. Sorry to call so early, but I figured you were an early riser, being a schoolteacher and all."

"I usually am."

"I wanted to fill you in on my conversation with Nancy Debevec."

"You talked to her?"

"She's in town and she called me," I said. "She gave me the low-down on 'F.G.Z.'"

"Good," Judith said. "Very good. When do you think you'll have a chance to meet with him?"

"With any luck, it won't be for another thirty, thirty-five years, at least."

I told her everything I'd learned about Zimmer and his case. I let her know that her father actually had an extensive file on the F.G.Z. case, and how it had mysteriously disappeared after his murder. I repeated his prediction that "Zimmer would go to jail, but the Forsythes would go to the gas chamber."

"We still don't have direct evidence of anything," I concluded, "but we're getting damned close. I'll speak to Zimmer's widow as soon as I can."

"Nancy," Judith said disgustedly. "She ought to be ashamed of herself."

"What's the problem?"

"She misled me and withheld information. It's practically obstruction of justice."

"No, it's not anything like that at all," I said. "You should be thanking Nancy. She's just stuck her neck way out for you."

"I don't agree, Mr. Gold. She threw me off track when she could have helped in finding my father's killers."

"Don't criticize Nancy if you're not willing to criticize him, too," I said.

"What do you mean?"

"Your father didn't exactly distinguish himself as a model citizen in this particular instance. He should've gone to the police after Zimmer was killed, to tell them what he knew. Instead, he took matters into his own hands."

"Listen, Mr. Gold," she said. "You can't talk about my father that way. How *dare* you criticize him!"

"Now *you* listen, Miss Sorin," I said. "I know you're mean, but I didn't think you were stupid, too. I respected your father a lot, and I wasn't seriously criticizing him. I was trying to make a point, an obvious point, that you're way off base in going after Nancy."

"I haven't 'gone after' anyone," Judith said.

"It sounds like you're ready to put a bounty on her head."

"That's idiotic. Imagine having mud slung at my father by a man like you."

"This 'man like me' just raised his hourly fees on the case by ten dollars. Have you already paid the bill I sent you?"

"No. I was going to do it this morning."

"Well, don't," I said. "I'll come by and pick up my fees, and I want the money in cash. Include an additional deposit of five hundred dollars while you're at it."

"I'm not going to pay that," she snorted. "You act as though you're the only private detective in town."

"I am — at least I'm the only one who hasn't already turned down your case. Maybe you can convince one of the other guys to take it a second time around."

"Nancy —"

"Go ahead — fire me. Fire me, and I'll go to my former brother-in-law and get twice what you're paying me, just to tell him what I've already found out. He can use the information to make sure nobody else finds out anything more."

"This is out-and-out blackmail," Judith said.

"It's perfectly legitimate free enterprise," I corrected. "I'm charging what the market will bear. If the price seems too steep, don't pay it."

"I think you really would go to your brother-in-law. You're a snake, Mr. Gold."

"Yeah, you told me so last Thursday night, or something to that effect," I said. "Make it a thousand dollars more on the deposit and fifteen dollars more per hour."

There was a momentary pause. "I guess I have no choice," she finally conceded.

"Sure you do — you can drop the whole case and let the Forsythes win. And before you commit yourself, let me add one thing more: If I find out you've given Nancy a hard time about what she did or didn't do, then I'm done working for you — and I'm going to keep every penny you've paid, whether I've earned it yet or not. Understood?"

"Why not?" said Judith. "You've asked for everything else."

"I mean it, Miss Sorin."

"You're very good at getting your pound of flesh, Mr. Gold. I hope you're half as good at dealing with your in-laws."

"Ex-in-laws," I said. "I'll be at your house for the money at around 3:30. Remember — fifteen hundred bucks, in cash, plus what you owed me from before." I hung up without saying goodbye.

I took a cigarette from my pocket and put it in my mouth. I needed a smoke, but the match wouldn't light, and after the fourth try I flung it to the floor. Then I broke the cigarette in two and pitched it toward the trash can next to Mrs. Skokow's desk. Half of it made it in.

"Goddamn it to hell," I said. It had nothing at all to do with the cigarette.

TWENTY-TWO

AT ELEVEN O'CLOCK, I met with a plumber from Parma who wanted me to find out whether his wife was making time with the mortician who lived up the street. As he was leaving my office, the intercom buzzed.

"Sig Danziger's on the line," Mrs. Skokow announced. "It's the third time he's called. I told him you were in conference, but he won't take no for an answer."

"Hello, Sig," I said after picking up the receiver.

"That secretary of yours, Benny — she ought to open a charm school."

"The two of you could join a mutual admiration society. What's up?"

"Meet me at Otto Moser's in an hour. You're buying. I've got a present for you."

"It's not a present if I have to pay for it," I said.

———

I got to the restaurant fifteen minutes early. Sig was already halfway through a corned beef sandwich.

"You said an hour."

"I couldn't wait," Sig shrugged. "You usually don't eat anyway, so I started without you."

"Why'd you have me come at all?"

"For that," he said, pointing to a thick brown envelope on the table next to his plate. "Names and addresses of all Elite Motorworks employees in Ohio, circa 1949. I couldn't get anything more recent."

"Is that the list from the wage-theft lawsuit?"

"Nope. That one was destroyed at the end of the case."

"Then how'd you get it?"

"Trade secret," Sig said. "Worth another sandwich, at least."

"Have another beer, too. It's on me."

"I know," he said.

I opened the envelope and took a look while we waited on Sig's second lunch. The list came as advertised, and then some — names, addresses, telephone numbers, positions, length of service. Zimmer's name appeared on the bottom of the second-to-last page.

"Thanks a lot," I said. "This is just what I needed." I saw no point in telling Sig I'd already gotten what I was looking for from another source.

"When was the last time you argued in the Sixth Circuit?" I asked while we were waiting for the check.

"That would have been the twelfth of Never," Sig said. "My practice is strictly state-side. Why do you ask?"

"I know someone who needs a lawyer. Maury Sorin was representing him before he got himself killed. It's a deportation case and it's coming up in a hurry. Know anyone who might take it?"

"Can the client pay?"

"If he can't, I will."

"Who is this?" Sig asked. "Some long-lost uncle?"

"Never mind," I said. "You know somebody, or not?"

"I know lots of people. What about Teddy Waxman?"

"Teddy's an idiot, Sig. My 'uncle' deserves better."

"Why don't you call Jim Roberts? You and he were pretty close in law school."

"Roberts is an assistant U.S. Attorney. His office is handling the case against my 'uncle.'"

"Even so," said Sig, "he's in federal court all the time. He'd know someone to recommend."

"I'm not too keen on asking the opposition who they'd prefer to face in court."

"Blood is thicker than water, Benny. Jimmy would send you to the right guy."

"I think I'll look elsewhere, just the same," I said.

I went back to the office just to tell Mrs. Skokow I was leaving for the day. It wasn't yet 2:00, but I intended to go directly to Judith Sorin's. I'd arrive more than an hour before I said I would. This was on purpose. I wasn't in the mood for the hand-to-hand combat I anticipated. With any luck, she wouldn't be home, and I could postpone the confrontation for another day.

To my misfortune, Judith was there to greet me when I arrived. "Please come in, Mr. Gold," she said. "I want to talk to you."

"Is it about the case?"

"Not specifically, no."

"You had your chance to talk to me about other things last Thursday night," I said. "If you don't mind, I'd like to just transact our business and get on my way."

"Mr. Gold, we have to stop treating each other with such disrespect."

"Listen," I said. "I said a thing or two this morning I wish I hadn't. But other than that, the disrespect has been completely one-sided."

"You made a pass at me, Mr. Gold."

"I just took you out to dinner, and it wasn't even my idea. If that's making a pass, I made a pass. Otherwise, you're nuts."

"See, there you go —"

"Miss Sorin." I was abrupt and loud with the interruption. "I'm not going to debate you. I'm also not interested in what you think of my behavior, now or anytime, because if I were, I'd have to jump off the Detroit Avenue bridge. You can think what you want, as long as you pay my fees."

Judith went inside her house and returned with a stack of bills in a white wrapper with "Society National Bank" printed on it. "Here's your money," she said as she handed it to me.

I counted out twenty fifty-dollar bills and gave them back to her. "Here," I said.

"What's this?"

"Like I told you. You got under my skin this morning, and I said some things I wish I hadn't. I'm sorry. It wasn't any way for a professional to act. The original terms of our deal apply. Sorry to have made you get the extra cash."

Most women would have used the opening to make an apology of their own. Most women would have at least said "thank you." Judith Sorin wasn't most women. I got back in the Schooner and headed home.

The Damiani kid was playing catch with his little sister in front of the building when I arrived. "Hello, Luigi," I said. "What's going on?"

"A delivery came for you this morning, Mr. Gold. My mom signed for it."

"That was awfully nice of her. Where is it?"

"In our apartment."

"Let's go see what it is."

The kids and I took the stairs up. I'd never been in their place, but before I could really look around, Luigi handed me a large white envelope with "ELITE MOTORWORKS COMPANY" engraved across the front and my name and address typed beneath that.

"Where's your mother?" I asked. "I'd like to thank her."

"She went to the butcher," Luigi's sister said. "She should be back soon."

I didn't want to wait to open the envelope. I thought for certain I knew what it contained.

"They actually went and sued me," I mused as I ripped the seal.

"Huh?"

"Oh, sorry, Louie. Just mumbling."

It wasn't the lawsuit I'd expected. Instead, the envelope contained a cream-white piece of stationery folded in half, along with a large photograph covered by a gauzy veil of thin paper.

I pulled the note out first. The text was handwritten in block letters and didn't include a salutation:

Remember, Benjamin.
Things don't always turn out so well
when you stick your nose in.
Enjoy getting reacquainted with your friends.
CF Jr.

I couldn't guess what the picture was. But I knew it wasn't going to be nice, and I didn't want the kids to see.

"Excuse me a minute," I said before walking through the entry to their living room and stepping to the side. Then I flipped the cover and took a peek.

It was a grisly scene — a heap of emaciated corpses, the bodies barely covered, with tortured expressions on most of the faces. "Ebensee 5/45" had been scrawled in the bottom right-hand corner, but Junior needn't have bothered labeling it. It didn't matter whether the photo came from precisely there and then. I knew what he was getting at.

For a moment, I woozily considered how he even knew about it. Elizabeth must've told him, I figured. She could've done so after the divorce. Junior might've become her confidant by then, instead of her nemesis — at least with respect to me.

I thought I was going to retch. Then I knew I was.

"I need your bathroom," I told the Damiani kids as I bolted toward the back of the apartment. But my head wasn't in any condition for bolting — it was as if I'd drunk three shots of whisky back to back to back. I started staggering and tripped on the living room carpet. I was in for another pratfall, like the one I'd done at Rosie's, but I had the feeling I might not get up so fast this time.

"Elizabeth," I cried as my feet went out from under me and I spilled forward.

I probably would've blacked out no matter what. But my forehead caught the corner of the end table next to the sofa on my way down. That cinched the deal.

TWENTY-THREE

I CAME TO on the living-room couch in my own apartment, and I immediately wanted to fall back asleep. I felt as though someone had carved a baseball out of the left side of my skull. It took me a moment to recall what had happened at the Damianis'. I couldn't tell how much time had elapsed since then; for all I knew, I'd been out for days.

I heard someone walking around in my kitchen, opening cabinets and running the water. I painfully turned my head in that general direction and saw Dr. Braunstein sitting in the chair next to the reading lamp, cleaning his glasses. He nodded when he saw I was awake.

"What are you doing here, Doc?"

"Your brother asked me to come," he said.

"Jake? How'd he know...?"

"Apparently the young man from the building called him."

"Okay. Yeah. But how'd Jake have your number?"

"That, you will have to ask your brother."

"Who's in the kitchen?"

"Your brother's wife," Braunstein said.

"Miriam? How'd she get here?"

"Your brother brought her. He was here too, but he went home with their baby to check on your nephew."

I turned toward the wall, as far as I could manage. My head was spinning, and it wasn't only on account of the spill I took. At long last, I'd had the reunion with my brother I'd been pining for — in a comatose state. His wife, whom I'd met for the first time only a few days earlier, came along and was now cleaning my kitchen. Meanwhile, my accused-commie headshrinker had made an impromptu house call. This was Dickens meets the Marx Brothers, with a touch of *The Goldbergs* added in.

"How long was I out?" I asked Braunstein.

"It is 8:30 now. I do not know exactly when you had your fall."

"How'd I get back here?"

"Your brother and the young man carried you."

"... That picture, Doc," I said. "It's a hell of a thing."

The photo was Junior's tribute to the incident that sent me off the deep end back in Europe.

I killed two prisoners at Ebensee by giving them chocolate when their bodies were too weak to digest solid food. It was an accident, of course, but that didn't make them any less dead. Many other prisoners died the same way when we liberated the camp.

I met my victims inside their barracks, after my buddy Gilly Gelfand announced that he and I were *landsmen* from America. They looked to be at least in their thirties, but Gilly later told me they were both eighteen and had been in this camp less than a month.

The encounter didn't last very long. They spoke little English, and I didn't speak any of the various languages they tried out on me. I was anxious to depart, given the swarm of lice crawling over their arms and legs.

Before leaving, I reached into my pockets for something to give them. I found a pack of smokes but figured they'd prefer the candy I had in my knapsack. They were devouring it as I waved and walked away.

The next morning, I came around and saw their bodies on the pile outside the barracks. A medic from our outfit explained what had happened, and I promptly went to pieces. I'd been teetering on the verge of a crackup for weeks by then, so it was probably a question of when, not if — and the Hershey-bar killings ended up as the trigger.

Gilly came to get me the next day after I turned myself in for murdering the two boys. The MPs were ready to have me committed then and there, but Gilly talked them out of it. Then I went missing overnight. They found me at noon the next day, curled up on the ground about a mile from the camp's main entrance. No one ever figured out how or when I got there. I wouldn't talk and barely reacted to anything. Within a few weeks, I was back in the U.S., in a psych ward on Long Island.

<hr />

"My head sure hurts," I told Braunstein.

"I brought my bag. I will sew up the laceration when you are ready."

"I thought you only worked on damaged egos, Doc."

"I was trained as a physician," he said, "even if the State of Ohio now says I am unfit to practice. I am not qualified to perform major surgery, of course, but this is merely first aid — and even a psychiatrist does not forget something so simple as stitching a wound."

Just then Miriam walked in from the kitchen, drying her hands on a dish towel. "Good," she said when she saw I was awake. "I finished cleaning out that refrigerator of yours. Some of that stuff belonged in a museum."

"I'm sorry," I said. "Thanks."

"Jake's going to bring some dinner for you when he comes to pick me up."

"He doesn't need to do that. I'm not hungry at the moment."

"You will eat," Braunstein said in the voice of a Prussian commandant. "You are far too thin, Mr. Gold. I do not think you would have fainted had you not been so malnourished."

"Doc..."

"We have been down this road before, Mr. Gold."

I tried to change the subject. "I'm sorry you and Jake got dragged into this," I told Miriam. "Luigi shouldn't have called."

"Nonsense," she responded. "He was scared stiff and didn't know what to do. Jake would've been upset with him if he hadn't."

"What made you think to call the Doc?"

"Jake knew about the incident at the concentration camp and put two-and-two together when I told him about the picture you were holding when you fell," Miriam said.

"How'd he know I was the Doc's patient?"

"He just knew — I don't know how."

"I think you should be quiet and lie still," said Braunstein. "I need to sew up that cut."

Braunstein gave me a shot of something, then showed me the gash in a mirror from his bag. It looked a lot smaller than it felt. After a few minutes for the injection to make me numb, he cleaned the wound and doused it with something that stank of iodine, then went to work.

"Your ex-brother-in law is a cruel man," Miriam said as the Doc was sewing. "What'd you do that got him so riled up?"

I started to explain about the Sorin case, but Braunstein interrupted. "No talking until I am finished, please."

I tried to relax and not think about how long it was taking. Miriam left the room for a few minutes and came back with the small suitcase I kept in my bedroom closet.

"I think you'd better come spend a few days at our house," she said. "I packed a pair of pajamas and some clothes for you."

"I'm not —"

"No talking!" said Braunstein.

"This way we can keep an eye on you," Miriam continued. "The Doctor said you shouldn't be driving or running around for at least a day or two, anyway."

When Braunstein finally finished his needlework, I nixed the idea of a sleepover. "It's way too much to ask," I said. "Besides, I don't like anybody taking care of me. It takes me back to a time I'd just as soon forget."

"Doctor . . . ?" Miriam asked.

"Your brother-in-law is a grown man," Braunstein said.

There was a knock at the door — five loud clops in rapid succession. I remembered that cadence from growing up. Even if I hadn't been expecting Jake, I would have known it was him. Miriam opened the door for her husband.

"Has Sleeping Beauty awakened?" he asked.

"See for yourself," I answered.

As Jake walked toward the sofa, I tried to stand up. My noggin rejected the idea, forcing me to sit back down before I'd made it halfway.

I would've had a hard time standing even if I hadn't hit my head. Jake's appearance brought on a crush of emotions — giddiness at seeing him, regret for the lost years, grief over my parents' absence, all roiling at once. I didn't know whether to laugh, shout, or cry.

Braunstein and Miriam kept it all in check. I had the sense they were carefully monitoring every detail of my reunion with Jake. It made me feel like an actor on stage who didn't know his lines quite as well as he should.

"Thanks for saving the day," I told my brother.

"Captain Marvel was busy."

"So who's watching the kids?" I asked after a momentary silence, just to say something.

"A neighbor," said Jake as he turned to his wife. "Speaking of which, tonight is Shirley's bowling night. We've got to be out of here in fifteen minutes."

"Huh…? Okay," Miriam said. "What'd you bring Benny to eat?"

Jake was holding two bags, one in each hand. "A burger from Mawby's," he said, holding out one of them. "And the usual side dishes."

"Good," said Miriam. She took Jake's delivery and headed for the kitchen. "I'll warm the food in the oven so it won't be stone cold. It won't take a minute."

"The hamburger might be a little heavy for Mr. Gold's stomach at present," Braunstein offered. "Not to mention the fried potatoes and the onions…"

"Never mind, Doc," I said. "If I'm going to eat, I might as well eat."

I gave my brother the once-over. He'd put on a few pounds, and his black hair had thinned considerably. He'd also become a four-eyes, with a pair of horn-rimmed specs resting on his nose. I was surprised. As silly as it sounded, I'd somehow expected Jake to remain impervious to aging.

"How many stitches did he take?" Jake asked Braunstein.

"Six or seven, I think."

"Will he have to change the bandage?"

"Ach. I forgot." Braunstein reached into his bag and pulled out some gauze and a roll of tape. He then gave me step-by-step instructions on what I needed to do with them and how frequently I needed to do it.

While he spoke, Jake examined the pictures on the credenza in the corner. There was one of my parents; one of my parents with Jake and me; one of Jake alone; and another of Jake and me, taken on his sixteenth birthday, just before we left for dinner and a show downtown. He might have picked up the last one for a closer look, but I couldn't look away from Braunstein for too long, so I wasn't sure.

"I think I will go now," Braunstein said when he finished with his instructions. "You are going to be fine, Mr. Gold, as long as you start eating a normal diet."

"Okay, Doc," I said.

"Mr. Goldstein, it was nice meeting you," Braunstein said to Jake. "Give my best to your wife."

"I can hear you, Doctor," Miriam called from the kitchen. "My hands are full, or I'd come out to say goodbye. Thanks for everything."

"Not at all," said Braunstein.

"Doc, I haven't forgotten about your case," I called to him as he headed toward the door. I certainly would've preferred to forget about it, but his coming to the rescue now only added to my sense of obligation. I felt compelled to let him know I was at least thinking about his situation.

"Mr. Gold," the Doc answered, "you do not have to concern your-self with that."

"I am concerned, and I'm not comfortable with the current plan."

"As I told you when we met last week, I do not believe I have any alternative."

Braunstein and I spent a few minutes discussing the appeal. I kept my comments as oblique as possible, so as not to reveal the Doc's predicament to Jake.

After Braunstein left, my brother and I were alone in the living room. "Jake..." I started to say. "I wanted to..."

"Goddamn it." He'd reached into his shirt pocket for a cigarette and found his pack empty.

"I think there's a box of Luckies in the top drawer of my dresser."

Jake made a disgusted face. "M, do you have any smokes?" he called to the kitchen.

"In my purse, hon."

"Where is it?"

"I don't know at the moment. Can't be far."

Jake sat down in the chair next to the reading lamp. He looked irritated, almost angry. I didn't know him well enough anymore to surmise what he was thinking, but he certainly wasn't in any mood for a heart-to-heart.

Miriam returned from the kitchen with the burger on a plate, nestled among french fries and grilled onions, and a tall glass of cream soda. "Here you go," she said. "There's more soda in the fridge if you finish that."

"Thanks. Just put it on the coffee table."

"We've got to hit the road, M," said Jake.

"Okay," Miriam said. "But tell your brother he needs to stay with us for a day or two."

Jake paused. "Benny's welcome, but he'll do as he pleases," he said quietly.

"Well, *that's* a heartfelt invitation," Miriam said.

"We've really got to go, M."

"All right, all right. Let me find my purse. And I want Benny to explain why that Forsythe creep is so upset with him."

"You know the Maury Sorin murder case?" I asked.

"He was that lawyer..."

"Right. His daughter believes my ex-in-laws arranged to have him killed, and she hired me to prove it. She must be on to something, because the Forsythes don't like the questions I'm asking."

"Why did they want to kill Maury Sorin?" asked Miriam.

"I don't know, but I'm hoping I'm about to find out."

Jake stood up. "If they killed Maury Sorin, they'll kill you, too."

"I hope not," I said.

"I hope you know what you're doing..." he replied without conviction. "Let's go, M."

Miriam walked over and kissed me lightly on the left cheek.

"Thanks for everything," I said. "To both of you."

"You're welcome," Miriam said. "I'm glad you're all right. I know it was a horrible accident, but if this is what it took to get you two talking to each other, well, I'm kind of glad it happened."

I smiled at her, then looked over at Jake. He was checking his watch as he went out the door.

TWENTY-FOUR

AFTER THEY LEFT, I took a sip of the cream soda and a bite of the burger, then pushed them away. I'd try to follow Braunstein's orders about eating more, but not right yet. Jake's icy demeanor had my stomach closed for business. Miriam was indulging in wishful thinking if she thought we were actually on our way toward reconciling. The only place Jake seemed ready to bury the hatchet was between my shoulder blades.

I was disappointed but not surprised. Jake had excised me from his life almost a decade earlier, and if he'd had any inclination to forgive and forget, it would've already happened.

I thought back to the afternoon at my parents' apartment, a few weeks after my father's funeral, when Jake gave me the kiss-off.

I was late for a client meeting at the Union Club and was on my way out the door.

"Where are you going?" asked Jake. "You're supposed to stay for dinner and help us with the insurance forms."

"I don't have time," I said, "and you don't need me to fill those out. If you can't do it, ask Herbie Schwartz's brother. I'll pay if he charges you."

"Fuck you," said Jake.

"Jake…" my mother said.

"Fuck you, Benny," he repeated. "You walk out that door now and you're dead to me. I swear I mean it."

"Really, Jake? Because I won't fill out some stupid forms?"

"Fuck you," he said a third time. "You were here maybe an hour, hour and a half the entire week we sat *shiva*. Your *shiksa* wife didn't come at all."

"She wasn't feeling well," I said.

"None of us were feeling well. It wasn't supposed to be a holiday at the beach. She should've paid her respects, especially since her father was the one who killed Pop."

"Goddamn it," I said. "That's not fair."

"You're right. The old bastard didn't do it alone. You and your Liz had a hand in it, too."

I started to respond angrily but stopped myself. "You want to accuse me of anything else?" I asked instead.

Jake didn't miss a beat. "We've known all along that your father-in-law was a Jew-hating bastard," he said. "Liz isn't much different, but she's so drunk most of the time, it's hard to hold her responsible for anything. But here's the clincher, Benny: It's not just your *goyish* wife and your *goyish* father-in-law. It's you, too. You're so goddamned turned around, you talk and think just like them."

"You ought to write novels," I said.

"You can't undo the circumcision, Benny. You are who you are."

"What I am is late for an important meeting," I said. "We'll have to finish this discussion later. In the meantime, call Herbie Schwartz's brother if you need help with the insurance. I'll pay for it, like I said."

I didn't take Jake's threat seriously. I figured it'd all blow over. In the weeks and months that followed, my mother begged me to make things right, but I wouldn't. Jake had thrown the tantrum, not me. He was the one with fences to mend.

I never had the chance to mend fences with my father. He died of a massive coronary the day after my twenty-eighth birthday, walking home from the newsstand up the street. He keeled over in front of my parents' building and was already gone by the time the ambulance arrived.

The night before, he and my mother had come to my house for my birthday celebration. Elizabeth's parents were there as well. The families got together once or twice a year, unless I managed to concoct a way out of it. It was always awkward and uncomfortable.

That night was no exception. Clayton Senior was less enthralled than usual with my parents' company, since he was missing his monthly poker game.

About halfway through dinner, the conversation turned to the War. I immediately knew we were heading for trouble. My father passionately hated and feared Hitler, and Clayton Senior passionately argued with anyone who felt passionately about anything. This contrarian streak made for lively repartee at the Club, where everyone in the conversation could afford not to give a damn no matter what the topic. My father, however, came from a different crowd.

"I read this week about mass killing of Jews in Russia," he said. "The Germans are lining up whole villages and gunning them down."

"I saw that report, too," Clayton Senior said after swallowing a bite of roast beef. "From some Communist group out of London. Not true. Not a word of it."

"How can you be so sure?"

"Just common sense, Mr. Goldberg."

"Goldstein," my mother corrected.

"-Stein, not -berg," said Clayton Senior. "I always make that mistake. But just think about it, Mr. Goldstein. Why in God's name would the Germans massacre a bunch of Jews? It doesn't help them militarily. It doesn't help them financially or diplomatically. It doesn't help them at all. That type of accusation is just a cheap and easy way of discrediting Hitler."

"Hitler is Daddy's friend," Elizabeth slurred.

"Not after he declared war on this country. But let me tell you something else, Mr. Gold...stein. You Jews don't do yourselves any favors with these constant accusations of anti-Semitism."

"How do you mean?"

"It's just so much malarkey," said Clayton Senior as he lifted another forkful of roast beef to his mouth. "I discussed the Jewish Question with Goering, one-on-one, right after the Nuremberg Laws went into effect. I told him point-blank that Hitler was playing with fire. I told him some very influential Jews had a direct line to Roosevelt, and if there was anything fishy about what he was doing, he'd find himself in the middle of an international conflict, maybe even a war. 'Don't underestimate the men who have the President's ear.' That's exactly what I told him."

"Exactly what he told him," Elizabeth repeated.

"And you know what Goering did? He laughed and said I'd been reading too much propaganda from the Jewish press. There was nothing racial at all about the Nuremberg Laws, he told me. It was economic, one hundred percent. The Jews had too big a piece of the German pie, and the people were calling for an adjustment. Hitler has nothing against your people. He did what any prudent leader would've done under the circumstances. And you can't argue with the results."

My father tried to fight back. "You deserve some of the credit for those results, Mr. Forsythe," he said. "Your company helped the Germans get back on their feet with all the manufacturing you did over there."

"We did do a lot of business in Germany before the War," said Clayton Senior, gulping some wine. "Our factories did well."

"It was after the War started, too. There was a story in the paper about that investigation."

My father was referring to the State Department's inquiry into whether Elite's European subsidiaries continued to deal with the German government after hostilities broke out. I knew for a fact that they had.

"That's all it was — an investigation," said Clayton Senior. "It went nowhere and amounted to nothing. There'd have been no investigation at all if it weren't for those same men standing behind Roosevelt, the ones I was just talking about. I built my company with my own money, Mr. Goldberg, without the help of international financiers. That makes some people unhappy, and sometimes they lash out. You understand."

My father was in over his head. Five minutes later, he stood up and announced that he and my mother were leaving.

"So soon?" asked Clayton Senior. "I believe there's birthday cake."

"I don't want no cake," said my father. "We got to go."

Three days later, I was at my parents' apartment with my mother and Jake, waiting to drive to his funeral. Elizabeth hadn't felt well that morning and said she'd meet us there. The phone rang five minutes before we had to leave.

"It's her," Jake told me after picking up.

"What is it, sweetheart?" I said into the receiver. "Does the driver need directions to Mount Olive?"

"I'm sick, Benny. Really sick. My head is just pounding. I don't know what I should do."

"Have you had anything?"

"Not a drop. I swear. I don't know what to do. I should be there, after the other night."

"Are your parents coming?"

"I don't think so," she said. "Did you ask them?"

"This isn't by-invitation-only."

"I don't know what to do," Elizabeth repeated. "The room starts spinning when I even try to stand up."

"If you're sick, you're sick."

"Your mother will be angry."

"No, she won't. And since when do you care?"

"I care today. I don't know what I should do."

"Forget it," I said. "I don't want to go to *two* funerals." I hung up before she had a chance to respond.

"She's not coming," I announced to the room.

"Honest to God," my mother said disgustedly. "Let's just go."

Elizabeth's no-show destroyed the last vestige of goodwill between her and my mother. They'd gotten along well enough at first, until my mother realized Elizabeth wasn't going to convert and exchange her life of privilege for the joys of Jewish second-class citizenship.

And then I told my father I was changing my name. "It's for professional reasons," I explained. "The clients at Grimm White only want a certain type of lawyer."

My father just shook his head.

"It's not like I'm the first Jew ever to do this. My friend Jerry Sanders was Jerry Saperstein until the third grade. And your friends the Rabbs used to be the Rabinowitzes."

"Bernie Saperstein is a *putz*," my father said. "And the Rabinowitz brothers were opening a scrap metal business. The shorter name saved them money on the sign."

I found out my mother had died from a letter Elizabeth sent nearly a month after it happened, a few months after D-Day. My wife was probably in one of her protracted drunken stupors and either forgot to write earlier, thought she'd already done so, or couldn't figure out what to say and just postponed the effort.

Jake didn't write me at all. He wasn't going to correspond with a brother who didn't exist. I knew he felt that way from the obituaries Elizabeth included with her letter. Each of them listed Jake as the sole surviving next of kin. Only he would have given that bit of misinformation to the newspapers.

As my division advanced through Germany, we began hearing lurid rumors about the concentration camps. Most of the GI's didn't believe them. I did, if for no other reason than that my father had warned of such things. He'd warned of such things, and Clayton Senior had mocked him for it — while I sat by. Now Pop was dead. So was my mother. She'd died before I could make amends for defecting wholeheartedly to Elizabeth's world. And Jake blamed me for all of it.

These thoughts continually churned through my head, all day, every day. And as they churned, distinctions blurred, concepts conflated, and the line between reality and delusion began to fade. Old Man Forsythe wasn't just sympathetic to Hitler — he was the Third Reich itself, and I was a collaborator, not just his son-in-law. The betrayal of my family somehow became one with the genocide perpetrated in the concentration camps, and I took on the guilt of a true murderer, as if I'd plunged a shiv into my father or fired a bullet at my mother's head. This craziness reached a climax when I killed those two boys with chocolate bars.

Pop-pop-pop-pop-pop. It was Jake's distinctive knock at the door. I jumped a little when I heard that he'd returned, and it hurt my head.

"Come on in," I said. "It's open."

"No, it isn't. We flipped the lock on our way out."

I got up and walked gingerly to the door to let him in. Jake wouldn't enter the apartment. He stood in the hallway facing me, with his legs slightly spread and his hands on his hips.

"Get your suitcase," he said. "You're coming with us."

"No, I'm not. Thanks just the same."

"I'm not in the mood to argue. Just get your bag."

"I thought you left," I said.

"Miriam and I were having a discussion in the car."

"You had to get home. Your neighbor who's watching the kids is going bowling."

"The neighbor who's watching the kids doesn't bowl. Now get your suitcase so we can get going."

"I told you no and I told Miriam no. Why'd you come back upstairs?"

"Because she thought I sounded less than sincere when I asked you to stay over. She thought I seemed angry."

"Tell her I didn't notice anything."

"Look, Benny, I'm not going to pretend. I wasn't home when Louis called. If I had been, we never would have come. Miriam was looking for a reason to get you and me together, and this gave her one."

"Did she tell you about the other day, when I stopped over?"

"David told me first. Then she had to."

"Why'd you call Braunstein?" I asked.

"Her idea."

"Listen, Jake, nobody's forcing you. Regardless of what Miriam says, if you don't want me around, it just won't be."

"I can't just pretend nothing ever happened, Benny. Our lives were never the same after you married that girl. The *mishegas* we went through — Mom and Pop became different people after that. Your in-laws made them feel small and dirty, and so did you. I can't forget about all that overnight."

"Overnight, Jake? Come on. It's been how many years?"

He shrugged. "There's no do-over on things like this. That's just the way I feel about it."

"To hell with you, then," I said. "I'm sorry for your wife and kids, but to hell with you."

Jake's face had turned instantly red. "Now wait a minute —" he said angrily.

"Everything you've said is true, Jake. I've known it for a long time now. That's what sent me to the psych ward and kept me off my feet for as long as I was. I couldn't live with what I'd done to Mom and Pop, and to you, too."

"Don't throw the psych ward in my face because I didn't come to see you."

"Didn't come to see me? You pronounced me dead and gone."

"I didn't —"

"Don't deny it, goddamn it, or I'll have to hit you. I don't blame you, Jake. What I got, I had coming — every bit of it. But when's enough enough? I'm sorry about Mom and Pop. Sorry's not a strong enough word. I'd do anything to make it right, but I can't undo the past. If you can't move beyond it, well..."

We stood looking at each other. "My head really hurts," I finally said, to break the silence. Jake didn't respond. I was trying to come up with another comment when we both turned to look at the pair of heels that were clicking their way down the hallway. They belonged to Nancy.

"I hope I'm not interrupting," she said when she got to the door.

"My brother and I were winding up a conversation," I said. "What are you doing here?"

"I heard you hit your head. I wanted to check out the damage for myself."

"Jake, this is Nancy Debevec. Nancy — my brother Jake."

"Pleased to meet you," they both said.

Her outfit consisted of white slacks and a tight red blouse that showed off her figure in all its glory. She looked like she'd gotten a lot of sun that day, and the dark tan on her face accentuated crags and wrinkles I hadn't seen the night before. Still, she looked terrific — beautiful, even. It didn't hurt that I was happier than hell she'd shown up. She could have looked like the Bride of Frankenstein, and I still would have found her ravishing.

"Why don't you come on in?" I said to Nancy. "Jake, you should go get Miriam and bring her back up."

"Is that your wife?" Nancy asked. "I'd love to meet her."

"We've got kids waiting at home," Jake said sullenly. "Maybe some other time."

"I hope so."

After Jake left, Nancy and I went inside and sat down in the living room. "I'm happy to see you," I said, "but how did you find me, and why did you come?"

"I ran into your FBI friends in the hotel lobby when I came back from dinner at my sister's," she said. "They told me you'd had an accident, and they gave me your address. I hopped in a cab and came right over."

"I wonder how the hell they knew..."

Nancy shrugged her shoulders.

"Do you think they followed you here?"

"I'm not sure," she responded. "I didn't see them, but I suppose they could make themselves invisible if they wanted to. And anyway, why would they need to follow me if *they* gave *me* your address?"

I excused myself to wash up and put on a clean shirt. Upon returning, I explained to Nancy exactly what had happened that afternoon with the photograph from Junior, my swan dive at the Damianis', and the rescue performed by Jake, Miriam, and Dr. Braunstein.

"Braunstein's our former client?" she asked.

"Yep."

"Your brother didn't look very happy before he left."

"He wasn't," I said. "We were discussing some unpleasant family history. He and I hadn't spoken since before the War."

"Yikes," she said. "What happened?"

"It's a long story."

Nancy watched while I pretended to eat the rest of my dinner.

We talked about my anticipated recovery time. She told me how she'd spent her day.

At around eleven, Nancy got up from the couch. "It's getting late," she said. "I probably should leave."

"Please don't."

"Really?"

"For some reason, I like having you around," I said.

"There's no accounting for taste."

I leaned over and kissed her on the lips. "There certainly isn't," I said.

I stretched out on the sofa with my head on her lap. I was out within five minutes and didn't wake up till nearly six the next morning. When I opened my eyes and looked around, I saw Nancy curled up in the chair across the room, sleeping soundly.

TWENTY-FIVE

ON TUESDAY MORNING I saw Nancy off on her train back to Chicago. Her sister and her sister's children came to Union Terminal too, and I was glad they did. The entourage protected me from what might have been an uncomfortable goodbye scene — Nancy mostly played with the kids until it was almost time for her train to leave.

Nancy had served as my personal Florence Nightingale in the days following my spill at the Damianis'. On Sunday, she dragged me to her nephew's baptism. I wrangled that appearance into an invitation to the family picnic the next day at Edgewater Park. My bandaged head prevented me from swimming, so Nancy and I spent the afternoon playing in the sand with the kids. That evening we went to dinner at Jim's Steak House in the Flats, then retired to my apartment to listen to jazz on the phonograph and do our own riffing of a different sort.

Nancy and I were standing alone on the platform when it came time to board her train. "Well, this is it," she said.

"Don't sound so glum. The world isn't coming to an end."

"That's reassuring."

"I'm trying to convince myself of the same thing," I said.

"Misery loves company, Gold," she sniffled.

"I really got used to yours." I leaned forward to give her a kiss.

I held her for a long time. "Thanks," I whispered before ending the embrace. "Thanks for everything."

Nancy got on the train, and the doors closed. A few moments later, she was gone.

I was going to miss her. She was a real person, for better and worse, who saw the world in full Technicolor — not black and white, like the daughter of her former boss. She had foibles and faults and had made some mistakes in her life. But she didn't run from them or pretend they didn't exist. She expected more of herself, and made me do the same, without a condemning lecture or an inventory of my various failings. I'd felt more comfortable with Nancy than I'd felt with anyone for a long time.

I was exiting the station onto Public Square when Number One and Number Two came up from behind me. I hadn't seen them since our rendezvous at the Hotel Cleveland.

"That was a touching scene," said Number Two. "Except I never made a habit of kissing my cousins that enthusiastically. Uncle and Auntie wouldn't have liked it."

"I bet you go to peep shows, too," I said as I kept on walking.

"We've got to talk," said Number One. "You've got to decide one way or the other whether you're going to cooperate."

"It's pointless for you to keep insisting you've got nothing to do with Braunstein," said Number Two. "We know he was at your apartment last week…"

"He sewed my head up," I said, pointing to the bandage on my forehead.

"You got us at the hotel, Mr. Gold, but no more silliness," said Number One. "Braunstein's a psychiatrist, not a real doctor. You were meeting with him about his case."

"If you say so."

"We know your 'cousin' was part of his former legal team. We've already told you we know who Judith Sorin is."

"I guess when Braunstein shows up in court and I'm not with him, you'll finally realize I'm telling you the truth," I said. "I'm not representing him. I'm not his lawyer."

"Even if that were true," said Number One. "you still could let us know what Braunstein's up to, who his friends are, what he's planning to do."

"You want me to spy on him?"

"That's an unpleasant way of putting it," said Number One.

"I'm confused," I said. "I thought you FBI guys were trained as attorneys."

"We are," said Number One.

"Then you must've been asleep in law school when they taught about attorney-client privilege. If Braunstein *were* my client, I couldn't share with you or anybody else the information I get from him. If I did, I'd lose my license, even if he really were a red."

"That doesn't matter," said Number Two. "Attorney-client privilege, I mean. This is a question of national security. The man's a menace. He needs to go."

"I get it," I said. "It's my solemn duty as a true-blue American citizen to rat him out."

"Again, a rather unpleasant way of putting it," said Number One.

"We've been talking to the lobby attendant at your building," announced Number Two.

"So now you're investigating me," I said.

"He tells us the building management wants you to move out. You've been asked to leave, but you insist on staying."

"I've always been the stubborn sort."

"He told us that some of your clients look like radicals," said Number Two.

"Hah. That punk wouldn't know a radical from a Rotarian."

"He also couldn't say for certain that he hadn't seen Braunstein come into the building for an appointment with you," said Number One.

"Braunstein? How would he even know what Braunstein looks like?"

"We showed him a picture," said Number Two.

I pulled a pack of Luckies from my inside breast pocket and lit one up. "Why don't you show him a picture of the Rosenbergs while you're at it?" I said as I exhaled my first drag. "Maybe he can't say for sure that they never dropped in, too."

"This is serious, Mr. Gold," said Number One.

"You never know. Julius and Ethel may have slipped by when he bent over to tie his Buster Browns."

"You're a regular Sid Caesar," said Number Two.

"I could say the same about you two," I replied. "But I'm getting really tired of your act. You don't have anything on Braunstein, or on me, for that matter. If you did, you wouldn't be badgering me for dirt on him."

"We're not badgering you," said Number One. "We're trying to get your cooperation in a case against a known Communist."

"I've had it with you guys," I said. "Next time you want to take a tour of my office, you better get a warrant first. And plan on arresting me if you want to continue this conversation."

"You're not out of this, Goldstein," said Number Two as I started to walk away.

"So you know that, too?" I answered. "After all these years, my secret alias comes to light. I can hardly wait to see what you find out next."

I realized Number One and Number Two would take that quip as a challenge. They glared at me with their arms crossed as I walked away from Public Square.

Twenty-Six

I MADE A POINT of stopping at the concierge station on my way into the Hippodrome Building. "I just spoke to your contacts at the FBI," I told Jonathan. "They say you made a wonderful stool pigeon."

Jonathan flushed. "All I did was tell the truth," he responded defensively.

"Sure you did. And I bet you're six-foot-five, too."

I went upstairs to an empty office. I'd sent Mrs. Skokow to Galion to get the scoop on Stuffleben and his connection to Elite Motorworks. There was method to my madness. Mrs. Skokow had never done fieldwork, but she was a Crawford County girl, born and raised in Galion, and still had friends, aunts, uncles, and cousins there. I thought those relationships would help get to the bottom of things more quickly than otherwise. I'd intended to accompany her, but my tumble at the Damianis' and recuperation with Nancy set me behind schedule by a couple of days.

I had some time to kill before my 1:30 appointment with Frank Zimmer's widow at their home in Shaker Heights. I began pacing the floor, scripting exactly how I would phrase my questions to her. I was anxious for this interview — the whole Sorin case hung on what I'd find out. I needed to know what Zimmer had on my ex-in-laws. It had to be serious — serious enough for the Forsythes to want him and his lawyer dead.

I was betting Zimmer's widow knew why her husband went to Maury Sorin. I also figured she'd want to help me out when I confirmed what she probably already suspected — that the Forsythes killed her husband. The trick would be convincing her that she wasn't putting her own head in the way of a bullet by filling me in.

Eventually I wandered out to Mrs. Skokow's desk to check the Zimmers' address on the Elite roster I got from Sig Danziger. The listing gave it as 3616 Glencairn, Shaker Heights — the same address I wrote down when Mrs. Skokow told me over the phone that she'd made the appointment, and the same one Nancy had given me at the Hotel Cleveland.

In looking at the roster, I wondered how Sig got ahold of it. It didn't contain any classified secrets, but Elite still wouldn't have wanted anyone outside the company to have a copy. I had half a mind to throw it in the waste basket and light a match, since I didn't really need it any longer.

I sat down on the couch across from Mrs. Skokow's desk and leafed through the roster, passing the time by looking for names of people I remembered at Elite. I'd just about exhausted the list when a name in the B's caught my eye:

BITKA Molly 1539 E. 69th Cleveland Oh. SU1-8424 Main Office STENO. Hired April '26.

"Unbelievable," I said out loud. "Un-goddamned-believable."

When I'd interviewed Molly Bitka about Maury Sorin's murder, she came across as nothing more than a little old lady with an affinity for chocolate cake. She'd heard of Elite, of course, but barely so. She'd put on a virtuoso performance. I hadn't suspected a thing.

But Molly's appearance on the Elite roster eliminated any doubt about the company's involvement in the Sorin killing. The coincidences were just too numerous to be coincidences. When Maury Sorin was murdered, he was handling a contentious case for a former Elite employee who had some kind of dirt on the company. The shooting took place in connection with a stick-up perpetrated by a guy who was so flush he bought his mother a new Olds for Christmas. This all occurred just a few days after someone had killed Sorin's client under equally dubious circumstances. Sergeant Stuffleben just happened to be on the scene to do away with Sorin's assailant, and he had an unsavory history with Elite. Now it turned out that Molly Bitka, the star witness, had a history working for the Forsythes, too — a longstanding one she had lied to conceal. None of this made any sense unless Elite had orchestrated Maury Sorin's death.

The way I put the puzzle together, Molly Bitka was an accessory to homicide. If my theory held, she'd do her future baking for the other cons at the Reformatory for Women at Marysville.

But first, Molly would have to live that long. The Forsythes were fastidious about tying up loose ends. Zimmer had been a loose end from whatever mischief he'd pulled for Elite, and they had him run down. Maury Sorin was a loose end begotten by Zimmer, and he met his maker, too. Grubb was next in the progression. Elite used him as their patsy to knock off Sorin because he'd have a believable motive, and because he was too hopped up to realize he'd be taking the next bullet. He was a loose end slated for tying from the moment the Forsythes hired him.

At some point, Elite would have to trust someone. Otherwise the murders would continue endlessly — first the two primary targets, then the targets' killers, then the killers of *those* killers, and so on *ad infinitum*. Molly Bitka must've shown unwavering loyalty over the years — my ex-in-laws apparently felt comfortable asking her to abet Maury Sorin's murder without worrying that she'd later blab about it or demand half the Forsythe family fortune to keep her lip zipped.

The stakes, however, had changed. I was asking questions that were too close for comfort. With the heat rising, Elite probably considered anyone who knew anything at all about the Sorin case a dangerous potential loose end.

That included me, of course. Given everything else I'd learned, my ex-in-laws had to be the ones who commissioned the effort to have me flattened on my way home from meeting Braunstein at the Alcazar. Rufus, as it turned out, hadn't been the only one who could've tipped them off about what I was doing. Molly Bitka was a much more plausible informant: I'd interviewed her before the attempted hit-and-run, and since she was already involved in the scheme, it only made sense she'd tell her bosses about the inquiries I was making into Maury Sorin's murder.

I wondered why the Forsythes hadn't tried to bump me off again. Maybe they were worried that others knew about my investigation and would come forward to implicate them if something happened to me. Maybe they regarded me as so feckless that I'd never find out the truth, even if they didn't bother having me whacked. Then again, there could've been a gunman waiting for me that very moment outside the building. The thought got my sweat glands pumping.

I picked up the telephone, dialed Molly Bitka's number, and announced my name.

"Yeah?" she answered sourly.

"I just wanted to double-check your story. You just happened to witness Maury Sorin's murder after leaving Union Terminal for a breath of fresh air. In a blizzard. As a reporter, I find this very intriguing."

"Get off it, Mr. Gold," Molly said. "I was in Elite's stenography pool the whole time you were married to Mr. Forsythe's daughter. I've known who you were from the beginning."

"I'm shocked," I said. "So why'd you play along with my make-believe?"

"If you wanted to make a fool of yourself, I wasn't going to stop you."

"You seem to have adopted my ex-father-in-law's opinion of me," I said.

"Mr. Forsythe always treated me just fine."

"Let's see how fine he treats you when you're indicted for helping murder Maury Sorin and the poor sap who shot him."

There was a momentary pause. "What in the world are you talking about?" she said slowly.

"Now you get off it, Molly. I know about the whole dirty business. I know your old boss had Frank Zimmer killed. I know he hired Warren Grubb to pop Sorin, and Vince Stuffleben to pop Grubb. I know all about Stuffleben's history with Elite."

"You're crazy," she said without conviction. "None of that is true."

"Sure it is, Molly," I said. "And you should be worried. The Forsythes have killed practically everybody else who knows about all this."

I waited three minutes after Molly hung up, then redialed her number. The line was busy, just as I expected. No doubt she'd called her handler at Elite as soon as our conversation ended, repeating everything I told her.

I'd stretched the truth a little, but that didn't matter. I had the goods on them. There'd be no denying Elite's responsibility for Maury Sorin's murder once I got the whys and wherefores from Frank G. Zimmer's widow.

TWENTY-SEVEN

I LEFT FOR Shaker Heights shortly before one o'clock. I knew the city from the years Elizabeth and I had lived there. Our house had been on South Park — a not-quite-a-mansion on a not-quite-an-estate. The Zimmers lived in a different part of town. Glencairn Road had thirty houses to a block on either side of the street, each one a brick two-story with a decent-sized yard and a free-standing garage. The neighborhood consisted mainly of professionals — lawyers, bankers, teachers, accountants. Most were young.

There was an old-model black sedan parked in the Zimmers' driveway when I arrived, so I left the Schooner on the street. Mrs. Zimmer answered the doorbell before it stopped ringing. "Did you have any trouble finding the house?" she asked perfunctorily as she ushered me in.

I followed her from the front hallway into her living room. There, on a navy-blue sofa, sat a wiry little man daintily holding a teacup in his left hand and a cookie in his right. Upon seeing me, he set the teacup down on its saucer on the table in front of him and stood. It was then that I noticed his turned collar.

"Mr. Gold, this is Reverend Floyd Pendergast of All Saints Church," Mrs. Zimmer said. "I've asked him to sit in with us, if you don't mind."

"Hello," I said as I walked toward the sofa with my right hand extended.

The Reverend didn't shake, presumably because of the cookie. He did bow slightly from the waist in my direction.

"Pleased to meet you, Mr. Gold," he said. His voice was a deep baritone, more befitting a man a foot taller and a hundred pounds heavier.

"Can I offer you some tea?" Mrs. Zimmer asked.

"No, thanks. I'm ready to get started if you are."

Mrs. Zimmer joined the Reverend on the couch. I sat facing them on a chair taken from the dining room. Mrs. Zimmer fidgeted nervously as she waited for the conversation to begin.

I started to ask my first question, but the Reverend beat me to it. "Mr. Gold," he said, "maybe you could tell us exactly what you're looking for from Mrs. Zimmer."

"Of course. Her husband was consulting with Maury Sorin about some dirty business he'd done for Elite Motorworks. The company wanted to keep a lid on it, and to do so, I believe it had both Mr. Zimmer and Mr. Sorin killed. I've corroborated a lot of the plot, but I still don't know what the original dirty business was that led Mr. Zimmer to seek out Maury Sorin's help. That's what I'm hoping Mrs. Zimmer can tell me. With that information, I think I can do something about it."

The Reverend and Mrs. Zimmer watched me intently as I gave my spiel. When I finished, they both shifted uncomfortably on the sofa and began studying the carpet at their feet. For a while, no one said anything.

"Is something wrong?" I asked.

The Reverend answered with his own question. "Can you tell us why you're investigating this matter?"

"No need to keep that a secret anymore. Maury Sorin's daughter hired me to find out what really happened to her father."

"I understand you typically work on domestic disputes, that sort of thing," he said.

"I do some of that, but not exclusively. Who told you that?"

"Isn't this assignment out of your bailiwick?"

"I don't think so," I said. "I wasn't aware I even had a bailiwick. Why the third degree?"

"You're asking Mrs. Zimmer to divulge some very sensitive information..."

"A man from Elite called yesterday afternoon," Mrs. Zimmer interrupted. "He asked me not to tell you anything. He said you were all wrong about what had happened, and had a personal vendetta against the people who own the company."

"They called about me?"

"Yes, they did. I didn't know what to do, so they suggested I consult Reverend Pendergast."

"You were once married to Elizabeth Forsythe, were you not?" the Reverend asked.

"Yeah, I was. Not only that — she was married to me."

"She divorced you, if I'm not mistaken."

"That's ancient history," I said. "And Elizabeth had nothing at all to do with Elite. It's her father and brother who run the company."

"The man who called said you always blamed them for the divorce," said Mrs. Zimmer.

"Who was this man?"

"He asked me not to say."

"And you're not going to tell me?"

"I've advised her not to reveal his name, yes," the Reverend said.

"Why?"

"Because at this point, I'm not at all convinced this is anything more than crass scandal-mongering."

I swallowed hard and concentrated on not telling the good Reverend to go straight to hell. They'd obviously decided not to cooperate. I wasn't going to lose my temper and give them something to justify the stonewall.

I turned to Mrs. Zimmer. "You know I didn't make this all up. Your husband went to see Maury Sorin about a serious problem. He brought him incriminating documents he'd taken from Elite. The company threatened him to keep him quiet; and they threatened you, too, and your son at college."

"They've explained that it was all a misunderstanding," Mrs. Zimmer replied weakly. "The man who called told me —"

"Remember, you're not supposed to repeat what he said," the Reverend interjected. "They were very emphatic about that."

"I wasn't going to give any details," said Mrs. Zimmer. "I was just going to say that my husband misunderstood what the company wanted him to do. It was a terrible accident that those men died …"

"Mrs. Zimmer!" The Reverend's deep growl shook the artwork on the wall.

"You're not telling me anything I don't already know," I said. "Not really. Maury Sorin thought your husband was going to send the Forsythes to the gas chamber. You don't get that for jaywalking."

"I think you'd better go, Mr. Gold," said the Reverend. "Mrs. Zimmer isn't in a position to give you what you want."

I looked at the Reverend, then turned to Mrs. Zimmer. "What's Elite paying you to keep quiet?" I asked. When she didn't answer, I repeated the question.

"How much? I hope it's a lot for your sake, given what they're asking you to do. And I figure you're getting a cut, too, Reverend.

Elite wouldn't have called you in unless they already had you in their back pocket."

The little man arose from the sofa and came toward me. "Get out of here, Mr. Gold," he said, "or — "

I stood up too, and took a step forward. "Or what, Reverend? You'll denounce me in a sermon? I'll leave, but don't push me."

The Reverend backed away. "Money isn't everyone's sole motivation," he said in a quiet, angry tone.

"Don't I know it. I'm on a personal vendetta. You all said so yourselves, so it must be true."

I looked at Mrs. Zimmer. Her face had turned crimson when I mentioned the payoff. "You should know why they're giving you the dough," I said to her. "You should know that unless you talk, they're going to get away with the whole rotten business. They'll have bought their way out of trouble, and they'll do the same the next time, and the time after that. There'll be a next time, because you'll have confirmed for them that it's just a question of how much. You can even kill a woman's husband in cold blood, and still, it's just a question of how much."

"We don't know what really happened..." she whimpered.

"We know enough," I said. "We know your husband killed someone as a result of what the company asked him to do. We know the company killed him and the lawyer who was willing to go to bat for him."

"Maurice Sorin was killed by a drug addict who needed money," the Reverend said. "What makes you think you know better than the police?"

"Because the police never looked at the murder as anything other than what it appeared to be. They never had any reason to. I did."

"You could be wrong," said Mrs. Zimmer.

"I could be, but I'm not. You're quite literally letting those people get away with murder."

"That's just rot," said the Reverend.

"And that's the opinion Elite is paying him to give," I replied.

"Mr. Gold, I can't believe you have the audacity to accuse me —"

"Save the speech, Reverend," I interrupted. "For all your huffing and puffing, you haven't denied it."

I thought Mrs. Zimmer might crack. She looked at the Reverend, took a deep breath, and started to say something — but then stopped. It was her conscience versus her bank account. The bank account won.

I was disgusted. "Thanks for nothing," I said to the two of them before turning my back and walking away. They started to whisper as I reached the front hallway, but I couldn't make out what they were saying.

I slammed the door when I left. It didn't make me feel any better at all.

TWENTY-EIGHT

I WENT DIRECTLY from the Zimmers' to a little bar I knew on Kinsman Road. The place had definitely come down a few pegs in the years since I'd been there, but Joey the bartender was still serving drinks, and the scotch was as good as ever — I spent three hours making certain of it. Joey wanted to call a cab for me when I got up to leave, but I insisted on driving home. It took nearly forty-five minutes, but I made it to my apartment in one piece.

When I got upstairs, I dragged myself into the kitchen to cook some dinner. Before leaving town, Nancy had made sure I honored Braunstein's mandate about eating more. But left to my own devices, I reverted to old habits. The fried eggs went straight from the stove into the garbage pail.

I was still agitated, even after all the booze. Mrs. Zimmer's decision to clam up was mostly to blame, but not exclusively. My get-together in Public Square with the FBI boys let me know that I had to extricate myself from the Doc's case, even though I wasn't actually involved in it. Then there was the situation with Jake. Miriam had called Friday morning to check on me, but I hadn't heard from either of them since. Jake had obviously decided to continue the Cold War.

At the bar in Shaker Heights, I'd momentarily considered going back to Mrs. Zimmer's house to see if I could catch her alone. I thought she might talk if the good Reverend Pendergast wasn't there to muzzle her. I needed her help if I was going to have any chance of proving that the Forsythes popped Maury Sorin. Motive was the issue: if my ex-in-laws committed the murder, why did they do it? I could only answer that question if I knew Zimmer's reasons for going to Maury Sorin. As far as I could tell, only Mrs. Zimmer and the Forsythes had that information. Unless she opened up, I'd be connecting the dots with invisible ink.

I understood why she'd bugged out on me. Her husband had tried to come clean about the Forsythes, and he ended up six feet under. She was on her own now, and probably needed the cash Elite was offering. My ex-in-laws had also turned up the heat, paying off a clergyman to see to it that she kept her mouth shut, or heaven help her.

I woke the next morning after 8:00 but stayed in bed, even though the hangover wasn't that bad. The only thing I had to do now was let Judith know her case had crapped out. I rolled over and dozed for another hour and a half.

I didn't make it downtown until almost lunchtime. Mrs. Skokow was at her desk, deeply engrossed in a telephone conversation that had nothing to do with work. I gave a half-hearted wave as I dragged myself to my office.

The stack of receipts sitting on my desk reminded me about Mrs. Skokow's mission to Galion. There was one for the train ticket, one from the Hotel Talbott, two from Carmel's Restaurant, and miscellaneous others. The hotel bill included five long distance calls to her home number. She and her husband talked more during her trip than they did face-to-face in a typical month.

"Andrews Dairy — $11.87?" I said to Mrs. Skokow, waving a receipt at her when she walked in five minutes later. "You must've taken half of Galion out for ice cream."

"Now, Boss, don't be stingy. I treated some of the people I'd been talking to about Sergeant Stuffleben. You yourself said it was important work."

"Not so important, as it turns out. Frank Zimmer's widow wouldn't spill."

"That's too bad," Mrs. Skokow said. "Why not?"

"The reason doesn't matter. Without her I'm up a creek."

"I didn't do so hot myself," said Mrs. Skokow. "The stuff about Stuffleben and Elite was pure rumor."

"What was pure rumor?"

"Stuffleben didn't do what they say he did. The Fire Chief himself told me so."

"You'd better back up," I said.

"There was a fire at the Elite Motors factory in Galion. The place was completely destroyed. Word on the street was that Elite hired Vince Stuffleben to set it for the insurance money."

"I didn't know Elite even had a factory in Galion," I said.

"It was a small plant that another company had owned. Elite bought it during the War to make parts for tanks they were manufacturing for the army. They closed it some time before the fire."

"When was that?"

"A few years ago," she said. "Wait a second..."

Mrs. Skokow left my office and returned a moment later with the front page from the April 4, 1949 edition of the *Galion Inquirer*. "Two Dead At Elite Motorworks Plant," read the headline just below the masthead.

"Where'd you get this?" I asked.

"From my Aunt Edna. She collects stories about murders, disasters, tornadoes — that sort of thing. She said I could bring this to show you, as long as we mailed it back to her."

"You'll have to tell her 'thanks,'" I said as I started reading:

A fire at the Elite Motorworks plant in town yesterday evening completely destroyed the factory and killed two employees trapped in a second-floor office.

"There was a lot of smoke," said Mrs. Albert Hornsby, of 318 N. Main, who'd driven out to watch the blaze. "Even at a distance, it was hard to breathe."

The Galion Fire Department responded to a call at 5:37 P.M. about flames coming from the rear of the plant, located on Ohio 19. By the time the fire trucks arrived at the scene, the west side of the factory was completely burnt.

The victims were identified as Horace Clement, 44, of 612 East Church St., and Edward Barfield, 53, of 92 Pershing. Both had worked in Accounts Payable for Elite before the factory closed in January.

Clement and Barfield had already perished when firefighters found them. It was not immediately known why they were in the building at the time.

The fire was discovered by Sgt. Vincent Stuffleben of the Galion Police Department on his drive home from work. "There was a lot of black smoke," he said. "I knew something was wrong."

After calling the Fire Department, Stuffleben broke into the factory through a window to see whether anyone was inside. He didn't know Clement and Barfield were in the second-floor office.

"I couldn't have gotten to them anyway," Stuffleben said. "The stairs were already half gone."

The cause of the fire has not yet been determined, said Fire Chief Doyle Amick. An investigation is ongoing.

"Did they ever figure out what caused the fire?" I asked Mrs. Skokow.

"Electrical problem."

"How do you know?"

"Straight from the horse's mouth, like I told you," she said. "Doyle Amick — the Fire Chief. I knew him from high school."

"So it wasn't arson?"

"Nope. I didn't get all the details, but Doyle was definite: Stuffleben didn't start it."

"Why did people think he did?"

"I don't know where the idea came from," Mrs. Skokow said. "But Stuffleben isn't a very well-respected man in Galion. They pretty much ran him out of town."

"I thought he still lived there."

"They kicked him off the local police force, anyway. People don't like him. He broke his wife's arm once, and his kids used to show up at school with black-and-blue marks."

"A true gentleman," I said.

"And a liar, too. They caught him once planting evidence on a suspect. He arrested some guy for robbing the drugstore. The pharmacist saw Stuffleben take things from the shelves and stuff them in the guy's pockets. It all came out at trial. After that, nobody believed a word he said about anything. He was lucky he wasn't arrested himself."

"That doesn't explain why people thought he torched the Elite factory," I said.

"It was fishy that he was the one who discovered the fire," she answered.

"He was coming home from work. What's fishy about that?"

"Stuffleben always had something up his sleeve," Mrs. Skokow said. "Aunt Edna said he'd steal change from a blind man's cup."

"After meeting him, I don't find that hard to believe."

"They figured Elite must've paid him so they could collect on the insurance," she said. "Somebody said they saw Stuffleben's police car parked at the factory the day before the fire. One lady heard he kept the insurance investigators from going over the place."

"Was any of it true?"

"No one could prove anything one way or another. But Stuffleben didn't set the fire. It wasn't arson. Doyle made that absolutely clear."

"You trust him?" I asked.

"Doyle Amick? His family's lived in Galion forever. If he says something, you can believe it."

That was too bad. If Mrs. Zimmer's refusal to talk had killed the Sorin case, the news from Galion desecrated the corpse. I'd sent Mrs. Skokow to get proof that Stuffleben was in bed with my ex-in-laws, but the only thing she'd found to connect them were rumors born from his status as the town pariah.

Still, I couldn't help being suspicious. In Vince Stuffleben, the Forsythes would've had a henchman as utterly rotten as they were themselves. He may have gotten a bum rap on the Elite factory fire, but he still could've been complicit in Maury Sorin's murder. Right then, I just couldn't prove it.

"I'm going over to the Blue Boar to grab a bite," I told Mrs. Skokow. "You can go on home. After lunch, I'll call Judith Sorin, then call it a day."

I ended up giving Mrs. Skokow the rest of the week off. I didn't want to work on anything other than the Sorin case, and there weren't any more leads I could think of to follow. Mrs. Skokow didn't have to come downtown to watch me stare at the wall.

At the restaurant, I got turkey and mashed potatoes and tried to figure out the quickest way to tell Judith her case had died. I was done being rude to her, but I didn't want to get into a heated debate about whether we knew enough to go to the prosecutor. We didn't actually know much, when it came down to it. What we had was inference and innuendo, not hard information. There wasn't enough to warrant even an investigation, much less a trip to the grand jury. I wouldn't have an easy time telling her all this in fifty words or less.

Thoughts of the Galion fire kept interfering with my speech-writing. It perplexed me that I was only hearing about it now. The Cleveland press followed Elite closely, and ordinarily would've given something like a fatal factory fire a lot of ink. I continued to scratch my head until I realized that the company's initial sale of shares on the New York Stock Exchange took place within months of the Galion blaze. Bad publicity would've depressed the market. The Forsythes must've called in a lot of favors to keep a lid on the story. If the papers outside Galion covered it at all, they probably had done so at the back of Section D, right between the classified ads and advice to the lovelorn.

The hush-hush treatment of the fire in Galion wasn't the only thing that had my wheels turning. While Mrs. Skokow hadn't connected Stuffleben to Elite, she did say something that seemed potentially significant — though at first I couldn't put my finger on why. The Galion factory went down in an "electrical" fire. Stuffleben didn't start it, but he was a blockhead who probably had trouble flipping a light switch.

Could the fire have been set by someone who was a real expert on fuses and wires and circuits — someone like Zimmer, a master electrician? The fire chief hadn't necessarily ruled out that possibility, as far as I knew. Zimmer's widow said there were casualties from the dirty work her husband did for the Forsythes. She might have been referring to the toasted bodies in Galion when she let that slip.

This hypothesis could bring the Sorin case back from the crypt. Still, I resisted the temptation to do cartwheels down the aisles of the Blue Boar. I'd had hunches before that turned out to be wishful thinking. I thought I was putting two and two together when all I really had was one and none.

At least it might be worth talking to Fire Chief Doyle Amick to check my math. I paid for the lunch I hadn't eaten and walked back to my office to put the call in through the operator.

Twenty-Nine

"What can I do for you, Mr. Gold?"

"I want to ask about the fire at the Elite factory a few years back," I told the Chief. "I believe you spoke to my secretary, Bernice Skokow..."

"Skokow? Oh, you mean Bernice Fillmore. That was her name in high school."

"Fillmore," I said. "At any rate, she told me about your conversation regarding the fire and Vincent Stuffleben."

"Listen. Vince Stuffleben was a bad egg. He'd steal change from a blind man's cup."

"I've heard it said."

"But there's no way on God's green earth he started that fire," said the Chief. "Not a chance in the world. I've got to tell you — it's damn strange you're asking about this now."

"What do you mean?"

"I guess you haven't heard. Stuffleben rammed his cruiser into an embankment on U.S. 30 day before yesterday. Dead upon impact, they say."

"Jesus. How'd it happen?"

"Nobody knows for sure," said the Chief. "His siren was on, but he wasn't answering a call. He was probably chasing some driver for speeding and just lost control. No suspicion of foul play or anything like that."

Well, I had suspicions — I'd already included Stuffleben on my list of likely Forsythe targets. Somehow, some way, the Forsythes had set up Stuffleben's crash to tie up another loose end from their string of criminality. I wondered how Molly Bitka would react when she learned of Stuffleben's unfortunate demise. I wondered whether she'd even be around to hear the news.

Eventually the conversation turned back to the Elite fire. I asked the Chief whether he'd ever figured out how it started.

"A short circuit in a piece of equipment from before the company owned the place, best we could tell," he said. "A lathe from the early Thirties. Apparently Elite continued to use it for this and that when the factory was still running. But they forgot to unplug it when they closed up shop, and it must've sparked."

"Why'd the place burn so quickly?"

"They kept the lathe near a storage area, which was mostly cleared out — but there was still some lubricating oil back there, and some other stuff. When that ignited, it was off to the races."

"How big was the plant, Chief?" I asked.

"Not big — only eight, nine thousand square feet," he said. "The place started as a foundry. A company that made parts for General Motors owned it for a couple of years. Elite bought it during the War to make hinges for tank turrets or some such thing. Employed about sixty people. Good for Galion."

"Can't argue with that."

"But the place was a fire trap," said the Chief. "If the company hadn't shut it down, we would have, sooner or later. One of our inspectors went out there the October before they closed it."

"Why was it a fire trap?"

"Elite bought the place in '42. There was no office space in the building, so the company built a second floor from scratch — a loft, made entirely of wood. They put in three telephone lines and a lot of electrical wiring."

"I'm getting the picture," I said.

"The company did all of this in a big hurry. It was never up to code, but we let it slide, because of the War and all. Elite said it would fix things up when business slowed down, but they never got around to it."

"Why didn't they renovate the place? I'm sure they could've used it for something."

"That factory was a relic," said the Chief. "Elite made do with it during the War, but it wasn't really suited for modern manufacturing."

"So the fire took an obsolete factory off Elite's hands," I said.

"I suppose you could put it that way. But at a heavy price, with those boys dying and all."

"Do you know why they were in the building?" I asked.

"Earlier in the week, the home office called Barfield and asked him to fetch some old invoices they needed for a report or something. They called him because he still had a key to the place. Clement was just keeping him company."

"Bad luck," I said.

"Yeah," said the Chief. "When they turned on the lights and fans, they probably caused a surge that shorted out that old lathe. No way of telling for sure, though. If it hadn't been that, it would've been something else, eventually."

"Chief, could someone have rigged the lathe to short out?"

"Now why would Vince Stuffleben...?"

"Not Stuffleben. But how about an electrical expert?"

"Sure, there's things you could do," he said. "We didn't see any sign of that, but it could be pretty damn hard to detect."

"Okay..."

"But even if you did that, you still couldn't tell for certain when the thing would blow. You'd need a magician for that."

"Or a master electrician," I said.

"I suppose so. Yeah..."

"So it could be done?"

"I'm not saying it couldn't," he said. "But it'd be damn hard."

The call ended. If nothing else, it confirmed Elite's amazing good fortune in getting rid of a plant it no longer needed. Two men might have fried, but the Forsythes wouldn't have lost much sleep over that, not with insurance proceeds to cover whatever compensation they had to pay the grieving families. As a business proposition, it was too good to be true — and I was sticking with my guess that it wasn't.

I got a busy signal when I telephoned Mrs. Zimmer. She picked up on my second try, and I went right at it.

"I know your husband went to see Maury Sorin about the fire he set in Galion. You and Reverend Pendergast stonewalled me, but I found out anyway. Your husband set the fire at the Elite factory, and two men died because of it."

"Oh my God," Mrs. Zimmer said.

"Maybe now you'll tell me what you know, so I have the story completely straight when I go to the police."

"What good will that do? Frank's already dead. He paid the price for what he did."

"But others haven't," I said. "It was for the insurance money, wasn't it?"

"I guess so..."

"Who else was in on it?"

"He talked to the younger Mr. Forsythe at the company," she said. "And there was a policeman in Galion who helped him get in and out of the building. That's all I know."

"How much did your husband get for setting the fire?"

Mrs. Zimmer hesitated for a moment. "Five hundred dollars," she admitted.

"That's it?"

"Yes. Five hundred dollars."

"I'm sorry." An apology seemed appropriate, but I wasn't sure why.

"You say you're going to the police?" Mrs. Zimmer asked.

"I'm going to talk to the Forsythes first. There's a few more details I need."

"You aren't going to tell them you found this out from me?"

I hung up without answering her question. Then I dialed the number for Elite's executive offices.

Junior's secretary didn't want to put my call through. "He's in a meeting and can't be disturbed," she said.

"I'll tell you what, sister — you'd better disturb him. I'm going to hang on the line for another minute, and if your boss doesn't pick up, my next call will be to the Prosecutor's Office."

"What do you want, Benjamin?" Junior said thirty seconds later.

"I'm just calling to pay my condolences. I heard there was a fire at your Galion factory a few years back, and you lost a couple of men. Vince Stuffleben tried to save the day, but it was too little too late, I guess. Now he's dead, too."

"So what's your point?"

"You know goddamned well what my point is," I said. "Maury Sorin knew it, too, and you killed him for it."

"We ought to discuss this face-to-face," Junior said.

"My thoughts exactly. I'll be by at 4:30."

"That's not convenient."

"All the better," I said as I hung up the phone.

THIRTY

THIS TIME JUNIOR was waiting for me in the Board Room. Clayton Senior was with him, along with Mr. Stanley, the Gorilla who served as Junior's personal security detail.

"Let's get down to business," Clayton Senior said. "I haven't got all day."

"You've got as long as it takes, old man," I replied. "This is going to be slow and painful."

"You're an obnoxious ass, Benjamin."

"You'll be calling me a lot worse by the time we're done here."

I was feeling my oats, all right. For what seemed like the first time in my dealings with the Forsythes, I was dishing it out and not taking it.

I'd been on the receiving end during my hour-long telephone conversation with Judith Sorin earlier that afternoon. "Call the prosecutor," she instructed me when I told her what I'd learned from Zimmer's widow. "You've got the evidence you need."

"No, I don't," I said. "I know why Zimmer was seeing your father, and I can connect him to Stuffleben, but I want to tie the whole thing together."

"There's no need for a showdown with your in-laws," said Judith.

"They're my ex-in-laws."

"It has nothing to do with the case. It's personal."

"You're wrong," I said. "But remember, you said you hired me because I had a history with these people. If it is personal, that's the way you wanted it."

And around and around we went. If the world needed a cure for happiness, the woman could've applied for a patent and cleaned up.

I'd bid my hello to Clayton Senior. Now it was Junior's turn.

"I really appreciated that lovely photograph," I said as I walked toward him. "It really had quite an impact. I thought I'd reciprocate." I then delivered a left-right combination to Junior's chin.

I'd started planning the attack as soon I hung up with Junior earlier that afternoon. I went back and forth all afternoon on whether I'd actually carry through with it. I was worried that Nancy might disapprove, and I wondered about what Elizabeth would think if she found out I'd cold-cocked her brother. I could've gone either way until I glimpsed my patched forehead in the men's-room mirror at the Union Trust Building. That made up my mind.

Junior fell to his knees after I slugged him. Blood trickled from the left side of his mouth, and he groaned miserably. The groan became louder when Junior put his hand to his lips and it came back red.

"You cut me, you son of a bitch," he yelped.

By this time the Gorilla was coming around the conference table and hulking toward me. I'd prepared for this contingency. On my way out of the office, I'd retrieved Mrs. Skokow's little .32 from her desk drawer. To my utter lack of surprise, she'd reloaded it since my visit from the FBI.

"I wouldn't be too hasty," I told the Gorilla as I pointed the pistol directly at his left knee. "Not unless you want to walk with a limp the rest of your life."

The Gorilla stopped about fifteen feet from where I stood. Junior cursed him for it.

"Goddamn it, he's not going to shoot you. He doesn't have the guts."

"Oh, no?"

I turned and fired a quick round toward the oversized portrait of Clayton Senior hanging on the far wall. The shot fortuitously hit the left breast pocket of his suit coat — right where his heart would've been, if he had one.

"Bullseye," I said. "Another lucky winner."

At the behest of the .32, the Forsythes and the Gorilla pulled chairs against the wall and sat down. I situated myself at the head of the conference table and turned to face them. Just as I started to talk, a security guard burst through the door.

"I heard a shot," he said. "Is everyone all right?"

"Everything's fine," Clayton Senior responded. "Our guest was just doing his imitation of a firecracker. You can go."

"If you say so, sir," the security guard said after hesitating a moment. He closed the door on his way out.

"Let's get on with this," Clayton Senior said to me. "What is it you think you know?"

"I know you paid Frank Zimmer five hundred dollars to set the fire in Galion," I said. "He sabotaged an old piece of equipment. He did a good job of it — no one suspected a thing. I know Vince Stuffleben helped stage the fire. And I know you killed Zimmer by having him run over when he started having second thoughts about what he'd done."

"That's slander," Junior retorted.

"It's not slander if it's true. You sons of bitches tried to run me over, too."

"You can't prove that," Junior said.

"Just like I can't prove you hired Warren Grubb to pop Maury Sorin and then used Stuffleben and Molly Bitka to bump him off."

I paused for a moment to take in the Forsythes' reaction. Junior put his hand to his forehead and shuddered. His father just stared at me. No one said anything for quite a while. I was confused — I didn't know exactly how the Forsythes would react to the report I'd be giving them, but I hadn't expected the silent treatment.

I tried to decoy them into talking. "Let me tell you something else I know. You paid off Grubb with illegal narcotics — speed — "

"That's a lie!" Junior blurted.

"Shut the hell up!" Clayton Senior shouted. "Just shut up, god-damn it!"

"How did you pay Grubb, if not with speed? Was it fifties or C-notes?"

"You see, Junior?" the old man said. "He doesn't really know anything. He's bluffing."

"You wish," I replied.

"Poor Frank Zimmer died a few days before the Sorin murder, did he not?" Clayton Senior asked after another momentary pause.

"Yeah. You know, because you killed him."

"If Zimmer was dead, why would I kill his lawyer, assuming I even knew he had one?"

"Come on," I said. "Sorin could still tell the prosecutors what he'd learned from Zimmer."

"Could he? I thought lawyers had to keep secret what they learned from their clients."

"They don't have to keep secrets if their client's been murdered and what they know will expose the murderer."

"If Mr. Sorin told what he knew, he'd have to reveal that Zimmer set the fire in Galion, according to the story you're telling. That'd make his client a murderer, too. You still think he would've revealed what he found out from Zimmer?"

"Who do you think you are — Perry Mason?" I asked testily. "You orchestrated all of these killings. I'm going to tell the prosecutor what I know."

"If you thought you had enough to go to the prosecutor, you wouldn't be here," Clayton Senior said. "Even if Maurice Sorin wanted to go public with accusations against us, he couldn't have proven anything without a witness, and he didn't have one after Zimmer died. Only a moron would kill him under those circumstances."

"You said it, not me."

"Tell me: Why in the world would I hire someone to burn down my own factory?"

"There probably were millions of reasons why," I responded.

"The Galion Fire Department didn't detect any foul play, but you know better?"

"I do."

"That was a damn costly mess for our company. We lost the building and everything inside, and had to compensate the families of those two fools who got themselves killed."

"Who are you kidding?" I said. "It *would've* cost you a lot, if not for the insurance. I'm sure Elite made a tidy little sum. Right before the public stock offering, too."

"You know, Benjamin, you really are a stupid kike," Clayton Senior said with a grin on his face. "A stupid, stupid kike."

I aimed Mrs. Skokow's pistol and fired another shot into the old man's portrait. "We'll see who's stupid," I said.

"We didn't have any insurance on the Galion plant. The carrier canceled our policy years before over the fire risk — you can't insure a building that isn't up to code. Nobody covered our losses. We had to eat them, and it hurt our bottom line plenty. It nearly made us postpone the stock sale."

Clayton Senior stood up and stretched his legs. Then he sat back down.

"The tale you're telling is a pack of lies," the old man resumed. "A filthy pack of lies."

"Yeah? We'll see."

"There are laws in this country that protect people from the likes of you," Clayton Senior said. "Junior talked about this the last time you were here, but now I'm promising it. For every time you've lied about us, there'll be a lawsuit. For every different person you spoke to, a separate case. And if any of them repeated the lie to others, there'll be more cases, all against you. We're going to destroy you, Benjamin, absolutely destroy you. Your law license — gone. Your license to do the crap you do now — gone. You won't work in Cleveland or anywhere else when we get through with you. You'll end up killing yourself, because that'll be better than the life you're left with."

When Clayton Senior finally exhausted his litany of threats, I walked slowly over to him and slapped his face with my open palm.

Or at least that's what I wanted to do — but I didn't. I wanted to slash his throat, too, or shoot him — the real Clayton Senior this time, not just the painting. But it wouldn't have helped the situation, and he'd have enjoyed it at some level — the slap, at least — since he'd have known he broke me down.

And he had. I hadn't necessarily changed my mind about what had happened to Maury Sorin. I also wasn't convinced I was mistaken about the Galion fire, except that I'd figured wrong on Elite's reasons for wanting to torch the place.

But the old man had made his point — the same point I'd been trying to impress upon Judith all along. What I thought or inferred about her father's death didn't matter. Neither did the objective truth. All that counted was what I could prove — and it wasn't much. The Forsythes could tear gaping holes in the story I'd tell to the prosecutor. There were no signs of arson, according to the Galion Fire Department, and Elite had no obvious incentive to set the fire. In the face of these facts, Zimmer's widow would seem like a hopeless crackpot if she repeated her second-hand confession — which she probably wouldn't, once the Forsythes reminded her who was buttering her bread.

Without corroboration, I couldn't explain why the Forsythes wanted to put Zimmer out of the picture. I also couldn't explain why Maury Sorin was still a threat after Zimmer died, given his obligation to keep quiet about what he knew. The prosecutor wouldn't touch this case with a ten-foot pole. There'd be no indictment, no trial, no convictions. The Forsythes killed Maury Sorin in cold blood, and the price they'd pay was nothing at all.

I'd pay a price, though. I knew Clayton Senior wasn't bluffing in threatening my demise, professional and otherwise. The bastard had a well-deserved reputation for ruthlessness. When he said he was going to get someone, he got them, and they stayed gotten. He'd been waiting a long time to have a go at me, and now I'd served myself up on a silver platter.

"You're not talking, Benjamin," said Clayton Senior. "You came for information to seal your case, and you ended up with the opposite."

"I've said what I came to say," I replied as I stood up. "We're done here."

"I'd leave too, if I were you. You could try begging for mercy, but it wouldn't help."

"Or I could just tell you to go fuck yourself."

"Such disreputable language…"

"You know something, Pops?" I said. "I'm still going to the prosecutor, insurance or no insurance. You can explain your alibis to him."

"We both know you're done, Benjamin."

I headed toward the door. "We'll see," I said. "Just remember, Clayton — there's no cocktail hour in jail."

I'd never before called my ex-father-in-law by his first name. Apparently, he didn't like it.

"You know, I had you pegged from the beginning," he said. "From the moment Elizabeth dragged you home. You were a mongrel then, and you're a mongrel now. Even your own family doesn't want anything to do with you."

I pointed Mrs. Skokow's .32 at his portrait and emptied it. "Like I said, Clayton, you can go fuck yourself."

I headed down a silent hallway toward the exit. The office had closed while I was in conference with the Forsythes. I didn't see a single person on my way to the elevators.

It took forever for the elevator to come, and I was in a hurry. I wanted to get to the payphone in the first-floor lobby as quickly as

I could, to call Judith and warn her not to repeat what I'd told her about the Forsythes and the Galion fire. That was for her protection as well as my own — Clayton Senior hadn't said he'd include her in his lawsuits, but it only made sense that he would.

On the ride down, I caught myself trying to think of ways to resuscitate the case. But it was hopeless. There were no witnesses left to interview, no new evidence I might uncover to turn the tide. Clayton Senior was right. I was done.

When the elevator opened on the first floor, the Gorilla was waiting for me with a baseball bat in hand. "I took the executive elevator," he said.

"Did you, now?"

I tried to bolt past him to the front door, but he stuck out his foot and tripped me. I went face-first into the tile.

"You should've saved some bullets in that gun of yours," the Gorilla said. "Then we would've left you alone. Wasting ammunition is unprofessional."

"Bad planning," I agreed groggily as I rolled over and tried to get to my feet.

The Gorilla dropped the baseball bat and helped me up with both hands. "I'll leave your head alone," he said. "It's already banged up."

"Mighty big of you."

I tried weakly to pull away, but the Gorilla restrained me with his left hand. He balled the right one into a fist and pounded me three times in the gut. The third punch sent me to the floor.

"Enough," I said after I got my breath back.

"Yes, enough, perhaps," the Gorilla repeated. "Mr. Forsythe didn't want me to break anything." He started to walk away but thought better of it, came back, and kicked me in the groin.

"Next time keep your hands to yourself," he said. "And leave your gun at home." Then he said something else, but I didn't catch it. I was concentrating on not blacking out.

I lay there for nearly half an hour before I took a chance and stood up. I had to lean against the wall for a little while longer, but eventually staggered through the lobby and out the front door.

When I made it to the street, Number One and Number Two were sitting in a black sedan parked in front of the Elite Motorworks building. They laughed when they saw me and started whispering between themselves. I was in so much pain that I considered asking them for a lift, but they sped off before I could open my mouth.

I eventually managed to hail a cab. I gave the driver the address of my apartment and told him I was going to rest until we got there. Then I laid against the backseat and closed my eyes. I didn't whimper or cry out once on the way home. I considered that my big accomplishment of the day.

THIRTY-ONE

I CRAWLED INTO bed as soon as I got to my apartment and didn't get up until two o'clock the next afternoon. I would've slept even longer, but the telephone rang and I felt obligated to answer. I figured it was Judith. Once the Gorilla ambushed me, I forgot all about getting in touch with her. I knew she'd expected to hear from me as soon as the meeting ended. I could only imagine the sweet nothings that would come from her mouth when we discussed why I hadn't called.

But it wasn't Judith. "This is the operator with a person-to-person call from Nancy Debevec to Benjamin Gold. Are you Mr. Gold?"

"Yes," I said.

"One moment, please."

"Gold? Is that you?" asked Nancy.

"The one and only," I said.

"I'm calling to check up on you. How's the head?"

"It's my least vulnerable part," I said. "I'm fine."

"You don't sound fine, Gold. Why are you home in the middle of the day?"

"I've got a meeting out this way and stopped off to change my shoes."

"A meeting on the Sorin case?" she asked.

"Another matter. Something new."

"How'd it go with Mrs. Zimmer?"

"It's a long story," I said. "Can I call you this evening?"

"You don't have to call. It's expensive. Put it in a letter."

Nancy gave me her address in Chicago, which I assured her I already had, since she'd written it down for me before leaving town. The conversation proceeded fitfully. I had things I couldn't tell Nancy, and just as many that I didn't want to tell her. I struggled through the minefield as long as I could manage, then said I'd be in touch soon and hung up.

I grabbed my cigarettes and a book of matches and made my way slowly to the living room sofa. Getting there was no small feat, given the searing pain that shot from my abdomen to my jaw and temples with every step. It felt as though the Gorilla had worked me over from the inside out.

I nearly gagged when I lifted my undershirt to inspect his handiwork. There were swollen welts on either side of my belly button, each the size of a baseball and the color of a ripe plum.

I hadn't enjoyed giving Nancy the brush-off, but I didn't want to talk to her or anyone else about what had happened. Maybe the humiliation would eventually pass, but I couldn't conceive of when. The Sorin case had given me the opportunity to nail the Forsythes — really nail them. I had the chance, but botched it monumentally, jumping before I looked and engaging in the sort of cheesy histrionics you'd expect from a Saturday matinee detective. Rather than bringing the Forsythes down, I'd probably emboldened them further.

I'd never really thought of myself as a small-time hack, but on the cab ride home from the Elite offices, I realized that's exactly what I was. I was the one to call if your husband was diddling his secretary or the maid had pawned the family silverware, but for anything more substantial, I was out of my league. The current debacle left no doubt about it.

Judith mercifully kept her yap shut when I got around to calling her. "I could do more digging," I said after recapping the meeting at Elite. "But I don't think it would accomplish much. We've pretty much reached the end of the road."

"How much do I owe you?" she responded.

"I think we're square."

"I'd appreciate it if you'd put my file in the mail."

"Okay," I said. Then I heard a click.

I immediately redialed Judith's number and started talking as soon as she picked up. "Our conversation wasn't finished," I said.

"Mr. Gold?"

"Yeah, it's me. I assume you're planning to take your case to another shamus."

"That's none of your business."

"Maybe not," I said. "But just the same, I want to make sure you tell my replacement exactly what he's getting into. The Forsythes want this matter over and done with."

"I'm not afraid of them," she said.

"You should be. They're not monkeying around. People have died."

"Including my father."

"Just let the new guy know what he's up against and let him make his own decision whether to put himself in the line of fire."

"Are you going to send me my file or not?" Judith asked.

"Of course I am."

"Well, then, goodbye," she said and hung up on me a second time.

I went downtown the next morning to make good on my commitment. When I got out of the elevator on the seventh floor, I saw a woman in a navy-blue dress standing outside the door of my office. Since I didn't have any appointments scheduled, I figured she'd gotten my name from the phone book and decided just to show up. I was less than overjoyed. Given my state of mind and body, I wasn't all that keen on listening to someone else's problems.

As I walked slowly toward the office, my eyes focused on the woman's bright silver handbag and the two diamond rings adorning the hand that was holding it. My stomach knotted when I looked up to check out the rest of her. I knew that face. The eyes, the nose, the chin — every contour of it was familiar, even after all the time that had passed.

"Elizabeth," I said. "What in the world are you doing here?"

"I need to talk to you, Benny."

All I could do was nod. I knew I wasn't dreaming, but I had a hard time believing what I saw. A ghost had materialized out of nowhere.

I unlocked the door and swung it open. "Come on in," I told her.

THIRTY-TWO

ELIZABETH FOLLOWED ME into my private office and sat in the chair facing my desk. She looked all right. She was heavier than she'd been before the War but not as heavy as she was during her flash visit at the hospital seven years ago. Her hair had grown out and returned to blonde. I was surprised to see crow's feet around her eyes. She hadn't aged in my thoughts of her.

I concentrated on keeping my yap shut as I went to open the shades and turn on the lights. I certainly had a lot to say but knew Elizabeth hadn't dropped by to hear my ruminations on the failure of our marriage.

She'd come on account of my showdown with her father and brother. That was the obvious explanation for her visit. I doubted she'd volunteered for the assignment, but I was irritated that she'd allowed herself to be dragged into it. I wondered what in the hell they sent her to tell me.

I pulled a bottle of scotch and two shot glasses from the bottom drawer of my desk and laid them out in front of me. "I know it's early," I said as I poured, "but it's a special occasion."

"None for me, thanks," said Elizabeth.

"Really?"

"I'm on the wagon."

"Good for you. How long?"

"Six weeks and counting," she said.

"Well, like I said, good for you." I drained my drink and hers, then put back the bottle and the glasses. "You know I saw your father and brother the other day," I said.

"That's why I'm here."

"I assumed as much."

"Benny, you —"

"Not so fast," I interrupted. The scotch had washed away my reticence. "I've got some questions I want to ask before you deliver your message."

"Benny, it isn't a good time for this."

"It's the only time," I said, and jumped right in. "What the hell was it with the quicky divorce?"

"How am I supposed to answer that question?"

"Try telling the truth. I'm back from Europe, laid up in a hospital, and you ditch me without any advance warning."

Elizabeth paused for a moment. "You and I weren't getting along before you left for Europe," she said. "Then we didn't see each other for over two years, and we weren't particularly nice to one another in our letters. I thought there was a rupture that couldn't be repaired."

"I really needed you when I came back."

"I know," she said.

"Why didn't you come to see me in the hospital more than once, for all of two minutes? Even if you were divorcing me?"

"There's no good excuse, Benny."

"Your parents were probably telling you to stay away."

"I can't blame them," she said. "I knew I should visit. When I felt guilty about it, I just drank more."

"I'm not venting spleen, Liz," I said. "I've thought a lot about this, and the whole marriage seems so twisted now. How in the world did you end up with a guy like me anyway?"

"What are you asking?"

"You pretended to be the rebellious youth, but what you really wanted all along was the life of the Forsythe heiress. I couldn't have been more ill-suited for that."

"You didn't seem so unhappy," Elizabeth said.

"I wasn't, at least not at first. But eventually reality came crashing down."

"We were living under my parents' thumb. It wasn't ideal."

"That's an understatement," I said. "But what happened? As soon as we got engaged, it was as if you became the society girl you said you never wanted to be."

"That's an overstatement."

"You went from being your parents' worst nightmare to the apple of their eye," I said.

"Except that I was marrying a Jew."

"Except for that, yes. But the Jew wasn't nearly as Jewish after the marriage as he'd been before."

"Depends on who you asked," Elizabeth said. "My father thought you were a purebred from start to finish."

"So what's your point?"

"I wasn't making one," replied Elizabeth. "You were."

"I was trying to find out why you married me when everything suggests you wanted somebody completely different."

"Did you ever think I might've loved you?" Elizabeth asked.

"Yes," I said. "At one time, I did."

"I've thought a lot about this, too, Benny. I know I was the one who got the divorce, but I've got my own regrets."

"Come on. About what?"

"Don't be so hard, Benny," she said. "It's not your nature."

"You canned me when I was at rock-bottom. I haven't heard from you in years. You can say you have regrets, but..."

"Aren't you responsible for anything that happened? You didn't have to take the job at Grimm White or go along with all the other things."

"What choice did I really have?"

"You could've put your foot down, Benny," she said. "We could've lived as Mr. and Mrs. Benny Goldstein instead of what we became. I would've done it for you. For us."

"No way," I said. "No way in the world."

"I would have, Benny," she said. "Like I said — I've thought about this, too, and I'm convinced I would have, if you had asked."

I knew I'd been all too willing to abandon my world and join the Forsythes'. But I didn't believe for an instant Elizabeth would've had it any other way, and I was hankering to argue the point. Elizabeth abruptly changed the subject before I got the chance.

"You need to leave town, Benny," she said. "Right away. My father and Junior are going to have you killed. You and your client, too — that Judith Sorin."

"What is this? Did they send you over here to rattle my cage?"

"If they find out I'm here, they'll probably have me killed, too."

"Come on, Liz."

"You of all people shouldn't find this hard to believe."

"If you're serious, you must've misunderstood something," I said. "Your father and brother have me right where they want me. I'm no threat to them."

"You're the one who misunderstands, Benny. They think you know way too much about that fire in Galion. They're afraid you're going to go to the police."

"With what? They had no reason to burn down their own factory."

"The fire was a means to an end," Elizabeth said. "Two men died, and it wasn't an accident."

It took a while for the news flash to register. "You're saying they committed arson in order to kill the two guys who were in the building?"

"Right. That's what I'm saying."

"How'd they rig it so the fire would start right when they came for the files?" I asked.

"I don't know anything about any files," Elizabeth responded. "Clement and Barfield went to the factory because they were expecting someone to show up with the payoff."

"Payoff?"

"They had something on Elite, something to do with billing irregularities. They were threatening to go to the newspapers right around the time Elite was selling stock to the public."

"Blackmail," I said.

"Uh-huh. They wanted a lot of money to keep quiet."

"So Junior and your father shut them up in a more permanent way."

"That's the way it sounds," Elizabeth said.

"How do you know all this?"

"I've heard them discussing it at the house. Last night, it got really serious."

"They talk openly about arson and murder right in front of you?"

"They think I'm too drunk to understand or remember," Elizabeth said.

"I thought you said you were on the wagon."

"I am, but they don't know."

"How could they not know?"

"Because I don't want them to," she said. "I play-act. My life's a lot easier when they think I'm soused all the time. They leave me out of what they're doing, which is exactly what I want."

I lit a cigarette for myself and offered one to Elizabeth. "No thanks," she said. "I'm trying to quit smoking, too."

"Next you're going to tell me you're joining a convent."

"Seriously, Benny, it's not safe for you here, or your client, either. Junior and my father figure she's going to keep pushing for answers even if you're out of the picture. You'd better call her and tell her to leave town."

"What exactly do you think they're going to do?"

"I'm not sure," she said. "But I know they're in a hurry. They were on the phone making plans last night until after midnight."

I excused myself and went to call Judith from Mrs. Skokow's desk. I didn't relish the prospect of speaking to her. She'd insist on details about exactly what I knew and how I knew it. I didn't want to share that information.

"You need to leave Cleveland immediately," I told her when she picked up the phone. "It's not safe to stay here."

"What are you talking about?"

"The Forsythes think you and I have learned too much about what they did. They've decided to do to us what they did to Zimmer and your father."

"You realize you're not on the case anymore," Judith said.

"That's neither here nor there."

"How do you know all this?"

"I'll tell you all about it some other time," I said. "Right now, you need to throw some clothes in a suitcase and get out of town."

"I'm not going anywhere, Mr. Gold. School starts on Tuesday, and I intend to be there to greet my class."

"Staying isn't an option."

"Nonsense," she said. "You refuse to tell me where you're getting your information. That makes me think — "

"MISS SORIN!" I screamed into the receiver. "JUDITH! Get this through your skull. They may already have people on the way to your house as we speak. I wouldn't have called if this wasn't real. Pack a bag and get the hell out of there *now*."

I could tell I'd shaken her. "Where exactly am I supposed to go?" she asked.

"I don't know, and for God's sake don't tell me," I said. "I'm pretty sure we have company on this line. Just don't drive to wherever you're going. Fly or take a train instead."

"Why?"

"So they can't get a bead on your car and catch you alone."

"So I'm just supposed to disappear forever?"

"Send me a telegram and let me know where I can reach you," I said. "I'll try to think of something in the meantime. Now go!"

When I walked back into my office, Elizabeth was smoking a cigarette and pacing in front of the window looking out on Euclid. "So much for quitting," I said.

"I heard shouting."

"That woman is a pill. I had to convince her it was in her best interest not to be murdered."

"She's going to leave, though — right?"

"Yeah, I think so," I said.

"How about you?"

"I'll lay low for a while, but I can't just run away," I said. "That's not a permanent solution. For me or for the Sorin princess, either."

"You're making a tremendous mistake," Elizabeth said, almost frantic.

"I've got to do something to bring this to a head, one way or the other."

"What can you possibly do?"

"I wish I had the guts and the money to put a hit out on them before they do it to me," I said. "Lord knows I'd be doing the world a favor."

"Benny..."

"Sorry, Liz," I said. "I don't suppose I have any choice but to go to the police and hope they'll listen."

Elizabeth finished her cigarette and put it out in the ashtray on my desk. She picked up her silver purse from the floor, then returned to her position in front of the window.

"You know the police won't help you," she said. "My father has them in his pocket."

"They'd have to do something if I had proof of what I was telling them."

"They'll just deny your accusations..."

"You could be the proof, Liz," I blurted. "You could come with me and repeat what your father and brother said about the Galion fire. You heard them admit they set the fire to kill those two guys. I bet you heard them admit to killing Maury Sorin, too."

"That's asking too much, Benny. My father and brother are bastards, but I'm not going to be the one who turns them in for murder."

"You'd be telling the truth and probably saving lives."

"They'd never believe me, anyway," she said.

She had a point. Clayton Senior and Junior were titans of industry, Elizabeth an inveterate lush. The cops almost certainly wouldn't take her side in a swearing match. Even under the best of circumstances, Elizabeth's story would sound like it came straight from a bottle of gin. But still — she was my last, best hope.

"You've got to do it, Liz," I said. "You've got to tell the police what you know."

We stood looking at each other. After a moment, her expression began to tighten, and I assumed her refusal was final. Then she looked as though she were going to cry, and I didn't know what to think.

"I'm not going to turn state's evidence against my own family," Elizabeth finally said. "But there's something else..."

"What are you talking about?"

"Copies of the papers Clement and Barfield were using to blackmail the company. The ones they were threatening to turn over to the press. I know where you can get them."

"Tell me more," I said.

"The file was at Elite's offices until yesterday," Elizabeth said. "But my father had Junior bring it home to store it in his safe. The file already got into the wrong hands once, and he wanted to make sure it didn't happen again."

"How am I supposed to get it out of the safe? I'd have to know the combination," I said.

"I know it."

"So you'll bring me the file?"

"I think you'd better come pick it up," Elizabeth said. "I'll need help getting it out of the house — I don't want to be seen carrying it around."

"You want me just to drop by? Invite myself in for tea?"

"You can come at night, after everyone else is asleep. No one will hear us."

"Then what?" I said, shaking my head. "Your father's going to come after you as soon as he finds out the file is gone. He's going to know you're responsible."

"I'm the last person he'd suspect," said Elizabeth. "He has no idea that I have the combination to his safe, or that I have any notion of what's going on."

"Are you serious about this?"

"Unfortunately, I am," she said.

The whole idea was cockamamie. Elizabeth's plan called for me to walk into the enemy camp without reconnaissance or backup, steal a secret file, then simply stroll out, all without being detected. Any number of missteps could doom the mission.

But I didn't really have any choice. I needed the police to intervene to protect me from the Forsythes. That wouldn't happen unless I could corroborate the accusations I'd be making against them. Neither of my two potential witnesses, Mrs. Zimmer or Elizabeth, would willingly cooperate — and Elizabeth wouldn't be taken seriously even if she did. By the process of elimination, the Galion papers were my only option unless I was willing to run away very far, very fast.

Judith said the file had gone missing once before — so it must've been the papers Zimmer filched from Elite and my ex-in-laws filched back from Maury Sorin's office. Sorin described their contents as a "smoking gun", and they frightened the Forsythes enough to kill, and kill again, to keep them secret. If I could get those documents, maybe I had a fighting chance of surviving.

"Will you be alone in the house tonight?" I asked Elizabeth.

"Junior's out of town. My parents might have dinner at the Club, but I don't know for sure."

"What time do they go to bed?"

"Eleven, most nights," she said. "Half past eleven at the latest."

"Then I'll be there tonight at midnight," I said. "I'll park up the street and come to the back door near the tennis court."

"Okay."

"Make sure you're there, Liz."

"I will be," she said.

"We'll have to be quick about this."

Elizabeth nodded and started for the door. I stepped in front of her and gave her a hug.

"I know you're taking a big chance for me," I said.

Elizabeth nuzzled her head against my chest. "You deserved better, Benny," she said, her eyes tearing up.

"You were just fine," I replied. "Just fine." For the moment at least, I meant it.

THIRTY-THREE

ELIZABETH LEFT, and I got ready to do the same. I couldn't find more ammo for Mrs. Skokow's pistol in her desk, so I put it back and got my own gun out of the safe. I couldn't remember the last time I'd used it. It was a .45 and seemed like a cannon compared to the little .32. For a moment I considered leaving it behind, but I decided that safe was better than sorry.

I turned off the lights, closed the door to my private office, and made my exit. I was waiting for the elevator when I decided to go back and retrieve my Minox camera from the top drawer of my desk. I figured that if possible, I'd photograph the Galion papers instead of taking the file out of the house. That way, Clayton Senior would never know anyone had seen the evidence until I confronted him with it.

The two-minute detour proved extremely unfortunate. When I left the office the second time, the Gorilla was leaning against the wall halfway down the hall, talking to a shorter but equally solid associate. Both were wearing black turtlenecks, black slacks, and gray sport coats. The Gorilla's sidekick was chewing on a toothpick.

"We meet again, sir," the Gorilla said.

"So I see," I responded with as much calm as I could feign. "What can I do for you boys?"

"We'd like to take you for a late breakfast," said the Gorilla.

"Or an early lunch," said the Sidekick. "We need to talk."

"We can talk right here."

"Why don't you make it easy on yourself?" asked the Gorilla.

"I'm going to start screaming bloody murder in about two seconds."

"So scream, if you want," said the Gorilla.

"I'll call the cops."

"Be my guest. What are you going to tell them?"

I was about to draw the .45 when a bell announced the elevator's arrival. The doors opened, and out stepped Number One and Number Two.

"Am I glad to see you fellas," I said.

"No funny business, Gold," said Number Two as they approached.

"Surprisingly enough, I really mean it. I'm ready to spill my guts."

"Good," said Number One. "Let's go inside."

"No. I'll talk, but I want to do it at your office, not mine."

"What's the difference?" asked Number Two.

"He wants to talk at our place, so we'll talk at our place," said Number One.

"Who are these guys?" asked Number Two, motioning toward the Gorilla and the Sidekick.

"Muscle, sent by the Forsythes," I said. "You know all about that, I suppose."

Neither of the agents lifted an eyebrow.

"Let's go," said Number One.

We all rode the elevator down and walked out the door onto Euclid. Number One and Number Two turned right, and I went with them. After half a block, I looked back to find the Gorilla and the Sidekick slinking behind us.

"Three's company, five's a crowd," I called to them. They kept on slinking.

"Can't you do something about those guys?" I asked my FBI escorts. The G-Men stopped and looked back.

"Get lost, gentleman," Number One said. "Mr. Gold has decided to come with us." His tone became a little louder when the Gorilla and the Sidekick didn't move. "I said, beat it. Now." We stood and watched the two of them turn and disappear around the corner.

"Let's get going," said Number One.

FBI headquarters was in the Standard Building, the same place Maury Sorin's office had been. When we got there, I kept walking.

"What gives?" Number Two asked angrily.

"Slight change in plans," I said. "I'm going to spend the day not getting killed. I'll have to talk to you boys some other time."

Number Two reached up and grabbed my neck. "You're not going anywhere," he said. "You're done playing us for a couple of saps."

"Are you arresting me?"

"No…"

"Is the FBI going to protect me from those two primates?"

"We're not your bodyguards," said Number Two.

"Then take your fucking hands off me."

"Let him go, Roy," said Number One in a defeated tone. "Let him go."

Thirty-Four

I HURRIED TO the garage where I'd parked the Schooner. "Anybody come in over the last few minutes?" I asked the attendant.

"People come in and out of here all day. It's a parking garage."

"I'm wondering specifically about two guys dressed in black, with gray jackets. One of them was pretty big."

"I don't pay much attention to what the customers are wearing. Only their cars."

I escaped the garage in one piece, no thanks to him. It was eleven o'clock, thirteen hours before my rendezvous with Elizabeth. That was a long time to play hide-and-seek with the Gorilla, the Sidekick, and whoever else the Forsythes had looking for me.

My first instinct was to drive to the West Side, park on some quiet side street, and fade into the scenery. It was a good plan in theory, but I was too wound up to spend the day just sitting in the Schooner. Next I thought of going to a bar, but I realized I couldn't be even partially loaded if I wanted to conduct my business at the Forsythes that night and get out alive. The zoo, a museum, the movies — all these possibilities crossed my mind. I even briefly contemplated going to the Catholic Church at Ninth and Superior and pretending to pray for as long as I could get away with it.

I ultimately decided to take a driving tour of nowhere in particular. I headed east from Downtown, on Route Two towards Painesville, and had the road pretty much to myself after I got out of town. When a car did appear in the rearview mirror, I slowed down so I could see whether one of the Forsythes' goons was behind the wheel. I knew I should keep my distance from anyone and everyone and stay out of range of any potential showdown to the extent I could. But my biggest fear was fear itself. I didn't want my imagination to turn every Packard and Buick into a life-or-death hazard.

I already had enough to worry about. I knew I'd be taking a long shot in going to the Forsythes' later that night. Potential problems abounded. I could have trouble getting into the house. The safe might not open. Someone could unexpectedly walk in on us. I didn't know how I would deal with any of these hazards. I was in way over my head.

I found myself blaming Judith Sorin for my predicament. I had assiduously avoided my ex-in-laws before she came into the picture. I'd witnessed their utter ruthlessness up close during my time as the Forsythe son-in-law and had no interest in confronting them over the despicable things they did as a matter of course. You had to have a death wish to do battle with the Forsythes — but somehow Judith had lured me into doing just that.

But being honest with myself, I knew she hadn't really lured me into anything. I took her case because I wanted to get back at Elizabeth's family, with full knowledge of the risks involved. I'd had several opportunities to walk away from the assignment, but I hadn't done so. And even though I couldn't claim a purely noble purpose in staying on the case, avenging Maury Sorin's murder was part of it — and he was noble, even if I never was. He had been Cleveland's equalizer, the last best hope for the little guy in trouble, the innocent in over his head. He was the David the Goliaths feared. He couldn't be bribed or intimidated; he spoke truth to power and didn't buckle under the influence of the Forsythes of the world. With Maury Sorin out of the way, there was one less reason for the fat cats to play things straight, one less obstacle to slow them down as they steamrolled toward their latest pot of gold. There had to be a check on their brand of impunity. If they could get away with killing Maury Sorin, they could get away with anything — and would.

In Painesville, I parked on the town square and went to a luncheonette for a hamburger I barely touched. Afterwards, I walked over to the county courthouse to look around. It was a nice old building, with columns in front and a green dome topped by an eagle spreading its wings. I tried a case there once — a breach-of-contract suit brought by the local newspaper against my client for overcharging on a new printing press. It was a unanimous verdict for the defense. I remembered talking to the newspaper's attorney after trial, on my way out of the courtroom.

"You had a tough case," I told him. "I don't think even I could've won it."

The memory made my face burn. What a conceited prick I'd been — a conceited prick who actually had nothing to be conceited about. I'd married a girl with a rich father. That was my single claim to fame. I'd been a successful gold-digger, and nothing else.

I got to thinking about Elizabeth as I paced around downtown Painesville. She seemed far more vulnerable now than she used to be.

She was different in a lot of ways. She'd never been a particularly contemplative person back then, but at some point over the years she seemed to have reflected thoughtfully on the disintegration of our marriage. I appreciated the effort, even if I didn't agree with the conclusions she'd reached.

The old Elizabeth wouldn't have intervened to stop her father and brother from their crooked machinations. She would've kept out of it, knowing full well they were monsters up to no good. Her family's rottenness was just her cross to bear, and she bore it. Sometimes I thought that was why she drank so much.

I probably should have spent the rest of the day in Painesville. It didn't appear that anyone had followed me there, and it was an unlikely place for the Forsythes to search for me. But I was jumpy. Staying put, even here, made me feel like a sitting duck. The Gorilla and his cohorts, I felt, would inevitably track me down unless I kept on the move. So that's what I did.

The gas gauge on the Schooner was hovering near empty. When the attendant at the station finished filling the tank, I asked how to get to Route Two going west.

"Left at the next light," he said. I thanked him and headed in that direction, back to the city.

THIRTY-FIVE

IT WAS MID-AFTERNOON as I approached Cleveland. With time to kill, I decided to detour to Euclid Beach. Of all the places the Forsythes might look for me in town, an amusement park seemed the least likely. The place was packed, which made it easy to fade into the crowd. I toured the grounds as part of the herd, going from ride to ride, game to game. I bought a popcorn ball and an ice cream cone along the way, taking a few bites of each before pitching them.

I waited in line for a spin on the Grand Carousel. After the ride, I made my way over to the arcade, where I spent nearly two bucks to win a Kewpie doll at ring toss. I gave the prize to a buck-toothed little girl who'd witnessed my heroics. Just then, her mother came by and swatted her behind.

"Here you are, Hillary," she said. "I've been looking for you for ten minutes." The hag spotted the toy in her daughter's hands and gave me the evil eye when she found out where it came from. I decided it was time to leave.

A black Oldsmobile sedan followed me out of the parking lot. I was only moderately concerned at the time, but five minutes later, at a stop light on Lake Shore, I noticed the Olds was still on my tail. The rearview mirror gave me a decent look at the driver, who was wearing dark sunglasses. I tried not to panic, but as I continued toward Cleveland, the black Olds steadily followed, staying close enough to prevent any car from cutting in between us.

Just past 156th, I turned right onto a side street, signaling well in advance so the Olds could follow suit, if it wanted to. I couldn't tell for sure whether I'd been marked, but I wanted to find out one way or the other. I parked up the street, then lit a cigarette and waited. At first, nothing happened, and I became convinced that my imagination had gotten the best of me.

Then the Olds came into view, moving steadily toward me after turning the corner from Lake Shore. My pursuer must've gotten stuck in the intersection, but he was back on course now.

The Olds pulled in diagonally to the curb directly in front of my Schooner, wedging me in. The driver got out and started slowly toward me. He was a short man in a rumpled gray suit, more than a little chubby, with a thin black mustache that entirely failed to make him look dashing. In his left hand he held a handkerchief, which he pressed against his forehead. In his right, he held a gun.

"I've been looking for you all day," the *shlub* said when he reached the Schooner, where I sat with the windows rolled down.

"What? Are you selling magazines? If so, I'm not interested."

"It's too hot to play games, Mr. Gold. You might as well just come along."

"Where are we going?"

I didn't listen to the *shlub's* answer. The .45 was sitting next to me, so close that I was probably blocking his view of it. I gauged whether I could pick it up and point it at him without getting shot first. It was even money at best.

"...So how about it?" he said.

"Sure..."

I grabbed the cigarette from my mouth and mashed it hard just beneath the *shlub's* left eye. He doubled over, yelping in pain. I seized the opportunity to seize the .45, which I pointed directly at him...but then I dropped it back on the car seat, since he was flailing around too much to pay any attention to it.

I didn't hang around to monitor his recovery. Instead, I put the Schooner in reverse and began a frantic backwards escape.

It was twenty-five yards to the corner, give or take, but I travelled at least fifty with all the zigzagging I did. It wasn't intentional, but even if he recovered enough to take a shot, he'd have had a hard time hitting me. At the end of the block, I backed into a driveway and pulled out facing forward. A few seconds later, I turned left onto Lake Shore.

My heart was pounding hard and fast. It reminded me of how I'd felt in Europe during our shootouts with the Germans. My hands were shaking on the wheel, and I was driving at least ten miles an hour over the speed limit. The *shlub* was down, but I hadn't put him permanently out. I needed to make myself scarce.

My route was circuitous and illogical. I moved generally westward, but purposefully avoided any rational course to anywhere. After half an hour, I ended up on Euclid Avenue in East Cleveland, with a straight shot back to town. My jangled nerves had settled, mostly. The *shlub* had gotten lucky once in finding me at the amusement park. I didn't see how it could happen a second time.

It happened. I'd gone three or four blocks when the black Olds pulled up alongside me in the left lane. "Pull over," the *shlub* shouted. "Pull over, now!" I felt like I was living in an episode of *Tales of Tomorrow*.

I didn't have time to indulge in paranoid musings. At the first opportunity, I shifted lanes and got out in front of the black Olds, then started bobbing and weaving through the traffic. My maneuvering would put a few cars between me and the *shlub*. Every time, he managed to squeeze his way back into position.

I caught a break at Mayfield, making it through the intersection just before the signal changed. At that particular moment, the *shlub* was two cars back. The blockade prevented him from running the light and keeping up — or so I thought. He just drove around it, passing the cars on the wrong side of the road and barreling across Mayfield with his horn blaring. He almost collided with a maroon Super 8 that was turning left onto Euclid, but ended up right behind me just the same.

At 105th, as I passed the Alhambra Tavern, I decided I'd had enough. I abruptly slammed my brakes and exited the Schooner with the .45 in my hand. The Olds grazed my bumper when I pulled up short, and was moving backwards as I approached. The Super 8's arrival on the scene brought the *shlub* to a halt.

I stopped around five feet in front of the black Olds, extended my arm, and fired two bullets directly into the front tire on the passenger side. Then I pointed the gun at the *shlub*, who I thought by then would have his own weapon drawn. But my surprise attack had apparently surprised him a lot. He held his hands in the air and shrieked *"No!"* as if I intended to do to him what I'd done to his tire. I just laughed before aiming and assassinating the Goodyear on the driver's side. Then I hustled back to the Schooner and raced away. The guy was a pretty hot driver, but he wouldn't get far in that car for a while.

I repeatedly checked the rearview mirror as I drove, looking both for the cops and the *shlub*. He would've had to hijack somebody else's ride to resume the pursuit, but given the persistence he'd already shown, I didn't put it past him.

I reached 55th and turned left toward Woodland. After considering the possibilities, I'd come up with a place where I could kill some time without the Forsythes knowing where to look for me. I was going to Rosie's.

THIRTY-SIX

WALKING INTO ROSIE's building, I passed a thin middle-aged man in a tan suit who almost certainly had been her last customer. His flushed face and mussed hair gave him away, as did his quick getaway up the street. He obviously was coming from somewhere he shouldn't have been.

I paced the hallway for a few minutes to give Rosie a chance to catch her breath. When I got around to knocking on her door, she answered immediately.

"Dick Tracy..."

I stepped quickly into the apartment and closed the door behind me.

"Don't blow your stack," I said. "After the last time I was here, you know I wouldn't come back unless I absolutely had to."

"*Had to?* What in the world are you talking about?"

"This is no joke, Rosie. My ex-in-laws have a hit out on me. I need somewhere to lay low for a couple of hours, and this is the only place I could think of that they wouldn't think of."

I filled Rosie in about my visit from Elizabeth, and her family's plan to turn me into a cadaver. I explained the scheme to photograph the papers from Clayton Senior's safe, and my run-ins with the Gorilla and the Sidekick, and then with the *shlub*. With each new fact, the worry on Rosie's face became more apparent.

"Jesus Christ, Dick Tracy," she said. "You're in way too deep."

"How many customers have you got the rest of the day?"

"Nobody till nine o'clock. Then two, back-to-back."

"I'll pay you one-fifty to call them off so I can stay here," I said. "Make it two hundred."

Rosie gave me an exasperated look. "You know," she said, "you pay me more for doing nothing than I get from doing business."

Rosie went into the bedroom to telephone her clients with the bad news about their cancelled appointments. I stretched out on the couch in her living room and tried to relax. It was a futile effort. I couldn't help thinking about everything that could go wrong at the Forsythes' later.

Rosie came into the living room with a bottle of gin and a glass. "No thanks," I said. "I've got to stay at my sharpest."

"You can have one, Dick Tracy. Just to settle your nerves."

I didn't feel like arguing. I downed almost the whole drink in one swig.

Rosie sat next to me on the couch. "No way you should be going to that house tonight," she said. "No way in the world."

"You think we'll get caught?"

"It's a set-up, darlin', sure as hell."

"I don't see how that could be."

"I don't trust that ex-wife of yours as far as I could throw her," Rosie said. "She's fronting for her daddy and her brother, without a doubt."

I tried to set her straight, but she didn't buy any of it. "A lion don't change its spots," she said.

"It's a leopard, Rosie. A *leopard* doesn't change its spots."

"Whether she's a lion or a leopard, hon, she's going to get you killed."

I poured myself another drink. Rosie's conspiracy theory wasn't exactly bolstering my peace of mind. I didn't *think* I was walking into a trap. Still, I sifted through the conversation with Elizabeth at my office, looking for some telltale sign of the double cross Rosie was predicting.

"You're way off base about Elizabeth," I finally said. "People change, and she's changed for the better."

"I hope you're right, for your sake, darlin'."

Rosie went back into her bedroom, and I managed to doze off for a few minutes. When I awoke, a baloney sandwich and a glass of milk sat on the coffee table in front of me.

"You're a mother hen," I said when Rosie reappeared.

"I don't want you getting killed on an empty stomach," she replied.

It was almost eight o'clock when I finished eating. "Thanks for the dinner," I said. "I'm going to get going."

"What? You don't have to leave for hours."

"There's a stop I think I should make beforehand."

"When did you decide this?"

"Just now," I said. "I've been mulling it over."

I pulled all the cash from my wallet and counted it. "I don't have the full two hundred," I said. "I'll have to come back with the rest."

"I know you're good for it," Rosie said, taking the wad. "If you're still alive."

She walked me to the front door. I leaned over to hug her, but she took a step back to avoid it.

"I just wanted to thank you for saving my neck," I said.

"You don't have to thank me. You paid for it."

"All right, then..."

I opened the front door, but Rosie closed it before I could exit.

"Wait here a second," she said. She walked into the back of the apartment and returned with a shiny set of brass knuckles in her right hand.

"What are you doing with those?" I asked.

"I assume you already have a gun," she said. "This'll give you a little backup."

"Thanks, Rosie. I appreciate it. But I really don't think —"

"Don't tell me no, goddamn it. It won't do any harm to have these on you, just in case."

Rosie handed me the knuckles, which I slipped into a side pocket of my trousers. "Thanks for looking out for me," I said.

This time she couldn't escape my embrace. I kissed her on the forehead, too. She didn't even complain.

THIRTY-SEVEN

I WASN'T EXPECTING a jubilant reception from my brother. He and I hadn't spoken since the other night at my apartment. Miriam checked in the one time, but not again. For all intents and purposes, I remained *persona non grata*.

I still thought I'd better let Jake know what was going to happen later that night. Fatalistic worrying got me nowhere, but I realized I couldn't count on leaving the Forsythes' as a living, breathing human being. Somebody needed to know about it beforehand. Otherwise I could vanish without a trace.

I parked the Schooner two streets away from Jake's, then got out and crept toward the house. I intended to make my entrance from around the block, through Jake's backyard, and tried to figure out which lot abutted his. I would've had a hard time performing this feat in complete daylight; in the dark, it was essentially eenie-mee-nie-miney-mo. My unfamiliarity with Jake's place made the task even trickier. I'd only glimpsed his backyard once, briefly, when I put David's bicycle away after his run-in with the *alter kacker*.

No one else was out on the street, but I still didn't want to dilly-dally. I picked out a driveway and walked decisively toward the back, as if I knew where I was going. I got lucky and only overshot Jake's house by two lots. With no hedges or fences in between, I adjusted my course and headed toward the back door.

I knocked quietly. For around twenty seconds, nothing happened. Then, to my relief, Miriam opened up.

"Benny!" she said. "What are you doing back here?"

"I like the view," I said. "Can I come in?"

"Of course. Please. But *Shabbos* dinner...we've already eaten."

"Maybe another Friday. I came to talk to Jake."

"He'll be happy to see you," she said, closing the door behind me. "So you've eaten?"

"No, but..."

"I'll make you a plate," Miriam said. "First I'll go get your brother. He's giving the baby a bath. Come wait inside."

I followed Miriam through the kitchen and into the dining room. From there I could see that the front drapes were drawn shut.

"Have you seen anybody unusual on the street today?" I asked.

"Not today, no," Miriam said. "But I know why you bring it up."

"What do you mean?"

"Two FBI men paid us a visit earlier in the week, right at dinnertime."

"Goddamn it," I said.

"It was a little spooky, but they didn't stay long. Jake talked to them on the back porch. They wanted to know what you said to Dr. Braunstein the day we were at your apartment."

"What did Jake tell them?"

"It wasn't much. He didn't know you were practicing law again. Jake said you told Dr. Braunstein you weren't happy with the current plans for his appeal and would discuss them with him later."

"Goddamn it," I said again, dropping my head.

"You couldn't expect Jake to lie for you, Benny. Not to the FBI."

"I wouldn't want him to lie," I said. "But I don't represent Braunstein, and never have, and I'm definitely not practicing law anymore." I gave a sigh. "I'm sure Jake told it as he remembered it."

Miriam stood silently for a few seconds. Then she went to get Jake.

I began wandering around the living room as she disappeared up the staircase. The place had the feel of my parents' apartment, though the layout was completely different. On the left side of the room, near the fireplace, a rust-colored sofa and matching chairs surrounded a dark brown coffee table. On the right side, there was a baby grand piano that was obviously old but still looked to be in pretty good condition. An impressionistic painting of an old Jew in a prayer shawl hung on the wall next to it, along with another painting I recognized as a Picasso print. An issue of *The New Republic* lay open on the piano bench. There was a toy truck next to the radio console toward the back of the room.

I went over to the piano and opened the fallboard. I was banging out "Chopsticks" when Jake entered the room, drying his hands on a pink towel.

"You're late," he said. "We've already eaten."

"So I've heard."

"No more bandage on your head, I see. How're you feeling?"

"Fully recovered."

Miriam walked in with David at her side. "Here's your nephew," she said.

I rubbed the kid's noggin. "Nice to see you again," I said. "How've you been?"

"Good," said the kid.

"I'm going to heat up some dinner for you," Miriam said. "In the meantime, I promised David you could tell some stories about his father."

I looked at David. "You really want to hear?"

David nodded.

Jake, David, and I sat down on the sofa, with David in the middle. I had trouble coming up with something appropriate. I ended up telling him about his father's heroics during high-school intramural baseball, and how he once won a bet by eating six pickles in one sitting. I thought the stories might loosen Jake up a little. I was wrong.

Miriam eventually came in to say my dinner was ready. "Tell your uncle goodnight," she instructed David. "It's bedtime for you."

"Can't I stay up?"

"No. Uncle Benny and your father need to talk alone. I'm going upstairs, too."

There was baked chicken and string beans and potato *kugel* waiting for me on the kitchen table in portions three times too big. Jake and I sat down, and I went to work on them. For once, I felt like eating.

"Listen, Jake," I said after a couple of mouthfuls.

"Don't start, Benny. I should've come to see you. You tried to patch this up the other night. Miriam and I have been fighting about it all week."

"Sorry."

"She agrees with the point you were making," Jake said. "I've been playing God."

"I never said that."

"I'm just punishing her and the kids when I treat you that way. And maybe punishing myself, too."

"You certainly have your reasons, Jake."

"I guess it's time I let it go," he said.

"It doesn't sound like your heart's really in it."

"I'm not sure it is. But my head is, and that'll have to do for now."

I didn't fully understand the last statement. I was certain, though, that Jake was making nice more to pacify Miriam than out of any interest in squaring things with me. I didn't appreciate that, and felt like telling him so ... but when Jake extended his right hand, I took it and shook.

"I need family, Jake," I said.

"I think what you really need is a keeper. The FBI paid us a visit the other night."

"Miriam told me. That's all bullshit."

"The two agents didn't seem to think so," he said.

I proceeded to change the subject, telling Jake what had happened in the Sorin case, and the scheme Elizabeth and I were planning to execute. When I finished, Jake leaned back against the kitchen counter and looked at me with his arms crossed and a scowl on his face.

"That's the stupidest goddamned thing I ever heard," he said.

Miriam returned just then from upstairs and misinterpreted what was happening. "I've had about enough of this, Jake," she said crossly. "Your brother made the effort to come see you. That wasn't easy, after the way you behaved last week. And you're still acting like some scolding parent —"

"Hold your fire," Jake said. "We've kissed and made up."

Miriam turned to me. I nodded.

"Kissed and made up," Jake repeated, "just in time for Benny to go and get himself killed."

I recounted my plans for the night to Miriam, who insisted I go to the police instead.

"As things stand now, the police wouldn't do anything," I said.

"They'd keep you from getting murdered," she said.

"For a little while, maybe. But after enough time passed, the Forsythes would come after me. I need solid proof, something that will put Senior and Junior away for life."

"Why doesn't Elizabeth tell the police what she heard?"

"She wouldn't be believed," I said. "And she can't rat out her own father and brother."

"I don't see much difference between that and what she's going to do tonight," Miriam said. "Besides, this way your life's at stake."

"It's at stake no matter what," said Jake. "Those bastards will never go to jail, even if you get the dirt on them."

"Probably not," I said. "But listen — I wanted you to know where I was going tonight. If I turn up missing tomorrow, you'll know what to tell the cops."

Miriam went and put her arm around Jake's waist. "You've got to do something," she said to him. "This is all too terrible."

I spared Jake the trouble of answering. "There's nothing he can do," I said. "But don't start planning my funeral yet. I'm planning on surviving the night."

Miriam eventually calmed down, and the three of us sat at the kitchen table, kibitzing about nothing important. Miriam made coffee, and I had a cup. As she poured a second one, I glanced at the clock on the wall. It read half past eleven.

"Is that right?"

Jake nodded.

"I've got to get going."

"Benny, I wish you'd reconsider," Miriam said.

"It'll be fine," I said. "Truly, it will. The Forsythes can't be expecting me. And I'm not the hero type — first sign of trouble, I'll be long gone."

I got up, nodded toward Miriam, patted Jake on the shoulder, and walked out the back door. As I cut through their yard, I wanted to believe they were watching me go, like parents seeing their son off to war. I damn near turned around to look.

I checked my watch instead. It was 11:40. I had twenty minutes to get where I was going.

THIRTY-EIGHT

THE FORSYTHES' HOUSE was on North Park between Lee and Shelburne. I arrived a few minutes before midnight. I'd forgotten how narrow and twisted the road was around there. Parking wasn't allowed on the street in front of their house, but their driveway still didn't have a gate — so I pulled the Schooner about a third of the way up the long driveway and killed the engine. No one would see me there. There were no lights, and the trees on the front lawn blocked the view from the house.

I took the .45 from the glove box and checked to make sure the Minox was still in my coat pocket. Then I got out of the car and started walking toward the back of the Forsythe house.

I hadn't taken two steps when a car ripped down the road with the radio blaring and horn honking. It came into earshot in a flash and left just as quickly. It had almost certainly been just some kids out for a joyride. It couldn't have been anyone else, really, but it spooked me just the same. I was tense — very tense — and became even more so when I saw a light through the drapes of an upstairs window. Elizabeth was supposed to be the only one awake. If others were as well, pulling off the job would become that much more improbable.

I was supposed to meet Elizabeth at the door that led from the den out to a patio next to the tennis court. To get there, I had to walk up the driveway, past the garage, and around the swimming pool. Windows from the kitchen and dining room looked out on the path I took. Both rooms were completely dark, but the moonlight made it possible for me to make my way.

Elizabeth wasn't there when I reached the door. Five minutes passed, then ten, but still she hadn't shown. I became convinced she wasn't coming. Something must've happened — either she'd changed her mind or she ran into God-knew-what kind of trouble. I wasn't sure whether to be angry, or alarmed, or both.

I was getting ready to head back to the Schooner when I saw something move through the door's window. As I was trying to figure out whether it was Elizabeth, I heard the key turn, and the door creaked open.

"Come in, Mr. Gold," said a whispering voice.

"Rufus!" I said more loudly than I should have. "What are you doing here?"

"Follow me, sir, as quietly as you can. I'll explain when we get where we're going."

Rufus took me down a maze of hallways I didn't fully recall from my days as a family member. We ended up in the vestibule leading to the front door, just a few feet away from the staircase to the Forsythes' bedrooms. Rufus paused and listened to make sure the coast was clear. We then tiptoed over the expanse of the living room and into Clayton Senior's study.

A small table lamp illuminated the room. It hadn't appreciably changed over the years. The walls were paneled with stained oak. There was red carpet, blue drapery, and a crystal chandelier hanging from the ceiling. Clayton Senior's desk sat toward the back of the room, with a telephone and a stock ticker on top. Behind it, on the wall, hung a portrait of Elizabeth's mother. The painting hid the wall safe.

"It's Friday," I half-whispered to Rufus after he shut the door. "Your night off."

"I'll be on my way as soon as you're situated," he said. "Miss Forsythe had some trouble with the family today and asked me to stay around in case she needed help."

"What kind of trouble, Rufus?"

"You'll have to ask her, sir."

"Do you know why I'm here?"

"Miss Forsythe started to tell me," he said, "but I stopped her. The less I know, the better."

"Where is she now?"

"She's upstairs, but will be down presently."

I sat in the chair behind Clayton Senior's desk while Rufus looked out the window onto the front lawn. After a few moments, Elizabeth quietly slipped in.

"Sorry I'm late," she said. "My father just wouldn't go to sleep. Thanks for letting Benny in, Rufus."

"Of course, Miss Forsythe," he answered. "I'll go now. The two of you best be careful."

After Rufus pulled the door shut, Elizabeth flipped on the overhead light. When she turned toward me, I saw that her eyes were swollen and red.

"Jesus Christ," I said. "Are you all right?"

"I'm fine," she responded unconvincingly. "It's been a long day."

"What the hell happened?"

They caught me at your building. It's been the third degree ever since."

"Who worked you over?"

"My father, my brother..."

"I thought Junior was out of town."

"He left late this afternoon," Elizabeth said. "Not before getting in his licks."

"They didn't hit you, did they?"

"No. At one point I thought they might, but it never quite got to that."

"What were they trying to find out?" I asked.

"They wanted to know where you were and what you were up to. They're convinced I know. The only way I got them to let up was to say I was meeting you for lunch at noon tomorrow. They plan to follow me and pick you up then."

"We've got to get you out of here, right now," I said.

"I can't leave."

"What do you think they're going to do when I'm not where you say I'll be tomorrow?"

"I'll say you stood me up," Elizabeth said. "I can convince them, I think."

"If you say so..."

Elizabeth pulled a slip of paper from her dress pocket and handed it to me. "The combination," she said. "Why don't you open it? I'm still a little shaky right now."

"I was wondering," I said as I looked at the numbers. "When you and I were together, your father always made a point of saying he was the only one who knew how to open that safe."

"He still thinks so," Elizabeth said, "but Mother wanted to see his will a few years ago, and he wouldn't show it to her, so she somehow got the combination."

"How'd you get it from her?"

"We were drinking sherry one afternoon and commiserating about how big a stinker my father was. She said, 'Here. You might need this some day.'"

I went to take the picture down and get to work. But before I did anything, I heard steps on the living room's hardwood floor.

"Elizabeth! Elizabeth!" It was Clayton Senior's voice. "Where in the hell are you? I wasn't finished . . ."

"Get under the desk," Elizabeth whispered to me. "Hurry!" I was halfway there before the words left her mouth.

"Elizabeth! Goddamn it!"

"I'm in your study."

I crammed in sideways under the desk. My knees were practically up to my chin. I heard the door of the study open, then I heard Clayton Senior grunt.

"What in hell are you doing in here?"

"What do you think I'm doing?" Elizabeth answered.

"Tell me, goddamn it. I don't want to play guessing games."

"I'm looking for the key to the liquor cabinet, that's what."

"Get it through your head," Clayton Senior said. "You can have as much as you want, just as soon as you tell me what I need to know."

"I told you, I don't know where he is."

"I don't believe you," said Clayton Senior. "I think you and he are close — very close. You wouldn't have been at his office otherwise."

"You're right, Father. I know his every move. As a matter of fact, Benny's here in the house as we speak."

"Goddamn it . . ."

"He's come for a visit, for old times' sake. He's back in the kitchen right now, making himself a sandwich."

"You think this is a big joke?" Clayton Senior said as he came around the desk to open a drawer. "That ex-husband of yours could very well destroy this family."

The old man was practically right on top of me. I heard the snip of scissors and the strike of a match. Then I smelled smoke. He'd lit a cigar.

"I wish we could've avoided all that ugliness from earlier," he said between puffs. "None of it would've been necessary had you'd told us where to find Benjamin."

"You'll just have to wait until tomorrow."

"Tomorrow may be too late," Clayton Senior replied. "A lot could happen between now and then. He might've already called that buffoon of a fire chief in Galion and told him what we did. He might manage to convince Zimmer's widow to come forward."

"Why don't you just kill them, too, and be done with it?"

"We've considered it," said Clayton Senior. "But Benjamin's stirred the pot too much. It'd be hard to do anything now without having to answer a lot of questions."

The son-of-a-bitch was still standing behind the desk. His feet couldn't have been more than a few inches from me. Sweat was gushing from my forehead. I strained to keep still, tensing every muscle so I wouldn't succumb to some involuntary spasm that would expose me.

Clayton Senior finally walked away. "I'm going upstairs now," he said to Elizabeth. "I've got the key in my nightstand. I'll gladly trade it for Benjamin."

"Terrific."

"You haven't had a drink since we brought you back this morning. You know you can't hold out much longer."

A few seconds later, I heard his steps on the living room hardwood. Elizabeth shut the door and told me I could come out.

"He's a true bastard," I said. "I'm really sorry, Liz."

The apology was inadequate for what I was putting her through, but I couldn't think of anything more to say. So I went to the back wall and took down the portrait of my former mother-in-law, exposing the safe. Its door was dark gray and looked to be about two feet by three feet. The dial was disproportionately large, around the size of a grapefruit.

"Might as well give it a try," I said.

I turned the dial all the way around two and a half times before entering the combination: Thirty-seven right. Thirty-one left. Twenty-two right.

Nothing happened. The handle on the safe remained firmly locked. I tried it a second time, then a third, with the same results.

"Maybe he changed the combination," I said to Elizabeth.

"He might have."

"Let me try it again."

This time, when I turned the handle and yanked, the door swung open. A light went on automatically, revealing a treasure trove inside. It was like something from a fairy tale. There were gold watches and diamond cufflinks, a gold bar, and a handful of brightly polished coins — some American, some not. Bundles of hundred-dollar bills sat alongside bundles of Canadian dollars, English pounds, German marks, and a few currencies I couldn't immediately identify.

I leafed through a stack of papers that included stock certificates, bonds, debentures, and a one-million-dollar promissory note. There was a brown sealed envelope marked, "TO BE OPENED UPON MY DEATH."

"You should take a look at this stuff," I said to Elizabeth, who was sitting in a chair in front of her father's desk.

"I'll pass, for now."

Among the papers, I eventually came to a folder with "Galion" written on the cover and ten or eleven pages inside. "I think this is it," I said.

"Good. Grab it, and you can get out of here."

"I've got to look through it first, to make sure it's what we're after."

"Well, hurry."

I sat down behind the desk and opened the folder. The first document I pulled out had addresses and phone numbers for Horace Clement and Edward Barfield, the former Elite employees who'd burned in Galion. Vincent Stuffleben's name also appeared, with a Galion address.

"This *is* it," I told Elizabeth.

The next document was a photostatic copy containing a slew of numbers — some in the millions, some in the hundred-thousands, some less than that. Some of the figures were added together. Others were multiplied. At the bottom of the page, "11,732,798" was written, underlined, and circled twice. I didn't know what the number meant.

I found the solution on a copy of an accountant's worksheet labeled "U.S. War Department/Galion". It had data for each month between June 1942 and September 1945. There were columns for "units billed," and "units shipped," one for "true cost" and another for "actual billing".

It took me five minutes or so to decipher what I was seeing. Elite Motorworks had billed the government for more parts than it made and shipped from Galion, and charged a higher price than its contract stipulated. The company became progressively bolder with its scam, bilking more from the government with each passing month. The "11,732,798" figure represented the total amount of Elite's overcharges during the three-plus years the contract ran.

The file included a letter the War Department had sent in December 1944 asking about "billing discrepancies". Also included was a response signed by Clayton Senior himself from the following month; he explained everything away and admonished the government for impugning Elite's "integrity and good faith".

Elite had perpetrated a monumental fraud. A telegram clipped to the back of the file connected the crime to the Forsythes' decision to incinerate Clement and Barfield:

BARFIELD CLEMENT INSIST 100K EACH OR ELSE INFORM PLAIN DEALER
NEWS PRESS ETC ABOUT GALION BILLING IRREGULARITIES WILLING
TO MEET AT FACTORY AWAIT INSTRUCTIONS TO PROCEED

The telegram was addressed to Clayton Senior and Junior, from "V. Stuffleben".

"I can hardly believe it's true," I said.

"What?"

"Clement and Barfield — the guys who burned in Galion. They really were blackmailing your father and brother."

"I told you. Does it say what it was about?"

"During the War, Elite overbilled the War Department for parts it was making. Clement and Barfield knew about it and were threatening to spill the beans unless they got a hundred grand each."

"That's awful, all the way around."

"Maury Sorin had his hands on these documents for a time," I said. "He called them a 'smoking gun'. Your father and brother think so too — they had Sorin killed to make sure no one else got a look at them."

"Let's close up and get out of here," Elizabeth said nervously. "I thought I heard something out in the hall."

"It's your imagination. Your old man's counting sheep by now."

I told her my idea about photographing the documents in the Galion File, then returning them to the safe. "That way no one will know I have the evidence until I spring it on them."

"I don't know, Benny. You've got to hurry."

"Relax," I said. "This won't take a minute."

THIRTY-NINE

I PULLED THE miniature camera from my coat pocket and cleared a corner of the desk for the photo shoot. "The lighting's a little iffy in here," I said to Elizabeth. "Maybe we should —"

"Goddamn it! How in hell did you open my safe?"

Clayton Senior was wearing a brown silk robe and a yellow ascot, and was glaring at me from just inside the doorway. Behind him were the Gorilla and the Sidekick, each with a gat in his hand.

"When I found you under my desk, I couldn't figure out why you'd be stupid enough to come here," he said. "Little did I know you'd come to rob me."

"You couldn't have seen me," I said.

"Seen you? I was practically tripping all over you. Once I knew there was someone down there, it wasn't hard to figure out who it was."

Elizabeth had fainted forward on the desk. Clayton Senior walked over, grabbed her head on either side, and began shaking it. "Wake up," he commanded. "Wake up now!"

The Gorilla tended to me. "Come around from behind the desk with your hands where I can see them," he ordered. I followed his instructions. He asked me whether I was carrying a gun. Without answering, I took the .45 from the inside pocket of my coat and handed it to the Sidekick.

In the meantime, Elizabeth had come to. Clayton Senior ordered her to go upstairs.

"What are you going to do with Benny?" she asked.

"This doesn't concern you anymore. Go to your room."

"Go ahead, Liz," I said. "There's nothing you can do."

"For once, I agree with him," Clayton Senior said. When Elizabeth didn't move, he nodded toward the Gorilla, who passed the signal on to the Sidekick. The Sidekick walked over, pulled Elizabeth out of her chair, and began dragging her toward the door. Elizabeth tried to resist.

"Don't make it hard on yourself," I told her. "Let him walk you upstairs."

Elizabeth audibly exhaled, and the Sidekick loosened his grip on her arm. Then they proceeded out the door.

The Gorilla had me sit on the floor with my back to the wall, next to the window facing the front lawn. He pulled open the shades and looked out before drawing them shut again.

"In case you're wondering," Clayton Senior said, "we're waiting for Junior."

"I wasn't wondering," I replied.

"He was at our place in Sandusky. He's bringing the boat back to dock it closer to town."

"So?"

"You're getting a burial at sea," said Clayton Senior, "or a reasonable facsimile thereof. These gentlemen are going to shoot you full of holes and dump your body into Lake Erie. They'll tie an anchor to your waist before you go overboard. No one will ever see you again."

"You wouldn't have to go to all this effort if your driver hadn't botched the hit-and-run on Coventry Road a couple weeks ago."

Clayton Senior grinned. "That was a mistake," he said. "I under-stand we made another one today, on Euclid Avenue."

"That *shlub* couldn't catch a cold."

"He came highly recommended by the security firm. Anyway, you turned up here on your own."

"I aim to please," I said.

"Tell me — what in the world did you come to steal?"

"That," I said, pointing to the Galion File on his desk.

Clayton Senior walked over and thumbed through its contents. "I'll be goddamned..." he said. "I'm not sure how she even knew about this, much less where to find it."

"I bet you lifted that stuff from Maury Sorin's office."

"As a matter of fact, we did. At least, most of it. We had to get it back after that bastard Zimmer stole it from us."

"How'd you ever let him get away with that?"

Clayton Senior bristled. "When the file went missing," he said, "we quickly identified Zimmer as the only possible culprit. Junior had the file out when Zimmer was in his office whining about the two reprobates who burned in the Galion fire. Zimmer must've seen him looking at it. The detectives we hired figured that he came back to the office after Junior left for the evening, to get a closer look at the documents — and then hid them under his coat and walked off with them."

"How'd you know to look for them in Sorin's office?"

"When we didn't find them at Zimmer's home, that became the most logical place they'd be. I don't know why I'm telling you all of this...but at this point, it doesn't really matter, does it?"

"There are only copies in the file, not originals," I said.

"The copies are what the blackmailers sent when they first made contact, to show us they weren't bluffing. They presumably had the originals in hand when they died in the fire."

"Why didn't you destroy the copies as well?" I asked.

"Our lawyers advised against it."

Clayton Senior picked up the Galion File and went through it a second time. "Elizabeth had to know the trouble she could've caused by letting you have this," he said.

"Face it, old man. Your daughter despises you. So does everybody else who doesn't get paid to tell you differently."

Clayton Senior's face turned bright red, but he quickly regained his composure. "You know, Benjamin," he said, "when they throw you in the lake, it'll take weeks for anyone to realize you're missing. I mean, who the hell will care, other than my lunatic daughter? You've got no wife, no kids, no close friends, no relatives who can stand to be in the same room with you. The only person you ever talk to is that fat Polack secretary of yours, and she hates your guts, too."

"Mrs. Skokow?"

"If that's the cow's name. You know she's been talking to the FBI. She helped them go through your files a couple of times, and even let them put a tap on your phone."

"Shit," I said. "Now they know about my affair with Jane Russell."

"She thinks you're an atheist commie, Benjamin."

"Jane Russell thinks I'm a communist?"

Sweat tricked down my forehead as I bantered with Clayton Senior. I wasn't kidding myself about the jam I was in. I didn't have any trick up my sleeve or some table-turning move I was waiting to spring. The best I could do was hold out for an opportune moment and make a dash for the front door, in hope that the inevitable bullets would miss. That would be more of a miracle than a long shot.

"I think I heard a car out front," the Gorilla said. "Your daughter might've called the cops."

"Nonsense. There's not even a telephone in her bedroom. It must be Junior you heard."

"So how do you know so much about Mrs. Skokow?" I asked the question as a diversion, in case Elizabeth had actually managed to get in touch with the police.

"We have our ways."

"It's too soon for your son to be here from Sandusky," the Gorilla said. "Someone really should go make sure we're in the clear."

"So go," Clayton Senior said.

The Gorilla motioned to the Sidekick, who'd just returned from escorting Elizabeth upstairs. "You'd better see what's what," he said. The mutt nodded and headed out.

We sat silently for a few minutes while the Gorilla rolled up the front window and peered out. The old man sat down at his desk and fiddled with a letter opener. Then a shot rang out.

"Hey, you!" we heard the Sidekick shout. "Get the hell over here!"

Two sets of footsteps ran up the driveway toward the back. We heard a faint thud and a fainter grunt.

"Somebody hurt somebody," said the Gorilla.

The silence returned for what seemed a lot longer than it probably was. Eventually the Sidekick returned to the study, pushing another man in front of him.

"This guy was nosing around outside," he said. "I thought I better bring him in."

I turned my head toward the captive, who had his head bowed and his eyes covered with his left arm. I didn't immediately realize that I was looking at my brother, Jake.

"What were you doing on my property, Mister, at this time of night?" Clayton Senior asked him. "Are you here to cause trouble?"

Jake lifted his head shakily and responded groggily. "Out for a drive," he said.

"So why'd you stop here, at my house?"

Jake didn't answer. Clayton Senior studied his face, then looked over at me before turning back. He'd met my brother several times, but apparently didn't recognize him now.

I couldn't fathom Jake's reasons for coming. Whatever they were, his presence made a miserable situation worse. Under hopeless conditions, now I had to plan for both of us to escape.

I was racing through the far-fetched schemes I'd already rejected, when I remembered the brass knuckles. I tried to make it look natural when I checked to confirm they were still in my pocket. I didn't know exactly what I was going to do with them, but an opportunity immediately presented itself.

"We'll have to deal with this joker later," the old man said to the Sidekick as he motioned toward Jake. "There's a bathroom at the end of the hall on the other side of the living room. Go lock him in there for the time being."

"Before you do that, you better let me pay a visit first," I said. "Nature's calling and won't take no for an answer."

"What are you up to, Benjamin?" Clayton Senior responded.

"What good would it do me to lie about that? I'll tell you what — wait a little longer, and you'll have proof that I'm on the level. I don't care. It's your carpet."

"Go ahead and take him," Clayton Senior said to the Sidekick. "But keep a gun on him the whole time, and if he takes one step out of line, kill him. I mean it, so help me God."

The Sidekick thrust the muzzle of his pistol into my back at least 10 times on the way to the lavatory. When we arrived, I went in and started to shut the door, but he stuck his foot out to stop it.

"Keep it open," he said.

"Are you kidding? There aren't any windows in here, and I'll give you the key. What the hell do you think I'm going to do, flush myself down the toilet?"

"Keep it open."

"Okay," I said as I unbuckled my belt and began dropping my trousers. "Have it your way."

"Oh…I thought… Hurry it up," he said as he pushed the door shut.

I figured I only had a minute or two, so I didn't try to choreograph the ambush. I knew, though, I'd have to knock the Sidekick out completely, as quickly and quietly as possible, to ensure that no one in the other room got wind of what was happening.

There was no time like the present. I flushed the toilet and turned on the faucet in the sink.

"Be out in a minute," I called to the Sidekick.

I fitted my right hand into the knuckle-dusters and made a fist. The metal was cold and heavy. I felt as though I could smash my way through a thick slab of concrete.

I shut the faucet and slowly opened the bathroom door. When I emerged into the hallway, I saw that the Sidekick was several paces away, oblivious to my presence and looking out a window. I cocked my arm as I approached him.

"Hey, you," I said in a loud whisper when I got within striking distance.

The Sidekick jumped and turned around. As he did so, I landed a haymaker squarely on the left side of his face.

The Sidekick exhaled in a deflating whoosh, and his eyes rolled backwards into his head. He started to wobble, but stayed on his feet, so I hit him again in the same spot, slightly harder. This time he went down in a heap.

The Sidekick was out cold. For an instant I thought I'd killed him, but he started breathing through his mouth, and his left arm flinched. I considered dragging him into the bathroom but ultimately decided it would take too long. Wherever he lay, the Sidekick wasn't going anywhere anytime soon.

I removed the knucks and picked up the Sidekick's gun, which he'd dropped on my first wallop. I also went through the pockets of his jacket to find my own .45. Then I went to rejoin my hosts. The trip to the john had taken less than five minutes, not long enough to raise any serious suspicion.

I took my shoes off before crossing the hardwood-floored living room, so no one heard me when I arrived back at the study. Clayton Senior still stood at his desk, thumbing through the Galion File. The Gorilla was leaning against the far wall next to Jake, who sat on the floor with his eyes closed.

The old man saw me first. "Benjamin!" he shrieked.

I would've been scared, too, at the sight of me. I had a pistol in each hand — one pointed at him, the other at the Gorilla.

The Gorilla was holding his own gun, which he immediately trained on Jake. "Drop them," he told me calmly, "or I'm afraid your brother gets it."

"That's right — we know who he is," squealed Clayton Senior.

I fired a bullet at the old man's feet. I meant it just as a warning, but I missed.

"Good God!" he yipped. "He shot me!"

"The next one kills him," I said to the Gorilla. "They'll probably give me a medal for it, once they find out what's in that file."

"You kill him, and I'll kill your brother," the Gorilla responded.

"Then there'll be three dead, when you join the party."

"Call an ambulance," Clayton Senior gasped. "I'm bleeding."

"That's what happens when you get shot, grandpa. Tell your man to drop his gun, and I'll call for help."

"Drop it, goddamn it, drop it."

The Gorilla laid his gun on the floor. I asked Jake to pick it up, which he did.

"Now what?" the Gorilla asked.

"I'm not exactly sure," I said. "I've got to make sure you don't give me any trouble."

"Why don't you let me drive Mr. Forsythe to the emergency room?"

"Uh-uh. I'm not going to let you run around on your own."

"How about...?"

"You're going in there," I said, pointing to the far corner of the room. There was a closet with a key in the lock.

It was barely big enough to accommodate the Gorilla. Before he went in, I had Jake empty its contents, which included several pairs of shoes, a wooden putter, a brief case, and a maroon dinner jacket.

"How about letting me take a leak?" the Gorilla asked as I was closing the door. "On the level — I really do have to go."

"Sorry, Stanley. I'm not going to end up like your friend out there in the hallway."

"What happened to him, anyway?"

"He's got a bad headache. He's sleeping it off."

I locked the Gorilla in the closet and tucked the key into my pants pocket. They'd have to break down the door when it came time to get him out.

"Let's see how badly you're hurt," I said to Clayton Senior as I walked over to inspect his wound. The bullet had ripped an ugly hole in his brown leather slipper. His foot was only grazed, but it was pretty bloody.

I removed his ascot and used it to make a tourniquet. "I've got bad news," I told him. "You're going to live. You may need some new neckwear, though."

"Please, Benjamin," he hissed. "I'm in terrific pain."

I stepped over to the desk and picked up the Minox and the Galion File. "I'll call for the ambulance after I find Elizabeth," I said. "Thanks for the evidence, old man."

I left the study to retrieve my shoes. Jake hung back to keep an eye on the shooting victim.

"What in the world are you doing here?" I asked my brother quietly when I returned.

"Miriam insisted I come," he said. "She said I had to do something."

"You almost got yourself killed."

"I was only going to wait in the driveway. At two o'clock, if you hadn't come out, I was supposed to go find a policeman. They must've heard me when I pulled up."

Jake and I stood for a moment, looking uncomfortably at each other. Then he told me he was going home.

"You think you can drive? Maybe I should call a cab..."

"I was a little loopy for a while, but now I'm just tired," he said. "I want to get the hell out of here."

Jake left without saying another word. I didn't talk either, even though I needed to thank him for trying to come to my rescue. There would've been too much emotion if I'd done that. It wasn't the time or the place for me to unravel. I also didn't know how Jake would react. He should've been thanking me, too, for saving his neck, but seemed only irritated at being wrangled into something he would have preferred to avoid.

I found Elizabeth in her bedroom, a third of the way through a bottle of bourbon.

"I had it put away, from before," she said. "I pulled it out when I heard the shot. I thought they might've killed you."

I filled Elizabeth in on what had taken place and convinced her she had no choice but to leave the house immediately. She was crying as we walked out the front door.

"I hope my father's going to be all right," she whimpered.

"I almost forgot," I said as I went back in to telephone for an ambulance.

The Schooner wouldn't start at first, but eventually I got it going. Elizabeth dozed off almost immediately. The motion of the car must've knocked her out. I wanted to sleep, too, but I knew it would be a while. I still had a busy night in front of me.

FORTY

I STASHED ELIZABETH at the Tudor Arms Hotel before going downtown to see the police. The bourbon and the trauma of the day had left her in a state where she could barely walk. I waited in her room till she fell asleep, then headed out.

It was around 5:00 A.M. when I finally made it to the station at 21st and Payne. In the lobby I was met by Lieutenant Monachino, the detective I'd spoken to a couple of weeks earlier. He was unshaven and hadn't completely succeeded in buttoning his shirt.

"I've been waiting for you, Mr. Magazine Writer," he said.

"What? Why?"

"The Forsythes' attorney called the Chief of Police and said you might be dropping by. The Chief needs his beauty sleep, so he asked me to handle it. Dan Corrigan from the Prosecutor's Office will be here any minute. He wants to see you, too."

"Have the Forsythes sent someone over?" I asked.

"No, and they're not going to," said Monachino. "They just wanted to let us know what you'd be bringing."

"They told you about the file?"

"They told us, all right."

"So…" I said after a pause. "Are you going to arrest me?"

"Not hardly," said Monachino as he pulled a cigar from his shirt pocket.

"Do they want you to?"

"Nope."

"Then why'd they call?"

"You hooked a big fish, pal. Don't expect to land it without a fight."

He tried to walk away, but I wouldn't let him go without the Galion File.

"This is going to knock your socks off, Lieutenant," I said. "Two former Elite employees were blackmailing the Forsythes over millions they stole from the War Department. The Forsythes killed them rather than pay up, and then killed Maury Sorin and his client when they were going to blow the whistle."

"If you don't mind," Monachino replied, "I'll keep my socks on till Corrigan arrives. He wants to be here when I go through this."

Monachino disappeared behind a door marked "No Admittance". I plopped down on a bench in the hallway and tried to assess the situation. The news was good, in part. I'd snuck into my ex-in-laws' mansion, stolen confidential documents, shot their patriarch in the foot, and walked out alive and uninjured. Yet instead of immediately filing criminal charges, they'd called the police to defuse the impact of the incriminating evidence I had on them.

The Galion File was, in fact, blockbuster stuff. With any luck, the Forsythes would be in handcuffs by the close of the weekend. But it ultimately depended on whether the powers-that-be had the backbone to stand up to them. Monachino was right: My ex-in-laws were big fish — among the biggest, in fact. They'd immediately gotten through to the Chief of Police to put the kibosh on the case against them before it even started.

I wanted to believe that even the Forsythes' influence had its limits.

The cops and the prosecutor couldn't sweep evidence as compelling as the Galion File under the rug. I wanted to talk to them as soon as possible, so they didn't miss the point.

They had other plans. Eight-thirty came, and I was still waiting. I ran out of ways to kill time, having paced the hallway like an expectant father till my legs couldn't take any more. Then just when I thought Monachino had forgotten about me, I saw him walking my way from the stairway at the far end of the hall. When he got close enough, he handed me the Galion File.

"Here," he said. "It's all yours."

"What gives? Don't tell me..."

"You'll have to talk to Corrigan," said Monachino. "He's the guy making the decisions. He'll be down to see you in a couple of minutes."

I fought the impulse to answer Monachino with a right cross. It had to be a misunderstanding, I told myself. No one from law enforcement could look at the Galion File and simply dismiss its damning import.

I was seething by the time Corrigan finally graced me with his presence half an hour later. I'd never met him before, but I knew who he was the instant I saw him strutting down the hall. He was short and stocky with flaming red hair — a fire hydrant in a sport coat.

"I'm Corrigan," he said without extending his hand to shake. "You're Gold?"

"No, I'm silver, with bronze toes and fingers. That's what makes my last name so ironic."

"Oh, a funny guy, eh?" he responded. "Let me get right to the point. The stuff you gave us isn't any good. It's a pile of crap, if you want to know the truth."

"If I can have five minutes, I'll explain how this 'pile of crap' proves the Forsythes killed Maury Sorin, and at least four other people, too."

"Maury Sorin?" Corrigan said. "The Maury Sorin case is closed, and has been for half a year. And there's nothing in your file that even mentions Sorin. We've been through the stuff three times now. The only thing that comes within ten miles is a passing reference to that Mansfield cop who shot Sorin's killer. It doesn't prove a thing."

"You're dead wrong, and I can show you why."

"I've heard all I want to hear about this nonsense," Corrigan said. "We were on the phone with the Forsythes' lawyers for two hours. They say their clients have no clue what this stuff is or where it came from."

"You can't be that goddamned stupid. They called to tell you about the file before I even got here. How could they have done that if they don't know anything about it?"

"Your ex-wife told them you dummied up those records to frame her father and brother," Monachino said. "She fessed up yesterday."

"I thought they told you they didn't know where the stuff came from."

"They said she'd changed her story today."

"This is all ridiculous," I said. "Why don't you slap those bastards with a subpoena and see whether they're still playing dumb under oath?"

"There's this little thing called the Bill of Rights," Corrigan said. "We can't force the Forsythes to incriminate themselves."

"If the file's what they say it is, they have no reason to take the Fifth."

"Listen," he said, "my office won't be serving any subpoena on that family."

"You guys have prosecuted cases with far less," I said. "What goes on here?"

"Figure it out, Gold. While you do, I'm going to enjoy what's left of my weekend."

Corrigan walked away. I just stood in the middle of the hallway, stupefied. It took me a minute or two to muster the initiative to walk to my car.

I knew as well as anyone that a different set of rules applied to the Forsythes of the world. But Corrigan was rubbing my face in it. He let my ex-in-laws shimmy their way out of a murder rap with a story so preposterous it was a miracle he didn't choke repeating it.

Why would Elizabeth help me "frame" her father and brother, years after our divorce? Why had she suddenly "fessed up" about the conspiracy? How did the Forsythes know I'd be coming to the police station? And if the documents were phonies, why weren't they having me prosecuted to the hilt?

Corrigan had to know things didn't add up. He should've at least done some digging, asked a few questions. Instead, the Forsythe name gave him all the answers in advance.

As I drove home, I tried to think of what I was going to tell Judith Sorin, and whether I could give her the green light to return home. I briefly wondered what the morning's developments meant for Elizabeth. The questions were impenetrable. I was too goddamned exhausted to contemplate the implications of what had happened or plot out what to do next. All I wanted was to climb into bed and sleep. That's exactly what I did when I finally made it to my apartment.

FORTY-ONE

I WAS GETTING out of the bathtub later that afternoon when the telephone rang. I wrapped myself in a towel and went to answer it.

"Mr. Gold, Tom Thomas from Grimm White. I'm calling about those documents you presented to the police this morning."

"You mean the documents I took from your client's safe?"

"The ones from the police station," he said. "I don't know where you got them."

"Sure you don't. How's the old man's foot?"

"I'm not prepared to talk about that."

"He probably didn't get shot," I said. "Just like I didn't take that file from his safe."

I tried to hide how surprised I was to receive the call. I knew the Forsythes would contact me at some point, but didn't think it would be so soon, and I certainly never expected their lawyer to do the talking for them. We had unfinished business, my ex-in-laws and I, and there was nothing remotely legal about it.

About an hour earlier, I'd been lying in bed, thinking about what to do with the Galion File. It didn't seem to matter much after what had happened at the police station. The file was sham evidence, to hear Corrigan tell it.

But sham evidence was in the eye of the beholder. It dawned on me that whatever the Galion File did or didn't prove about Maury Sorin's murder, it unmistakably documented the billing scam Elite had perpetrated on the Army. I had to think the federal government would look unkindly on that kind of fraud, particularly when it was committed by a defense contractor currently being paid millions to manufacture the latest turbojet engines. Revelations from the Galion File might convince the Air Force to end that arrangement. The Justice Department could also sue to recoup the money Elite had gouged, along with interest — and maybe even prosecute a criminal case against the Forsythes.

Given these possibilities, I began to wonder why the Forsythes didn't have the police confiscate the Galion File the minute I showed up at the station. But then I realized that doing so would have required them to claim that the documents in the file actually did belong to them — openly linking Elite Motorworks to the very evidence they were trying to suppress.

The Galion File still posed a threat to the Forsythes. They obviously realized this, even if I hadn't done so immediately, and they weren't going to acquiesce to my continued possession of it. The Gorilla and his colleagues would no doubt corner me soon in some isolated place to explain in their own inimitable way exactly why my best interests required its return. I'd have to act before that happened if I wanted to get the file to the Feds.

"We're going to need those documents back, Mr. Gold," T-Squared told me.

"I'm not surprised to hear you say so. But unfortunately, I dumped them down a sewer this morning on my way home."

"I find that a little hard to believe," he said.

"Nevertheless…"

"I have a proposition for you, Mr. Gold. The Forsythes are prepared to pay fifty thousand dollars for the file. You can have the money immediately, in cash."

"Fifty grand? For the file I didn't steal from them?"

"Don't be coy," he said. "That file could cause a lot of trouble if it fell into the wrong hands."

"Or stayed in mine."

"That's precisely the point."

"What if I wanted more than fifty thousand?" I asked.

"How much more?"

"I don't know. Seventy-five thousand? A hundred, maybe?"

"That's a lot of money. But I'm not saying no. We're open to negotiation."

"It's too bad I don't have the file," I said.

"How long will you need to get it back? My clients want to wrap this up as quickly as possible."

"Why don't we get together around six o'clock this evening? I should know what the situation is by then."

"Okay, I guess," Thomas said. "You obviously know where our offices are."

"Yeah, I know where they are, but you need to know where my apartment is, because that's where we're meeting."

"Mr. Gold..."

"I get home-court advantage this time," I said. "And come alone. The place isn't big enough for the whole entourage."

After the call, I went into my bedroom and got my bathrobe. Then I retired to the living room couch and tried to figure out why the Forsythes were choosing to pay to get the Galion File back rather than using fists or bullets. My guess was that they figured they should lay off — for a while, at least — after the to-do that morning at the precinct. If anything happened to me, they'd be the obvious suspects.

So the Forsythes decided they'd have to buy me off to get what they wanted. They assumed I'd jump at the deal, given the single-minded greed they regarded as my defining characteristic.

The truth was that nothing restrained me from indulging my own self-interest in this affair. I was a free agent, without any remaining commitment to Judith Sorin. Grab bags like the one Thomas Thomas was offering didn't come along every day. They *never* came along. No one could reasonably expect me to pass up a hundred thousand dollars in favor of turning the Galion File over to the U.S. Government.

I wondered what I would really accomplish by going to the Feds. The whitewash that morning at the police station showed the type of influence my ex-in-laws could wield. The U.S. Attorney was probably just as susceptible to their persuasion as Corrigan had been. Even if I turned over the Galion File and Elite was prosecuted for the billing scam, the company would mobilize its usual battalion of lawyers and public relations men to quell the threat.

I almost had myself convinced. But I couldn't help remembering my diatribe a few days earlier against Mrs. Zimmer for allowing the Forsythes to buy their way out of a murder rap. It felt like I'd be doing the exact same thing in taking the deal they were offering me now.

I returned to my bedroom and got dressed, then straightened the apartment. It was already past four o'clock. Thomas Thomas would arrive in less than two hours.

FORTY-TWO

TOMMY THOMAS SHOWED up at my apartment in a three-piece suit and a shiny pair of oxfords. "Damn it, Thomas," I said. "I didn't know this was formal. Maybe I'd better go put on my Brooks Brothers pinstripe."

"You're fine," he grumbled, finding no humor in my humor.

Whatever his mood, I was high as a kite. I'd been so jumpy waiting for him that I decided I couldn't do without a drink. There wasn't any booze in the apartment, so I went upstairs to see Mrs. Rosenthal. Unfortunately, all she had was the bottle of Manischewitz normally reserved for *Shabbos* dinners.

"Any port in a storm," I said. She didn't say whether she got the pun.

I finished the wine in less than half an hour. It tasted like grape juice but still did the trick.

Thomas Thomas followed me into the living room and sat down on the couch. I pulled up the chair from across the room, then sat down myself.

"What'd you decide?" he asked.

"I'm willing to sell," I told him, "but it's going to cost more than you're offering."

"I said we're willing to discuss the price."

"Add another zero. Five hundred thousand bucks."

"Half a million dollars?" he shouted. "That's a ridiculous amount of money."

"I don't think so, Thomas," I said. "By the way, please know that when I call you that, I'm using your last name, not your first. I wouldn't want you to think I'm being too familiar."

"I'm sure my clients won't pay that much."

"Then it's been nice talking to you. Sorry you came to the other side of the tracks for nothing."

"Would you take one hundred thousand?" Tommy Thomas asked after a short silence.

"I would if you added another four hundred thousand to it."

"You won't negotiate at all?"

"It's never been my strong suit," I said. "Besides, I'm already compromising. The way I figure it, the file's actually worth a full million, at least."

"You're pulling these figures out of your ass," he grumbled.

"They have to come from somewhere."

T-Squared fussed a little while longer. Then he told me the Forsythes would pay the five hundred thousand.

"Excellent," I said. "We've resolved that part of the transaction."

"What are you talking about?"

"There are other matters we need to take care of."

"I don't know what you mean," he said.

"I'm about to tell you. Your clients are going to pay Judith Sorin a million bucks for killing her father."

"Mr. Gold, you're out of your mind!"

"You're not the first to make that diagnosis."

"First of all, the Forsythes didn't kill Maury Sorin," said T-Squared. "It's a slanderous accusation."

"They killed him, all right," I said. "They may not have told you explicitly, but I bet you know it. They killed several others, too, to keep secret what's in that file."

"My clients will not pay Judith Sorin one million dollars," Thomas Thomas pronounced.

"She gets the money, or I keep the file. And it's not just the million. They've also got to pay me a $250,000 fee for negotiating the settlement."

"On top of the million?"

"Yep. A total of one-point-two-five million to settle with Judith Sorin," I said.

"You've got to be kidding."

"I kid a lot. It's my usual form of communication. But I'm not kidding about this."

"You've overplayed your hand, Mr. Gold," Thomas said as he started to get up from the couch. "I think we're done here."

"Sit back down, counselor," I said. "You know your clients can't have me walking around with that file. We've still got to discuss what Elizabeth Forsythe gets."

"Elizabeth Forsythe?"

"Don't act so surprised. We used to be married, you know."

"I'm well aware of that," he said.

"You're also aware that her brother controls the trust that holds all her Elite Motorworks stock. As part of our deal, he's going to have to dissolve that trust and transfer all its assets outright to his sister."

"No way," said Thomas Thomas. "It simply can't be done. There'd be outrageous tax consequences, for one thing."

"I have every confidence the esteemed trust-and-estate attorneys at Grimm White will figure out how to handle it," I said. "If there's a tax bill, your clients will just have to pay it."

"Why in God's name do you want to terminate the trust?"

"Would you want Junior to control all your wealth, after everything that's happened over the last few weeks? He was an asshole to begin with…"

"I'll pass that along," Thomas Thomas said snidely. "But it's going nowhere."

"What's the value of the trust?"

"You have no right to that information."

"Tommy, please," I said. "Let's not pretend we're conducting some kind of legitimate business deal here."

"Around five million dollars at the end of the last quarter," he grumbled after a moment's hesitation.

"That's better. Tell Clayton Senior and Junior they're going to pay me a ten-percent fee for negotiating its dissolution. That's another half a mil, if I'm not mistaken."

"You are truly out of your mind, Mr. Gold."

"You're repeating yourself," I said.

Thomas Thomas began writing on his legal pad again. "That's half a million for the file, half a million for breaking up the trust, and one-and-a-quarter million, with fees, for Judith Sorin. Two-point-two-five million in total, not including the cost of breaking up the trust."

"You're good with numbers," I said. "I would've needed an abacus to make that calculation."

"I can tell you now, you're not going to get what you're asking for," said Thomas Thomas.

"And I'm telling you, it's take-it-or-leave-it, pal. Clayton Senior has till noon tomorrow to let me know."

"Goodbye, Mr. Gold. I'll see myself out."

Thomas Thomas called me shortly before ten o'clock that same night. "The Forsythes want to have you prosecuted for extortion," he said.

"So call the cops. I've got Lieutenant Monachino's number written down somewhere. Give me a minute and I'll go find it."

"Now hold on, Mr. Gold. They're not happy about it, but they'll accept your offer."

"The complete package?"

"The complete package," he confirmed. "Naturally, it's going to take a few days to draw up the paperwork, and a bit more than that to dissolve the trust."

"All right," I said, "but skip all the *whereas's* and *heretofore's* and *thereon's*. Don't forget, I'm a Grimm White alumnus. I know all the tricks."

I immediately called Elizabeth to let her know about the deal I'd negotiated for her. She was bewildered by the news.

"You mean I won't have to ask Junior for money?"

"That's right," I said.

"No matter how much I want?"

"Uh-huh. And you can do what you want with your Elite stock."

"Like what, for example?"

"Like sell it," I said. "Or use it to elect someone to the Board of Directors to represent your interests."

"Aren't Junior and my father going to be angry about this?"

"I certainly hope so."

Elizabeth thanked me for what I'd done, once she understood what I was telling her. Judith Sorin reacted far less appreciatively. We met Monday evening at her home, after she returned from her weekend in hiding.

"You're not my lawyer, Mr. Gold, and never have been," she said. "You're not even working as my investigator anymore."

"No one's going to force you to take the money," I said. "If you don't want it, just say so."

"Money's never been the point of all this. I told you from the start that I wanted to see your in-laws behind bars for killing my father."

"And I told you from the start that they're my ex-in-laws," I said. "I did my best to convince the police and the prosecutor to take up the case, but they didn't bite."

"So that's it?"

"I think the Forsythes will pay in the end."

"They have an endless supply of money," Judith said.

"Just the same."

"I don't know what you're getting at, Mr. Gold, and I really don't care. Give me that file, and I'll present it to the police. Then maybe they'll — "

"Listen, toots," I said as I headed for the door. "I'm selling the file back, one way or the other. Let me know what you want to do."

Judith waited two days to call. "I accept," she said. "When can I expect my money?"

FORTY-THREE

"You have fifteen minutes, Mr. Gold."

I stood, strode to the podium, and unfolded my notes. "Thank you, your Honor," I said uncertainly. After clearing my throat, I started explaining to the three Sixth Circuit judges why they'd be giving Good Doctor Braunstein a raw deal if they booted him from the country.

It was late October, roughly two months after the showdown at the Forsythes' and my meeting with Thomas Thomas. I'd come on as Braunstein's counsel only a few weeks earlier. I'd asked for a three-week postponement so I could prepare; but the government objected, and the court nixed my request.

I didn't have any illusions about how I'd do. I was bringing my legal career out of mothballs after nearly a decade to argue a complicated appeal against sophisticated, well-trained lawyers, in a field of law far outside my experience. I wasn't aspiring to eloquence or some brilliant turn of phrase in presenting Braunstein's case. If I could get through the essential points in coherent English, I'd consider it a success.

For the longest time, Braunstein had insisted upon representing himself. I told him in the strongest possible terms just how bad an idea that was. Eventually he relented, and when I couldn't find another lawyer to take the case, I stepped in to fill the breach.

I couldn't let the Doc get deported without doing something. I owed him an incalculable debt — he'd put me back together when the damage seemed irreparable. Now I needed to reciprocate in his hour of need. I could tell myself from now till kingdom come that I wasn't the same selfish punk I'd been when I married into the Forsythe clan; now it was time to prove it — to do the right thing for once, even if I didn't personally benefit from it. I had to put up or shut up.

Our case was last one on the docket for the day. The courtroom was empty except for me, the government's lawyer, and Number One and Number Two, who sat in the back row of the gallery.

Opposing counsel was young, fit, well-groomed, well-spoken, and completely confident in what he was doing. He characterized each of his arguments as "irrefutable", "indisputable", or "beyond debate". The judges nodded in agreement with many of his pronouncements.

I tried to fight back. "The party Dr. Braunstein belonged to in Vienna may have had socialist leanings, but it wasn't tied to the Communists."

"Should your client have disclosed his membership in applying to come here?" asked the judge on the right.

"He's not accused of withholding that information, your Honor."

"There's deception by commission and deception by omission. The Communists are masters of both."

"Of course you're right," I said. "But you're suggesting Dr. Braunstein lied about being a Communist because he didn't voluntarily reveal his membership in a party that had no Communist ties. Respectfully, your Honor, the logic doesn't hold up."

"Counselor," said the judge on the left, "You can't seriously question the danger posed by the Communists in our midst. Don't you think we should rather be safe than sorry?"

I answered by talking about the evil of guilt by association, the constitutional presumption of innocence, and America's unparalleled commitment to due process and freedom of speech. It all sounded pretty compelling to me, but the panel gave no indication that they agreed.

"You've got thirty seconds left, Mr. Gold," said the judge in the middle. "Better wrap it up."

After the hearing, I called Braunstein from a payphone on the first floor of the courthouse. I chose my words carefully. I honestly didn't think things had gone too well, but I saw no point in burdening the Doc with my pessimism. When he asked for a prediction, I told him the case could go either way.

"I cannot thank you enough for your help," Braunstein said. "How long do you think it will take the judges to rule?"

"A few months, at least. I'll let you know as soon as I hear."

Number One and Number Two were waiting outside the courthouse when I exited. I wanted to walk right past them, but they wouldn't let me.

"You lied to us, Mr. Gold," said Number One. "You represented Dr. Braunstein all along."

"Believe whatever the hell you want."

"You're a goddamned red," said Number Two. "They ought to put you and your client on the same boat to Russia."

"You know what?" I told my two friends. "I'm not a Communist. I'm not even a registered Democrat. You both can go fuck yourselves, as far as I'm concerned."

I knew I was making things worse with enemies I'd rather not have. But I was on their hit list already, and my standing wasn't going to improve no matter what I did. Besides, there wasn't much Number

One and Number Two could really do to hurt me. I was financially secure. The Maury Sorin case had made me a wealthy man.

FORTY-FOUR

I STAYED ON in Cincinnati for two extra days after the Sixth Circuit hearing, mostly just to sleep in my hotel. It had been a hectic few months, with the high drama of the Sorin case followed immediately by the frantic preparation for the Court of Appeals. I needed the rest.

Before starting back for Cleveland, I put in a long-distance call to Jim Roberts, the Assistant U.S. Attorney who'd gone to law school with me. Roberts had heard about my argument in the Braunstein case.

"I was only moderately atrocious," I said.

"Actually, they told me you pretty much held your own."

"Jim, I've got evidence of a multi-million-dollar scam a supplier ran on the Army during the War. The company's still doing business with the government. I was wondering whether you guys want to take a look at it."

"Millions of dollars? Of course we do," Roberts said. "What kind of evidence is there?"

"A mix of things. The government's own records will corroborate the fraud, once I show you where to look."

"Who's the supplier?"

"I'll tell you when I see you," I said. "I guarantee you'll recognize the name. It's the crème de la crème."

Of course, the terms of sale of the Galion File expressly prohibited me from keeping any copies or telling anyone about the
file's contents. I secretly awarded myself a waiver on that part of
the deal — in fact, I'd never intended to honor it. Waiting for my
meeting with Thomas Thomas that afternoon in my apartment,
I realized that I didn't have to choose between taking the money
and taking the high road. I could sell back the Galion File and still
turn the Forsythes in, simply by emulating them. My ex-in-laws lied
and cheated and connived as a matter of course. In this particular
instance, I'd do the same.

I still had my Minox camera with me from the previous night.
A few minutes before T-Squared rang my doorbell, I finished taking
a snapshot of every page in the Galion File. I developed the film
in the darkroom at a friend's house two weeks later, the same day
I met Thomas Thomas at his office to turn over the file and sign
the contracts he had drawn up. I printed two copies — one for the
U.S. Attorney, the other placed in a safety deposit box I'd rented
specifically for that purpose. I wanted to make sure the Forsythes
didn't trump my double cross with one of their own. If the first copy
of the file disappeared, there'd be a backup.

I knew the Forsythes would come after me once I exposed them.
But as I saw it, they really couldn't hurt me too badly. If they sued
for breach of contract, they'd be trying to enforce an agreement to
suppress evidence of multiple felonies. Good luck with that — courts
don't aid and abet the commission of crimes. If your contract is
illegal, you've got no claim for enforcement.

The Forsythes, of course, were capable of exacting vengeance in
less refined ways. Clement and Barfield, Zimmer, and Maury Sorin
would all attest to that. But if the U.S. Attorney took up the case

against Elite, I would become an important witness in an ongoing federal prosecution. The Forsythes couldn't bump me off under those circumstances, since the Feds and everyone else would immediately realize who did it.

I spent the Saturday night after I returned to Cleveland at the same bar on Kinsman where I'd gone after my meeting with Zimmer's widow. I was drinking scotch, and plenty of it. It was a celebration, in part. Two-point-two-five-million was a lot of money, any way you looked at it. I'd inflicted a serious pinch on the Forsythes' wallet.

The Forsythes' pain ran that much deeper because I was receiving so much of the cash. My ex-in-laws definitely didn't want to be my ticket to easy street. They believed I'd only married Elizabeth as a means of reaching that destination. She may have divorced me on the cheap, but now I'd arrived anyway.

I congratulated myself on my moxie: I saw an opportunity to exploit the Forsythes, and I seized upon it.

That was one perspective on my conduct. It was equally accurate to say I'd committed a brazen fraud by selling back the Galion File with the secret intention of also turning it over to the U.S. Government. As I drank my scotch, I couldn't stop thinking that only a con-man or shyster would pull this sort of stunt. I also fixated on the notion that fraud doesn't become any less fraudulent just because the victims had it coming to them.

I considered how the Forsythes would react when they found out what I'd done. I realized they'd take it as confirmation of the conniving, avaricious stereotype they ascribed to me the minute they heard my last name was Goldstein. It was that happy notion that kept me at the bar on Kinsman till closing time early Sunday morning.

FORTY-FIVE

WHEN I RETURNED to the office on Monday morning, I nearly tripped over the letters piled inside the door beneath the mail slot. There'd been no one tending to the correspondence since Mrs. Skokow jumped ship after I confronted her about collaborating with the FBI.

Mrs. Skokow's blubbery face turned crimson when I repeated what Clayton Senior had told me. I thought she was going to cry, but she got ahold of herself and went on the offensive.

"Darn right I talked to them," she said. "And I let them look around, too. I'm a law-abiding citizen. You wouldn't object if you were one, too."

"You've changed your position on things. At first you said you approved when I used your pop gun to chase those guys out of here."

"I didn't approve, at least not after I got the chance to talk to them. I didn't know anything about the Braunstein case. You hid it from me."

"I didn't hide anything," I said. "I hadn't agreed to represent him at the time."

She harrumphed. "That's what they said you'd say. But you're still going to Cincinnati."

"You're being ridiculous."

"Listen. I'm a loyal American — "

"And a law-abiding citizen," I interrupted. "Don't forget that."

Mrs. Skokow stomped to the front of the office and began packing up her desk. Half an hour later, she presented me with a check written on the firm's account to cover her wages till the end of week.

"Why should I pay you through Friday?" I asked. "You're leaving today."

Mrs. Skokow began to argue, but I mooted the point by signing the check. She handed me her keys and turned to leave.

"Don't think I won't tell the building what goes on up here," she said as her parting shot.

"Good. They can tell me when they find out."

<hr/>

The heap of letters included one from Nancy. "I'm hoping you lost my address," she wrote, "and I'm not getting the silent treatment for some other reason. So here it is again, with my telephone number..."

I hadn't lost anything. I'd been a busy man the last several months, and hadn't found time to get back in touch.

But that was only part of the explanation — a small part of it. My initial delay in contacting her led to further delay, given my growing embarrassment over how long it had been. I also wasn't looking forward to telling Nancy about my money grab in wrapping up the Sorin case. I myself had trouble stomaching the wheeling and dealing I'd done. I didn't think Nancy would react any differently.

I went to a phone booth around the corner and had the operator dial Nancy's number. The FBI was presumably still tapping my line, and the Forsythes might've been doing so as well. This was going to be difficult enough without having an extra audience.

"Well, hello there," Nancy said when she heard my voice. "You must've gotten my letter."

"Lucky you sent it. I'd lost your address."

"Yeah, lucky I sent it," she said. I couldn't tell for certain, but I suspected she saw through the lie.

"So how are you?" I asked.

"Can't complain. More importantly, how are you? What ever happened to Judith's case?"

I spent the next half hour answering that question. I hit all the highlights: the revelation about the torched factory; the showdown at Elite's offices; Elizabeth's materializing out of nowhere; my theft of the Galion File; and my double-dealing in simultaneously selling the file back to the Forsythes and turning it over to the U.S. Attorney.

"Jesus Christ, Gold," Nancy said when I finished.

"I don't know exactly what you mean by that, and I'm not sure I want to."

"I just mean, that's quite a story."

"I'm worried I didn't handle the situation with as much integrity as I should have."

"Because you lied to your ex-in-laws?" she asked. "They're scum."

"Not so much the lying, as raiding their cookie jar in the process."

"So you took their money. They'd have done the same to you."

"I'm not sure they're the appropriate standard-bearers for honorable conduct," I said.

"I took money for telling you Frank Zimmer's name. Am I bad, too?"

"The two things aren't remotely comparable."

"Don't forget that you got money for Judith, and Elizabeth Forsythe too," she said. "You weren't in it only for yourself."

Nancy continued trying to convince me of my unadulterated heroism. It didn't work, but I appreciated the effort.

"This is costing you a fortune," she said nearly an hour after our call started. "We'd better say goodbye."

"When are you coming back to Cleveland?" I asked.

"The trains run in both directions, Gold. Chicago's not so bad. We have sidewalks and streetlights, and the restaurants stay open after dark."

"I'll try to remember that," I said. The call ended on that sarcastic note.

I made it through half the mail before going to the Hippodrome Theater downstairs for a matinee of *High Noon*. In the film, Gary Cooper sacrifices his honeymoon with Grace Kelly to confront a gunslinger with murderous intentions. He doesn't resort to subterfuge in doing his duty. He doesn't get rich, either. Critics were giving the picture four-star reviews. It only made me feel worse.

FORTY-SIX

THE U.S. ATTORNEY's Office wasted no time in putting together its case against Elite. The Forsythes received the summons and complaint just in time for Christmas. The case didn't mention their five-man killing spree, but it still caused quite a stir. An editorial in the *Plain Dealer* described Elite's conduct as a "shameful money grab". The *Cleveland Press* accused the company of "indulging in the worst extremes of corporate greed," while the *Cleveland News* called for an "immediate and thoroughgoing" review of billings on all of Elite's government contracts.

New Year's came and went, and I hadn't heard a peep from the Forsythes. Eventually I got the call I expected from Thomas Thomas.

"You won't get away with this," he told me. "We had a deal, and you flagrantly breached it."

"I don't know what you mean."

"Yes you do, Mr. Gold. The Forsythes paid you an exorbitant price for that file. You took their money and then gave a copy of it to the government."

"Ohhh, you're referring to the lawsuit," I said. "Maybe they figured out Elite was stealing on their own."

"That didn't happen," replied Tommy Thomas. "They've shown us the evidence they have, and the only place it could've come from is that file."

"From what you're telling me, that's just a guess."

"Who do you think you're jerking around here?!" bellowed a new voice.

"Mr. Forsythe is on the extension," T-Squared explained.

"Hello, grandpa. How's the foot?"

"Grandpa, my ass," Clayton Senior said. "You double-crossed us, Benjamin. I'm going to sue you to kingdom come."

"I sincerely doubt that. But if you do, it'll be your funeral, not mine."

"You're a liar and a crook."

"I learned from the master," I told him. "You've always done unto others, Pops. Now I'm doing unto you."

Clayton Senior railed at me for another few minutes before he and Thomas Thomas hung up. The call invigorated me. I enjoyed putting the screws to the old man. He'd never considered the possibility that I might cheat him on the deal for the Galion File. He undoubtedly wanted to send me the way of Maury Sorin, but he couldn't without compounding his own problems. My sudden demise would only brighten the spotlight already shining on the Forsythes' illegal conduct. Clayton Senior could fume at me over the telephone, but he couldn't do much else.

In public, he and the rest of the family were keeping their yaps shut. The government's lawsuit elicited no boisterous denials of guilt or threats of grave repercussions for slandering the Forsythe name. Elite's official response seemed almost contrite, acknowledging the "seriousness of the allegations" and promising to "look into the matter". I took the muted response as a good sign: by all appearances, my ex-in-laws were flummoxed.

But the joke was on me. I found that out when Jim Roberts called me at the beginning of February.

"I wanted you to hear it from me first," he said. "The Forsythes are settling the case. My boss is going to announce the agreement tomorrow or the next day."

"You're kidding…"

"It's a fantastic result. They've agreed to pay everything they stole, plus interest. They're even making a public apology."

"What about the guys they burned in Galion? What about Maury Sorin?"

"We ordinarily don't prosecute for murder," he said. "That's a state-law offense."

"Isn't there anything you can do?"

"We sued for the money they bilked from the government, and we're getting it all back. Case closed."

After hanging up with Roberts, I immediately dialed Dan Corrigan at the Prosecutor's Office. "I've still got that file," I told him. "Maybe you're willing to take on the Forsythes, now that the Feds have done it first."

"You're whistling in the wind, Gold."

"They murdered five people in cold blood."

"Says you," Corrigan answered. "Get it through your head — I'm not filing homicide charges against the Forsythes, or any other kind of charges, for that matter."

"Is that final?"

"As final as it gets," Corrigan said as he hung up the phone.

FORTY-SEVEN

A FEW WEEKS later, the Sixth Circuit ruled in Braunstein's case. The decision neither booted him from the country nor affirmed his right to stay. The court instead remanded the case for a second trial on whether any "bona fide connection" existed between the communists and the "parties and organizations" that Braunstein had "concealed". The Feds had passed on their opportunity to present evidence of this kind the first time around. The Sixth Circuit had no good reason for giving them a do-over, but then again, at least it didn't order Braunstein's deportation. I'd take what I could get.

"The district court will probably schedule your hearing sooner rather than later," I told Braunstein. "We've got to get right to it."

"You have done enough, Mr. Gold. I cannot ask you to continue as my attorney if I cannot pay you."

"You're stuck with me, Doc, for richer or poorer. No point in arguing about it."

I arranged to have lunch with Sig Danziger the day after the Sixth Circuit released its decision. I was leaving town for a while, and I wanted to see him before I departed. We met at the Theatrical around noon. While we waited for our meals, I handed Sig a bank check for five thousand dollars.

"Jesus, Benny," he said. "That's a lot of dough. What's it for?"

"I did all right on the Sorin case. You helped me, so I thought I would share a little."

"'All right'?" said Sig, staring at the check.

"It was a nice fee."

"I won't say no, Benny. You don't have to do this, but I won't say no."

Elizabeth telephoned late the same afternoon, just as I was leaving the office. The call didn't exactly thrill me. In recent weeks, she'd become increasingly insistent in demanding my attention. She seemed to have hopes of resurrecting our marriage, but that was a lost cause. She'd just saved my life, and for that I was deeply grateful — but still, I had no interest in taking a second spin on a malfunctioning carnival ride.

The previous week, Elizabeth had cornered me into having lunch with her at her new apartment on Shaker Square. Love was in the air, but it didn't involve me. Elizabeth had rekindled her romance with the hooch, downing almost a full bottle of wine during the meal after two martinis beforehand. I practically had to carry her into her bedroom. I'd seen this act before. Elizabeth was the same slobbery drunk I left behind when I went into the Army.

The phone call today was more of the same. "Welllll, it's my long-lost husband," she said when I picked up the receiver. The slur in her tone and her slow cadence let me know she was fully lubricated.

"Guess what?" she said after a few moments of disjointed small talk. "I'm taking a cruise to Europe, and you're coming with me. It's all decided."

"I don't think so, Liz," I said.

"Don't tell me you have to work."

"It's just not a good idea."

"Well, I think it's a marvelous idea," she said, "and I've already bought you a ticket. We sail out of New York a week from Thursday. We can take a train or fly there the day before. Your choice."

"You'd better return the ticket, Liz. I'm not coming."

"I figured you'd say that," she said sadly. "That's why I didn't really buy the ticket."

"It was a nice thought, anyway."

"You should reconsider, Benny. We'd really have a terrific time. Terrific."

That night I had my biweekly dinner at Jake's. Miriam had put the ritual in place shortly after the midnight adventure at the Forsythes'. Jake and I had never really discussed the incident. I went to see him a few weeks afterwards to thank him for trying to save the day. I came prepared to talk, but had a hard time getting started, and Jake did nothing to assist — the conversation lasted all of five minutes. We shook hands, and I left.

At dinner that night, Jake's cold shoulder initially seemed to be thawing. He actually put in his own two cents when I was telling David stories about our childhood. But then he clammed up again. His contribution to the conversation at the dinner table consisted of an occasional nod or head-shake.

As I was leaving, I told Jake I would be out of town for a while and would call when I returned. "Have a good trip," he said. He didn't ask where I was going, and I didn't tell him.

I packed a suitcase that night before getting into bed. I fell asleep quickly but woke up after a few hours, fully alert and raring to go. My train left at two o'clock in the afternoon, and I had work to do beforehand. I wanted to get on with it.

I arrived at the office early and made a neat stack of the various papers I needed to review and file. I was rumbling with excitement, but forced myself to go slowly, to avoid mistakes I'd have to clean up later. I wrapped everything up by noon. With nothing left to do, I walked over to the Terminal.

The place was more or less empty. It was midday, mid-week in early March — not a busy time for travel, apparently. After getting my ticket, I went to the bar for a drink, which I made a double. I then doubled the double by having another, contemplated a third, but instead gave the waitress an overly generous tip and started toward the platform. At a newsstand along the way, I stopped to get a copy of the afternoon *Press*.

"Goddamn it," I said when I saw the front-page headline.

"Is everything all right, sir?" asked the man at the counter.

"Fine," I said, tapping the newspaper. "I just didn't think they'd find out quite so soon."

The man leaned forward to see what I was cackling about:

ELITE OWNERS ACCUSED IN ASSASSINATION PLOT

Lawsuit charges Forsythes in slaying of local attorney Maurice Sorin

When I filed Judith's wrongful death case that morning, I hadn't noticed any reporters in the courthouse. It was just as well, I'd thought. I'd be long gone when the bombshell detonated. I guess some court reporter was faster and sneakier than I'd expected.

Judith Sorin had committed to suing the Forsythes the previous week, after I delivered her own personal copy of the Galion File. She was more than willing to proceed. All along she'd told me she wasn't afraid of my ex-in-laws. As it turned out, she wasn't.

I really hadn't wanted to recruit her for a crusade against the Forsythes. I would've preferred to keep her completely out of it.

But I ended up with no alternative. The U.S. Attorney's case had fallen flat. The settlement was a "fantastic result", as Roberts had said — "fantastic" for the Forsythes. It would certainly cost them millions, and they certainly hated paying it, particularly on top of what I'd extracted from them. Even so, writing the check would hardly imperil the family fortune. And it was worth every penny to them. Settling the case kept the full extent of the fraud the Forsythes had committed on the War Department under wraps, along with the killing spree they'd engineered to cover up their crimes. The case would be an ephemeral blip on their otherwise exemplary record. The bastards would make back all they had to pay and more, in no time flat.

I couldn't leave it at that. My ex-in-laws were thumbing their noses at the principles to which Maury Sorin had devoted his career. With the U.S. Attorney too feckless to go to trial, and the local Prosecutor's Office too beholden to the Forsythes to do anything at all, Judith became the last hope to give them what they had coming.

She'd have to overcome one huge hurdle right off the bat. In exchange for the million bucks she got from the Forsythes, Judith had waived whatever claims she had against them. Tommy Thomas would go to court as soon as possible to argue that this clause pre-empted any suit based on her father's murder. And it probably did — except that the Forsythes had represented in the agreement that they had "in no way caused or contributed to the death" of Maurice Sorin. T-Squared had acquiesced to this language when I proposed it, confident that Judith would never have evidence to the contrary. With the Galion File in hand, along with the other information I'd assembled, we had at least a fighting chance of proving the Forsythes defrauded Judith into signing the deal by lying about their innocence. If we could establish that much, Judith's waiver would disappear.

Judith, of course, initially wanted someone other than me to be her lawyer. Her first choice as counsel, however, took one look at the case and immediately became too busy to handle it. The other attorneys she contacted came up with similar excuses.

"They're obviously afraid to take on the Forsythes," she explained when she came to ask for my help.

"Yet again, you're stuck with me."

"You know, my father wouldn't have been afraid to take on a case like this."

It bordered on a compliment. But then she added, "of course, he never would've sold back that file as you did."

The *Press* article said that Claytons Junior and Senior were "unavailable for comment". The reporter did manage to track down Elizabeth, who said "the allegations could be true, as far as I know." I doubted she was sober when she offered up that morsel, though I really didn't care.

I scrambled to a payphone and called Thomas Thomas. "Can I speak to him?" I asked the secretary who answered.

"He's in conference, sir. May I take a message?"

"Sure you can," I said. "This is Benjamin Gold. Different first and last name. This morning I filed a lawsuit that's going to make Mr.

Thomas very angry. I'll be out of town, but if he wants to talk about it, I'll tell you where he can reach me."

The secretary took the name and address of my hotel. "Is there anything else for Mr. Thomas?" she asked.

"Yeah. Tell him 'don't bother to call' if he wants to discuss settlement. This case is going to trial."

"I'll give him the message, sir."

A few minutes later, I boarded my train. Within half an hour, we were on our way.

"Where are you headed?" the lady sitting across the aisle asked me.

"All the way to Chicago," I said. "Mud City..."

That's where I was going, for two whole weeks. Someone once told me the restaurants stayed open after dark. I wanted to see for myself.

THE END

ACKNOWLEDGMENTS

I GOT HELP and encouragement from various people in writing this book. Thanks to Peter Pattakos, Jim Rosenthal, and Ellen Kramer, who slogged through early drafts of the manuscript and provided helpful insights. I also received incisive comments from those who read later drafts, including Pat Cigetich, Stevie Weismann, Julie Brekke, David Brekke, and Melissa Quartner Brekke.

Where would a Jewish boy be without his mother? My mom, Maxine Cohen, who is a published author in her own right, reviewed and commented on multiple drafts of the book. So did my wife, Marci, whom I abandoned many nights and weekends while I tended to my writing.

My law partners, Jim, Ellen, and Jason Bristol, deserve special thanks for allowing me to yammer on about the book when we all should have been working. And my deepest gratitude goes to Don Radlauer and Yael Shahar of Kasva Press, who provided invaluable assistance in honing the story and editing the rough prose. The book never would have come together without their insights and advice.

About the Author

JOSHUA COHEN lives with his wife, Marci, in Cleveland, Ohio, where he practices law at a small firm specializing in complex civil litigation. He grew up in San Antonio and attended the University of Texas both as an undergraduate and for law school. Josh is an avid fan of film noir and crime fiction from the 1940s and 1950s. *The Best Assassination in the Nation* is his first novel.